HOOD FETISH

Derrick and Latroya Johnson

D & L Uptown Novels
Dallas, TX

Printed in the United States of America

ISBN: 9781793093677

It takes a strong committed woman to believe in a dream that has no roots. The courage she shows in watering the soil of a man with high expectations and wants, advertises the strength she really possesses.

I think ALLAH, the creator, for placing my wife Latroya Peters Johnson, in my life. At times I wanted to give up she was there. At the times I wanted to stop, she was my push. As our journey continues, I pray that our success, happiness and faith constantly blossoms.

In addition, I would like to thank my dad, Derrold Hunt for being there when I needed it most. You showed me that blood is always thicker than water.
'Preciate you man!
Last but not least, to my aunt Jean, a.k.a. Wilma Shelton. You watched me come from bad to good and never gave up once. Now you can smile that I finally figured out how to live the right way and that's through the worship of Allah, the one true deity.

To my supporters thank ya'll very much. It only gets better from this day forward. God bless us all!!!

AS. SALAMU.ALAIKUM
May peace and blessings be upon you.

"Panthers! Panthers! Panthers!" The noise in the stadium was unbearable. Everyone was screaming their lungs out. _"Bears! Bears! Bears!"_ Cheers and chants were coming from both sides of Lowes basketball court. This was a big night. The night that someone would make a mark in history and become the champions of this division, a high school basketball game. Representing the north Dallas area was the Hillcrest Panthers and competing against them was the South Oak Cliff Golden Bears, who were equally as good. Both teams had an undefeated record, but the edge was going toward the Panthers, mainly because of one player. He stood 6'7 and weighed 230 pounds. People were comparing his athletic skills to that of LeBron James. At this very moment scouts from different colleges sat in the stands, waiting to see him perform.

Tracy Mc Davis was the star shooting guard of the Hillcrest Panthers. He earned his nickname because of his style of game, which favored that of NBA'S most dominate player- T-Mac! Tracy looked toward the stands impatiently. He smiled when he locked eyes with his mother and longtime girlfriend, Ja' Zarri. The excitement shown on both women's faces forced him to hide his true emotions. He waved, and they quickly returned the motion. T-Mac's frustration went down a notch but not enough to calm him completely. He placed his towel over his head and tried to mediate. "Where this nigga at man!" T-Mac asked himself. This was the biggest day of his life and the most important person in his life, wasn't here. He shook his head. "Damn where you at!"

Several people approached him and gave him encouraging words. T-Mac looked up when he heard his coaches voice and briefly, his true feelings were hidden. "What's up T-Mac? Why the long face on a night like this? I've been watching you since we stepped out the locker room. T-Mac looked away slightly before answering, "I'm cool coach, jus' a little some'em on my mind is all. "He paused. "Step off I'll be ready."

Coach Henry nodded, we'll let's get some shots in. "He grabbed Tracy's shoulders. They both stared at one another. Coach Henry's eyes said words his mouth was trying to formalize. "Listen son, yo' future is in yo hands. You gotta get whateva's distracting you from yo mind. Deal wit' what's happenin' now." It was apparent that this African-American man wanted to see the younger black generation succeed. The odds for that in these drug and gang infested neighborhood were slim to none. Coach Henry pushed him toward the court. "Gone out there an' get yo' mind right. Ms. Mac didn't come here tonight to see you fail." He winked his left eye at T-Mac. Tracy smiled and jogged on the court. He was showered with the welcoming sound of his name. "T-Mac! T-Mac! T-Mac!"

Vince Mc Davis, owner of Street Approved Records, sat in the parking lot waiting on his connection. Viper, as the streets of Dallas Texas knew him, all thanks to his deadly attitude, glanced at his diamond bezel Rolex watch. The time was out of sync with where he was supposed to be. His baby brother had a big game tonight and in no way, for, or fashion was he going to miss it. Again, he glanced at his watch, then looked around at the positions of his shoulders. Their cars sat in a semi-circle, facing the phone booth, at the side of the store. This is where his chameleon painted 600 Mercedes-Benz was. Viper looked around some more in search of any signs of the police. Even though this car would have no illegal activities inside, it was an attraction drawing monster. At this moment, the Mercedes was transforming from violet to candy apple red. "Where these bitches at Doug?"
Doug raised up and searched the parking lot before speaking. "I don't kno' but we can bounce. It's they lost, not ours."

Viper thought about the statement, which was true, but this was the weed that drove the whole city wild. At 6,000 a pound, only the hard hitters could get a trustworthy connection. He was considered one of the big boys, not because he purchased 150 pounds of O.G Kush at a time, but he was always business oriented. "Naw we gone give'em a bit longa. Then I'm rollin regardless. My baby bro is expectin' me." Doug nodded. The stage was set, no need to say a word.

"This is astonishing!" The Hillcrest Panthers are being out played. Their down by 10 points at the end of one and their star player, Tracy Mc Davis, only has 4 points. It seems like an upset in the making. Wit' so many expectations exceeded this year, how will this turn out? Are the Panthers goin' to tuck their tails and allow the Golden Bears the opportunity to climb to victory. This is only the beginin' and still more quarters to come …" The announcer was yelling.
"Everything's aight team!" Coach Henry spoke to his team. "Mo' defense these next quarters." If they can't score, then they can't win! Now keep yo' hands up an' yo' feet movin'. "He looked at Tracy, "We give our all an' nothin' less. "The second quarter whistle blew, and the team returned to the floor. Get it togetha' nigga! T-Mac told himself. This game could make or break him in his selection into the top college programs. Knowing this, he pushed the thought of his brother's whereabouts, from his head. When the game started again, he slowly tried to work himself into a zone. Holding the ball, T-Mac dribbled to the right, crossed over left and pulled up for a jump shot …. bucket. Smooth! The crowd stood up showing their support for him. The next play had much of the same resorts. T-Mac stole the ball from the opposing guard and raced toward the goal. He slammed it home and was fouled. Three-point play and the referee's whistle blew.

After two consecutive baskets, the Golden bears lead was cut to 5 points. They decided it was needed for a time-out. "That's it defenses wins' championships! "Coach Henry screamed. The shine in Tracy Mc Davis's eyes changed as he looked toward the stadium's entrance. Viper walked in, accompanied by Doug and Chip, his bodyguards. Everyone stared at him. He was a hometown celebrity. His freshly faded head, wearing a Dallas Mavericks hat with matching jersey. It hung over his 6'1 200-pound frame nicely. The VV's diamond neckless that dangled from his neck, hung to his Red Monkey Jeans, which sat over the tan Timberland boots on his feet. Viper was dope boy fresh and Street Approved Records was in the building.

Viper spotted his mother, then him and his team headed in her direction. T-Mac stood up as his brother spread his arms. What's up were the unsaid words. T-Mac returned the motion. Seeing the energy passed between them, Coach Henry smiled. There was nothing else to said. "It's yo' night champ!" Tracy Mc Davis took to the court in the second half and things never was the same. It was like a Tasmanian devil had hit the spot and instead of being small, it stood 6'7.

"The turn of events was spectacular. Tracy Mc Davis scored an outstanding 35 points, 10 rebounds, 10 assist and became the game's MVP. The Division a Championship will be one to remember. The Hillcrest Panthers came back from a first half stumble to win in the second half, with a score of 74-73. A last second shot by Tracy Mc Davis gave them their win. The NBA should be excited for this player…"

Tracy Mc Davis smiled as he sat watching the late-night local news on the T.V. His brother hugged him, while his mother and girlfriend looked on. "You keep doin' you an' I got the rest." Viper said, "Your too good fo' this lifestyle so become some'em beta." His two trophies sat on his mother's china cabinet. There was so much to look forward to and all he had to do was stay focused. Tracy smiled again, success was right around the corner.

Chapter One

Viper was 25 years old and known around the city for his exotic weed sales. He supplied houses in three major parts of Dallas, which consist of North, South and Oak Cliff area. In these spots nothing less than an ounce at $700, was sold. These areas he forcefully put weed in and made a lot of small-time hustlers mad. With the people he'd surrounded himself with, Viper could care less about who's toes he stepped on because he knew nobody could compare to his moves. He walked around his record label before heading toward the back. There, Doug and Chip were supervising the rest of the crew, as they separated and rewrapped ounces that were coming off the scales. "What it looks like Doug?" Viper asked as he stepped into the label's storage compartment. "It's cool but we gone be here awhile." Doug smiled. "Tre an' Kim weighin' an' RaRa rewrappin' some pounds. All the work is being done though."
Viper nodded before walking toward Chip. "Chip what's happenin'?"
Chip looked up from his spot, which was surrounded by boxes. He was the main wheel, when it came to shipment. He had to make sure everything was greased and bleached correctly before they were placed in the boxes. With 150 pounds, this was no easy task. One slip and it was over.

Chip took his gloves off and stood up. "Shid I'm iceboxin' boss but- "He paused, thinking his statement though. Viper's temper could be sparked by the smallest thing. He was the man and he made sure the world knew it. "We might need a little mo' help baby. You gettin' bigga then you think. "Viper studied the man for a moment. Not only was he a smart dope boy but he also was the owner and CEO of this record label. Street Approved Records was creating a buzz in the mix tape world. Especially after signing the   newest member of the label, G.T. Everyone was requesting the latest tapes and urban wear sold out of his shop. "Yea you right baby." Viper finally said. "It's hard to trust these boys. I'm good wit' ya'll, but you can always quit." He smiled a smile that showed no emotion.

Chip understood exactly what was being said. "Do the job or be replaced!" I feel you on that tip...jus' a thought."
"Good to hear it though. "Viper turned to leave the room. "Doug come fuck wit' me. Chip this yo' world, aight'?"

Both men entered the room simultaneously. Viper stepped to the side, closed the office door, and walked toward the bar. Doug took a seat and watched his boss quietly. Nothing was said for several minutes, then suddenly, "What you drinkin' Doug? An' look behind that chair an' grab that bowl full of Kali Mist." While moving toward the desk to retrieve the happy plant, Doug spoke with his back turned, "Pour me up some Grey Goose....an' what's da blessin' fo'?" Doug knew, that if they were smoking, they weren't returning to the storage room until the work was finished. Their smell alone would contaminate the wrapping process. Viper handed his right-hand man a glass. "my nigga what's up wit' yo' boy Chip? Is he gone be aight? I'm payin' em' straight, I kno'? Doug smiled. This was typical of Vince since they broke away from the Mexicans and started purchasing from the Jamaicans. "He cool baby. It's on me if- "

Viper was in his face before the words were complete. This made Doug drop the cigarillo he was rolling. "Nigga fuck that. There's too much at stake Doug! He's your problem, not mine so I shouldn't have to worry about him, feel me?" Viper yelled, Doug nodded, afraid of his voice now. Viper eased back and continued. "This is us!" He waved his hands around the room. "You helped me build this. One-week link could fuck it all up. "Walking toward the window, Viper looked out. His Mercedes, a Dodge Ram truck, BMW, Dodge Charger, and a Lexus Jeep sat in front of the record label. "roll the fire up nigga, don't go pussy on me now." Doug laughed. He knew that even with the temper Viper had, he always packed fare." Viper I'll holla at him first thing smokin'." He fired up the finished cigarillo. Viper said nothing, as he walked to the stereo and turned it on. He sipped his Grey Goose and listened to his newest artist G.T. the title was, "Remember A Gangsta," and already people were looking for the album to drop.

"Left me to die, thought I was dead an' gone/ I'm hard as a headstone/ a savage 'bout my cabbage, even when my breads gone..." Viper nodded as he listened. He turned the volume down a notch and spoke. "This nigga in my way to pull out so I gotta push him. "Doug passed the plant to his boss and settled back in to listen. This man was one of the smartest street hustlers in the city and when he spoke, something always came from it. "Listen!" Viper turned the system back up." *...Shiesty bitches be on my dick, tryna steal my venom/ talkin' down my game, mad cause I' wit 'em/ but I jus' smile diamonds everywhere/shoes on da coupe cost three stacks a pair..."* Doug shook his head. "yea da boy nice. What's da haps though?"

Viper passed the Kali Mist back. "He street, kno' da game an' all but he ain't fuckin' aroun', which is why I signed him." He sipped from his glass before resuming. "Plus, da nigga cool wit' my baby bro. T-Mac on his way to college an' I told him I'd help da nigga. My words bond."

Doug knew this was true. "So, what's next". The sentences he was forming where cut all short. The Kali Mist was pulling his brain toward the ceiling and back down toward the floor, all in a motion. "I want 50 of them pounds broke down an' sold by da gram. That's on you where you move them at... here!" Viper reached behind him and grabbed a bag, then tossed it in Doug's lap. "That's 20 stacks. Get a house and an apartment somewhere. That's enough to pay fo'' everything an' pay da workers fo' da spots," Viper looked at the cigarillo. I gotta put this shit down! He laughed. One mo' thing. Afta' I finish this drop we got, I should be ready to pull back, feel me?"

"That's what's up?" Doug said. "I like that idea too baby. Clean money is da perfect way to stay alive. "This time Viper nodded. "You kno' how it is, mentioning my name, brings da whole city out.... So, I'm a use that to make millions da right way." He pulled out his cellphone and pushed speed dial. The phone rang a few times and then a woman's voice came on the line. "Hello baby, I've been waitin' on yo' call."

Yea right! Viper thought. "Kitty I'm on my way an' straight up, I'm ready to fuck, so clothes off befo' I get there."

"Ain't we demandin' but I'll comply. "Kitty giggled.

You betta! "20 minutes' bye. "He hung up before she could respond. Viper stood up, grabbed his keys, and   headed toward the door. "You in charge. Make sure shit right an' closed up. I'm gone get my dick sucked, kissed an' loved. "both men laughed.

"I got'cha baby. "Doug said.

"I'm out. "Viper left the room and closed the door. There was no more to discuss, the boss had spoken.

Chapter Two

Tracy Mc Davis sat in his 2010 Dodge Challenger, trying to surpass the shock of this morning. He'd woke up to the sound of his brother's voice urging him to go outside. The dawn sky had just rose and oranges' red could be seen for miles, "Nigga get up!" Viper yelled while snatching the sheets off his brother. "What man, damn!" T-Mac responded. "Momma tell this sucka to gone on!" He tried to retrieve the sheets from his brother's hand. "Nigga it's too early fo' this shit."

Viper, who was dressed in a silk short set, begin to laugh. "Alright nigga since you bitchin' out on me." He looked over his shoulder to make sure his mother wasn't in earshot distant, while he cursed. Viper continued to talk. "you won da championship an' I got you some'em, but you don't want it." He paused to let his words settle in. "I'll take it back champ. "Viper laughed again.

T-Mac was listening to every word. His brother was the only dad he'd known his whole life. Their father had disappeared when they were younger. Nobody ever mentioned his name, but Vince looked just like him, with his light brown complexion. Their mother often said Vince was a splitting image of their dad from the look, down to his attitude. This was something his brother liked but at the same time despised. "Vipa what you got?" T-Mac was raising out of bed, when their mother's voice screamed. "Vince who car blockin' me in? I gotta be at work. I'm already runnin' late boy...all these damn cars poppin' up at my house." Viper shook his head at his mother's frustration. "It ain't mine. Tell T-Mac to move it. I don't kno' why you won't quit that job anyway!" He yelled back.

"I'm not goin' there wit' you no more." She paused. "Somebody come move this damn car, so I can go!"

It was a known fact that his momma wasn't with the fact that he hustled but she didn't complain. Samantha Mc Davis was one that did few unchurchly things to put food on the table for her boys. "Vince!" She yelled again. Viper looked at his brother, who now had a smile cresting his lips. He tossed a set of keys to him. "Go move yo' shit chump. This all to shit on them niggas an' bitches, fo' sho'."

Now Tracy was sitting in the parking lot looking around the inside at his interior. The inside was piano black with woodgrain, leather headliner, and diamond pattern bucket seats. It also had a customized multimedia in the dash. He couldn't stop the smile on his face and in his eyes. His brother had done it again. The challenger was painted pearl white sitting on some Asante 22's with Pirelli low-profile tires. Shaking his head in amazement. T-Mac slowly ignited his vehicle to a bunch of envious stares. Shitting on them, is what he was doing. He threw his backpack over one shoulder and walked in the cafeteria, where he usually chilled.

Ja'Zarri, his longtime girlfriend and G.T. his neighborhood friend, approached the table he was sitting at, with two other students. "Hey baby!" Ja'Zarri said as they came closer. T-Mac looked up from his book and cinnamon roll. "What's up?" He reached his hand out. "I heard yo' demo nigga. You got at that bitch." G.T. smiled. "Yeah I gotta stay focused. Vipa got me in da studio every day when I'm out of school."

T-Mac laughed, then raised up to allow Ja'Zarri a chance to sit in his lap. "You kno' how that is..." He paused to kiss his girl's cheek. "He's a perfectionist, but you on point anyway." G.T. displayed his jewelry filled mouth again. Diamonds and gold teeth outlined his street image. His braided hair and Polo unit topped off with the Street Approved Record chain. What T-Mac liked about him was the fact that his short 5'7 frame was outshined by his personality. Even though he came from a dope filled area of the city, G.T. was trying to use his verbal skills to upgrade his lifestyle, instead of crime.

G.T looked at his watch. "Man, class finna be in, you gone be out today at lunch?" He asked. T-Mac curled his lips up. "Nigga that's what I do. Practice make me the beast I am. "He laughed arrogantly. Ja'Zarri hit him on the shoulder playfully.

G.T. nodded. "I feel da same way bout this music baby. "He rubbed his chin. "I saw that Dodge Challenger you pulled up in. That bitch sweet." Again G.T. nodded. "Vipa told me he was gone cop it fo' you. I'm next on da list so watch out." Ja'Zarri looked at T-Mac in surprise. "You rollin' now an' you ain't tell me?" she asked. Suddenly the bell rung, and it was time to head to class. "I'll fuck wit' you. I'm tryna holla at Shierra fine ass. "G.T. said and walked away. T-Mac and Ja'Zarri followed in the same direction. "Bye." Ja'Zarri said, and walked up a set of stairs, leaving Tracy to walk with himself and his thoughts.

The spring weather in Dallas, TX was close to summer heat, that would come soon. It was lunchtime at Hillcrest High. Ja'Zarri was in a pair of Chanel sunglasses with her hair pulled back in a ponytail. Her mocha skin tone shined over the off-white Louis Vuitton blouse and shorts she wore. The wrap around calf high black Prada sandals showed off her French pedicured toes. "T-Mac watched her as he prepared to get his 200 shots in. She was model material at least and celebrity status at best so it was a brainer that her 5'6 frame holding 135 pounds, was a showstopper. "Zarri!

"T-Mac yelled as he dribbled the basketball. "Boy shoot, I'm a throw it back to you. "This was her way of letting the nearby girls, that often came to watch him practice, know he was taken. "No! move fo' you break a nail. "T-Mac laughed as she placed her hands on her petite waist. "Aight I warned you. "He gracefully pulled up for his first shot, an eighteen-footer and drained it home. The ball came in at an angle causing her to flinch away. Laughing, T-Mac hustled to retrieve the ball and shot again. She flinched again, as she tried to catch the shades that fell from her face.

All the nearby people giggled at her expense. T-Mac never stopped his practice shooting. Having learned her lesson, reluctantly, Ja'Zarri moved away from the court. "I told you. "T-Mac yelled behind her. 30 minutes later, he sat on the bleachers between her legs, wiping sweat from his unshirted chest. "Hey T-Mac wit' yo' cute self. "A light skinned chick yelled, from a crowd of girls, walking by. He waved back.

"Tramps." Ja'Zarri said to him. He laughed at the act, knowing she hated those moments more than anything. "Girl you a mess. Where G.T. at? Wit' his little bittie ass."
"He walked in the snack room earlier, but I continued out here to help you practice. "Ja'Zarri smiled at her joke.

T-Mac stood up and stretched. "I'm finna' go see if he still over there. It's bout' 10 mins befo' class, you want some'em to drink?"
She looked at him with no shirt on but before she could speak, he spoke. "Keep that bullshit to yo 'self. Now do you want some'em or not? "She pouted sexually causing him to move down the walkway, away from her. Ja'Zarri yelled after him. "Bring me a slushy! "Throwing up his thumb, T-Mac headed toward the snack room to quench his thirst.

As he turned the corner, he saw two boys about 6'0 feet each, holding G.T. against the wall. The other guy held his chain in his fist, with his face inches from G.T. "Lil-bitch ass nigga I'm a keep this fo' that money…. punk ass nigga!"
"Hey! "T-Mac yelled as he approached the three men. "What's up G.T.?" "Bitch ass nigga mad cause I hit 'em on da dice. "G.T spit blood to the concrete. "T-Mac shook his head because he knew how G.T. got down. If the dice wasn't loaded, he wasn't shooting. It just was surprising that the lames had caught him, "Let him go niggas. "T-Mac said calmly. His 6'7 230-pound body demanded respect. "An' give me that necklace back fo' it gets ugly. "The men looked at each other for a while arranging their thoughts, then complied.

The smaller of the three, tossed the necklace to the ground and spoke. "I'm a catch you later bitch ass nigga. "In one motion, G.T. punched him in his face. "If we gone do it, let's exchange blows now! "he yelled. The two men locked up like pit bulls in a pen. The dark-skinned dude stood a few inches taller but the swiftness of G.T. made up for this lack of height. The other two men looked at the fight, then back to T-Mac, who was now accompanied by a few of basketball teammates and decide they'd do better staying clear. "Get money nigga!" T-Mac yelled. "get it boy!"

Suddenly the fight was over, but the crowd was still growing. Both men where breathing hard and they shared a good understanding for one another. "What's up hoe ass nigga?" G.T. yelled between breathes.

"Shid what's up? "The other man said as he stepped forward. He was stopped by the sound of the school bell. T-Mac grabbed his friends' shoulder and handed him his chain. "You made yo' point. Let's bounce baby. "He commanded in a low tone. Nodding, G.T., begin walking away. I still hit you hoe ass niggas! He laughed.

"Yo' T-Mac!"

"What's up baby?"

"Preciate cha. You eva need me, I'm comin'."

"That's what's up."

I'm down for you so ride with me/ My enemies your enemies/ Cause you ain't never had a friend like me/ Nobody knows where we'll be/ My enemies your enemies cause you ain't never had a friend like me..." Tupac Shakur.

Chapter Three

Viper bagged out his two-story home in Oak Cliff. He was in his sky-blue Dodge Viper, talking on the phone. Today was an important day because interviews had to be done and another club had to be rented in order to throw a concert. "Doug what's some news I can use?" He stopped at the corner of Camp Wisdom Rd. and continued conversating. "I'm comin' from da house. Meet me at da label."

"I'm about a block away from da spot. How long you gone be?
Doug knew what he had to say wasn't to be said over the phone.
"Kim say it's good an' business movin' fasta' than usual."
"That's good!"
Viper said while pushing the bottom to his CD charger, in search of Young Jeezy.
"Did you take care of that I asked da otha' day?"
He still was sitting at the corner, in no hurry to move. Holding the remote to his system, Viper adjusted the no hands device in his ear, to fit more comfortable.
"Yeah I'ma get at you on that when you make it this way, ya' feel me?"
Doug replied. "I'm pullin' in da spot right now so how long you gone be?

Viper ran the Kali Mist filled cigarillo across his nose, before firing it up.
He answered. "Nigga I gotta scoop G.T. up an' head to K104 radio station."

He inhaled hard, then exhaled. "Afta' that I gotta go see if them niggas gone charge me to rent Crushed Berries fo' Friday. "Viper looked around to make sure no one was getting and crazy ideas. This Dodge Viper, on chrome 24's Giovanni Blitz, has been known to give niggas the heart of frogs and they seem to jump. Seeing everything was clear, he continued talking. "You jus' be there when I come, ya dig? We got business to go over, real talk."

"I'm here baby. They here so take yo' time. We'll finish this discussion lata'." Doug talked while heading inside the record label. "I'm out then. "Viper hung up and turned up his four 12-inch Audio subwoofers. His customized trunk did no raddling, as he eased the volume to 10 notches. Young Jezzy begin to spit. *"I'm goin' out da same way I came in/ Hard than a mu'fucka/Real street nigga, I ain't nothin' like these other suckas (naw) How much da club cost, I might this mu'fucka/have da Feds parked right outside this mu'fucka...* "Viper laughed as he sang along. *These niggas can't touch me!* He laughed some more then jumped into traffic, heading toward 67 freeway. Once there, he opened the engine up to 100 mph and dropped the top.

"Hey what's up Triple D? This DJ Slickwitit, at yo' favorite radio station k104, an' we got the hottest underground rapper G.T. an' Dallas's best-known CEO Viper, from Street Approved Records in the house., give a shout out fam'."

"A what up Dallas. This Gangsta T, known to da land as G.T. Ya'll call up an' show yo' boy some love. It's hot in here." G.T. replied.

Viper spoke next.

"Dallas what it do, what's poppin', what's crackin'! Whateva' make ya' smile. Street Approved Records in da house.
Befo' I turn it back ova' to my man G.T. let me give a shout out
To my baby brother, the All State shootin' guard of the city,
Street   Approved!"
Yeah, Yeah that's right Street Approved Records in the house wit K104 an' DJ Slickwitit. Let's get some calls."
"Hey G.T. Hey!" A woman screamed over the line.
"Hold on baby. "DJ Slickwitit said "What's yo' question baby?"
"My name Kristie an' when yo' tape comin' out?"
G.T. replied. 'Keep yo' ears to da street baby. This summer mine.   You gone be at Crushed Berries to see me, huh?"
"Yeah an' can ya'll play my song off yo' mixtape, "Comeback Coochie."
"Right afta' this new Twista song we'll see if you really got that Comeback Coochie."

DJ Slickwitit said. "Ya'll make sure to be at Crushed Berries.
"It's gone be off the chain."
Viper spoke once more.
"Dallas let me see you out there in numbas'. Fo' da first 200
women, I'm given away signed Street Approved shirts.
An' da bar free 'til 11 o'clock."
"You heard it here first on K104. More afta' this."

Viper and G.T. came to a screeching stop in front of the
Street Approved record label.

Both men jumped out and walked into the building. Kim his
studio manager, was sitting behind the desk dealing with
some paperwork. She spoke.

"I heard ya'll niggas. That's what's up!" She held her hand up
for a high five.

They followed suit. "Where Doug Kim?" Viper asked

"In there wit' Chip." She pointed toward the office door.

"G.T. it's time, an' Kim when I come out remind me, I need
to talk to you." Viper walked, his baggy Sean John unit,
swaying with the movement. He entered his office and
slammed the door." Doug, Chip what's up?" Both men
nodded their reply.

"Get out my seat nigga!" Viper laughed, as the two men, Doug
and Viper, switched places. He begins talking once his feet
was on top of the desk, showing off some Gucci Air Force
ones. "So, what's up wit' you? "Viper asked.

Doug took his time before speaking. "I opened up an
apartment in da greedy Grove. An' I got a house, which I put
burglar bars on, in da Cliff. "He looked at Chip, who was
now sipping on a glass of Ace of Spades. "I got two hoes to
run them spots cause it's gone be a lot of sittin'. These niggas
tend to get restless, feel me? "Viper nodded but said nothing.
Doug continued. "We should bring in bout' 3 mill, once
everything done."

Chip whistled at the numbers. This caught Viper's attention.
"How those zone house goin'?"

"Everything on my end. Ain't neva been wrong, ain't gone
start now."

Chip replied. "I'm on RaRa an' Tre tight."

That's what's up. I need to hear that. We got a goal. I want all this done so we can focus on da legit side of shit. No playin' at all. Business that's all I'm about this month. "Viper looked at his watch. He had to finish this, so he could go mess with the production on some tracks. "There's 50 pounds an' I'm gone move those whole so da numbas ya'll talkin' need to be right, ya hear?" They agreed. "Now leave an' send Kim in here."

Seconds later, Kim a 5'2 well built, mixed breed women entered. She was Columbian and Black. Viper watched as she softly closed the door behind her. Her Prada, low cut blouse, showed off her belly ring, which hung to the top of her Prada denim pants. Kim's Gucci stiletto boots gracefully moved her toward the desk, where she stood in front of Viper. Reaching for his bowl, he pulled a cigarillo out and sparked it up. After two pulls, he reached it out to her. She expected it, then spoke.

"What's on yo' mind boss?" Kim said teasingly as she inhaled the exotic weed.

"I need you girl, fo' two reasons. One, I need you to make a transaction fo' me."

He looked at her. The Kali Mist had her eyes low and sexy in less than a minute. Powerful Shit!

"What's the second thing? "Kim asked in a husky voice.

Smiling, Viper pushed the button that turned on the stereo system and reached for the blanket covered plant. He took a pull.

"You kno' da rest boo. "Butt naked Please"!

Without any urging, Kim stood there with nothing but a silk pair of Prada panties on. Her body was mesmerizing. This was something they often indulged in, free of expense. No strings, no worries, no attachment, just the way he liked. "So, where you want it"? Viper smiled harder as he discarded his own clothes. Lyfe was singing the words that were true. *"Even when yo' hustlen days are gone/ she'll be by yo' side still holdin' on/ Even when those 20's stop spinnin'/ An all those gold-digging' women disappear/ She'll still be here..."*

"Right here!" Viper said.

Viper sat behind his desk reading some newly received paperwork. His gold Versace glasses were smoothly on his light brown face. The top of his Sean John unit was hanging on the back of the chair. He only wore his diamond covered chain, which had the logo on it, over his G-Unit tank top. His muscular body pushed against the fabric as he leaned forward. The sexscapade with Kim had relaxed him and it helped him to concentrate on the matters that were important. Leaning back, Viper placed both hands behind his head and begin to think. I need new talent! G.T. was creating a major buzz but something was needed after him. Nasty boy and Brianna, His other artist, were selling a few singles but they weren't ready for any big role just yet. He exhales, took his glasses and placed them on the desk. This was where he'd have to earn his keep. Viper looked toward the door but quickly pushed the thought of Kim out his mind. Business Time! Crushed Berries he decided would not only be a concert for G.T. but he'd also sign the guy that could beat or complete against his artist, in battle rapping. Viper sparked the half of cigarillo up that was left in the ashtray and smiled. That was a brilliant idea because that was G.T.'s specialty. If someone could compete on that level, then they were worthy of a deal. He inhaled and put his Versace glasses back on before he could resume his reading, his sidekick phone vibrated in his pocket. Without thinking, Viper grabbed it and begin talking, all in one motion. "Aw what up! "He spoke impatiently.

"Ey mon! It'z been a minute since chu holla'd mon.

"Redman!" Naw homie, it really ain't but what's up tho?" Viper leaned back and placed his feet back on the desk to relax. He smoked his exotic and listened.

"Chu usually holla b' fo da next shot mon. "Redman's heavily accented voice said.

"Iz something else happenin'?"

Who this nigga thinks he fuckin' wit!" man peep game, I'm doin' me on my end. "Viper paused and contemplated his next words. "It might be a little longa' or it might not be at all. It all depends how I turn out, feel me?"

Redman begin to chuckle. His laugh was a heavy one, which matched his dark-skinned face. He was a handsome man but that was over shadowed by his deadly style of living. Redman had been a part of over 100 men's early arrival in heaven or hell, for that matter.

"Chu kno' mon. I really like chu style. Chu stand firm to chu an' not many do dat." Redman continued. "But we like family...I need Chu.... An' chu need me mon."

Dealing with Redman was a plus and a minus, all in one. Two bulls never live in the same pen. Nothing good could or would come out that. Viper said nothing for what seemed like centuries. Instead, he smoked the remaining cigarillo and thought. Not being a person to allow anyone to dictate his actions, Viper temper was boiling. Say baby, I'm real busy at this moment so I'm a let you go. Answer when I call, feel me? "Again, Redman chuckled."

"I heard chu gotta concert."

He let the statement sink in, before speaking.

"I'll be chere mon. Talk to chu den." Then line disconnected.

Viper shook his head. "Who this Island nigga think he fuckin' wit!" It was time to put more goons on his payroll because trouble could brew. Viper pulled his drawer back and grabbed his shoulder holster, which held a 40. Caliber pistol inside. He slung it around his arms and snapped it shut. Next, he places his Sean John jacket on. He looked around his office in frustration. Niggas! Not finding what he was looking for, Viper picked up the phone and dialed. Seconds later a woman answered the line.

"Hello."

"Momma how you doin'?"

"Fine baby, an' you?" She asked. Viper scratched his chin.

"I'm fine. Where T-Mac at?"

"Hold on a minute, he in the room wit' that girl. Ain't no tellin' what they grown self doin'. Hold on though'"

It wasn't long before his baby brother's deep voice graces the receiver with volume. "What's up bro?"

"Man, I want you to come fuck wit' me baby."

T-Mac asked. "Where you at?" Viper laughed. His brother was willing to drive his new car.

"Naw I'm a come scoop you. Plus, Friday G.T. in concert. We goin' cool?"

"Hell yea, it's cool. I'ma leave Zarri here. Her an' momma be aight'. Let me jump in da shower. Bye!" He hung up. Viper disconnected

and already he was feeling better. His little brother could always do

that for him. He got up and left out his office, walking with swag of a millionaire. "Kim I'm gone. Tell Doug I said we need some mo' hands."

"Aight." Kim responded to the back of his shirt, as the door was swinging shut. "That nigga a mess." Kim said and laughed.

Chapter Four

Tracy McDavis rolled out of bed to the soft sound of music. His head was pounding from the hard night of partying with his brother. He glanced at the clock. 10:09 am This was late to him because he'd developed a habit of rising early, in order to get a few miles and shower, before school. Today that wasn't the case. No miles would be ran and no school would be attended. I'm cool. Test ain't 'til next week! He moved toward the bathroom, using his middle and index fingers, to massage the sides of his head. It felt like someone was hammering a nail straight through his brain. Drunk too much, but it was fun! Tracy laughed to himself, as he turned the faucet on.

He stuck his hand under the water and splashed his face several times, trying to wake himself up. His body smelled of women's perfume and liquor. The smell alone brought a smile to his face. Dallas Gentleman, a major strip club in Northwest Dallas area, was another world, used to please men. It was filled with some of the most beautiful women around the state. You could close your eyes and pick out a dime piece. Having fun with his brother was something Tracy always enjoyed. He looked up from the sink to see his brother standing in the doorway. "Take a shower an' come down stairs. We have some're to discuss, aight?" Tracy nodded but didn't speak.

After his shower, Tracy throw on a pair of Air Jordan sport and walked bare feet, across the thick emerald green oriental carpet to the first floor of the house. It always amazed him at how big and beautiful this house was. Mahogany any wood furniture covered the living room area, while gold platted mirrors lined the walls. Over the brown brick fire place was a wall size 52' plasma T.V. His brother's style was everywhere, even in the kitchen, where he stood on white marble floors. The entire eating area was Black N Decker from the stove to the refrigerator. Whoa! He said to himself as he fixed a bowl of Honey Comb Cereal.

With his bowl in hand, Tracy enter his brother's personal office and took a seat in the empty chair in front of him. Viper looked up at him, smiled, and put his head down. There was a lot of papers in view. After several minutes, Viper leaned back and began talking. "Hey baby I see you still a cereal head."

"I found these on yo' icebox nigga!"

Viper laughed. "You kno' you right. You have fun last night?" He rubbed his chin, before continuing. "Nigga you fucked up 20 stacks, you kno' that huh?" Tracy spilled some milk with his sudden motion.

"You serious?"

"Dead serious. "Viper looked at him. Tracy was shaking his head in frustration. It was funny how an eighteen-year-old kid could run through money and never know it. "Nigga you aight. I wanted you to have fun. "Tracy nodded but he still wasn't convinced.

Viper looked around for a moment trying to arrange his thoughts. He had to school his brother on the business part of his life just in case anything happened to him. The record label was fool-proof, co-signed for by his mother, who was a registered nurse of 20 years. All loans went through her but were all paid off quickly. He was CEO, which made him legit all the way around. Viper placed both hands on his desk and begin talking. "Listen fam. I have my will made out. All my things go to you, wit' you tendin' to mom. "He paused. Tracy said nothing "I know you goin' to da league, but you need to understand some of this business just in case I come up missing."

Tracy laughed as he down the milk in his bowl. "Man, who gone fuck wit' you? Plus, that Nigga buy anything money is what I'm gone use fo' us. "He smiled and wiped the moisture from his chin. "That's what I want you to do but here are some copies of all my business plans. Take it an' learn it too!" Viper pulled his drawer back and pulled out some pre-rolled NYC Diesel, then ran the cigarillo under his nose. He got up and stepped to his walk-in closet. "Come here T-Mac! "Viper called from his position. "What's up bro?" Tracy stood towering over his brother.

Viper punched a few numbers and slowly the side wall moved outward. His eyes moved from the money back to his brother.

"Damn baby!"

He knew his brother had money but not to this degree. "That's about 3.5 million bro."

"Viper smiled." That's why I'm comin' at you like this. You kno' what else I do, so no need to go over that. "He fired up the cigarillo in his hand. "Jus' make sure you keep those copies and read'em. Everything from da contracts to my safe code is there." Tracy shook his head in agreement. "Afta' school tomorrow, come by da house. It's G.T.'s debut album an' we gone be in da spot. Rememba' I got some secrets. "Viper said seriously still staring in the safe.

Tracy replied. "Fo sho' "Damn he on! (adding) "An you always full of surprises."

Viper closed the safe and walked back to his desk. He didn't try to pass the weed to his brother, knowing he wouldn't take it. "Sit down so I can go ova' things wit' you. It' a must you understand this shit. "He could see in his brother's eyes. Tracy was focused now. "This gone be awhile, so you might as well get comfortable."

Gangstas, Hustlas, Ballas, Cap-pillars/ who I be, the nieghberhood drug deala/ A young soldier that's bout it, bout it/ we comin' up on you suckas, we gettin' rowdy....." Master P started rapping over the speakers built in his office walls. This was his life and it was a must, he got his brother caught up to pace. Life was to short, not to plan ahead.

Chapter Five

The man awoke to the sudden scream of his daughter. As quickly as it begun, it stopped. He struggled to focus his view through the slits that once were his eyes. He shut them back at what he thought he saw. No this can't be happenin'! The smell of blood, gasoline, and cigar smoke reeked through the air. He opened his eyes again quickly to the sudden touch on his naked body. Nothing was said by the dark-skinned man just an evil smile sat on his handsome face. Seconds later he stared, then he spoke. "Chu woke mon?" The man shook his head yes. "Dat'z gud."

Frantically, the man looked around, not for help though because he knew that nobody in the world could save him now. His eyes were in search of his wife and daughter. The wire that binded his wrist and ankles, was cutting deep in his flesh. Its pain was excruciating but what hurt more was his wife nude body wearing a Jamaican necktie. Her beautiful body was lifeless, with her eyes staring into horror. No! He thought to himself. What have I done? His legs were aching none stop, from the broken kneecaps he'd endeared. The hand slap him lightly on his face.

"Wake up mon...I need chu to see dis. "His thick accent floating in the air. "Dis iz chu life mon. "He chuckled.

Opening his eyes again, he tried to focus. It was hard, but he begins to see faces and forms through the dimly lit room of his home. Dread headed men stood around with AK-47 assault rifles. The one that kept tapping him on his face wore a fade and looked out of place, everything from his clothes to his shoes, everything except his smile. That smile which gripped a cigar between its lips, was perfect for this scene. "What do you want? I gave you everything I had. "The man pleaded, while resting on his side. He was squinting from the pain. "Yes, chu did but- "He laughed for a second. "chu did it too late. Nobody fucks wit' Redman an' live to talk 'bout it, mon."

"Why my wife? An' where's my daughta' they had nothing to do wit' us!" The man yelled. "Why?"

His voice cracked with rage. Redman laughed some more. "Chu killed dem not me. Look!" He waves his hand toward the tub in the bathroom. Floating was a small frame, still dressed in a Dora Explorer sleeping gown.

"Noooo!" The man yelled in a crying tone. "Why?" He whispered. Then tears streamed down his cheeks.
"Chu ask me, no chu ask chuself mon." Redman replied. "Neva fuck wit me bizness."
He fired up his cigar and took a hard pull. With the flip of the wrist, Redman tossed the remainder of the match toward the bed causing a fire to form. Redman watched until he was sure the fire was in full height.
"Now bitch nigga......go visit chu family- "He paused." .... whereva dey at."
The reflection of the flames was in his eyes as he turned to leave the scene. "Make sure dis iz finished. I have sum' where to be. "Redman called over his shoulder as he exited the house. The sight was a scary sight as though the devil was walking out of hell.

Everything from urban wear to casual clothing was present in the parking lot of Crushed Berries. People were moving to and from their cars, trying to secure a place in line and draw attention themselves as ballers. Triple D was out in numbers to support the latest local star. The underground mixtape was breaking records and causing a buzz that the whole city wanted part of. Z Ro and Big Pookey of Houston was in the building. Both men, setting the mood for G.T. to grace the stage. It was already an unbelievable turn out and the crowd didn't seem to be stopping. Dallas was in the house for sure. K104 radio station, along with 97 was broadcasting live. They were giving the radio world, play by play announcements of the Friday night club scene.

DJ Slickwitit was in the front of his van talking rapidly into his microphone. "If you ain't out here, you wrong an' you know you wrong. There're so many hot ladies out here, I can't stop sweatin'. An' women, the men is fly like an eagle. Come out Triple D there's still some room. CEO of Street Approved Records Viper an' his monsta rapper G.T. are in the building! Come out, we need ya baby"

The tone was more than expected but felt just right as Viper turned down the radio. He looked at his team and smiled. Kim, Doug, and Chip sat in the soft European leather sofa, while G.T. and Viper's brother occupied another 24-karat gold rimmed smaller sofa. Viper stood and looked around the customized Mercedes Benz luxury coach van. He purchased it for this very occasion. "Team!" Viper begins.

"This da big moment an' we gone show'em who run this rap game. "He paused and looked at G.T. "You ready champ?" This yo' night." G.T. smiled showing the diamonds in his mouth.

"Nigga I been ready"

Everybody laughed good heartedly at his response. The whole crew knew how much had been put into this project. "That's good because I think you da next Texas legend. "He put his hand out. The rest of the crew followed suit by resting theirs on top of his. "Street Approved Records!" He yelled. The others begin to pop bottles of Rosa and chant the same words. While the volume of his team Rosa, Viper took his other hand and hug his brother. "We came along way. I love you bro."

"I love you to bro." Street Approved! Street Approved! Street Approved! The shout grew louder. Tonight, was the night.

Viper and his crew sat in V.I.P watching G.T. grace the stage with song afta' song. It seemed like after every cut his energy level grew more intense. Every word had the crowd waving and rocking from side to side. He was the little big man and the way he charmed the people was magic in the making.... *Bitches on my dick tryna be my wife/maybe it's da' chain/or simply cause I'm fly/My swag can't be matched like a G-Unit suit/ so if you ain't down wit' my click/ Bitch you can get da boot...,"* verse after verse he delivered a fire bar. Viper poured a glass of Ace of Spade. "That nigga da shit, fo' real baby. HAAA!" He yelled drunkenly.

A heavy knock came on the door. "get that Kim!" Viper ordered. Kim opened the door and without seeing the face, he knew the voice. Viper turned around and walked toward Kim, who was using her 5'2 frame to block the entrance way. "Vipa ey mon! Chu lady friend want let me pass. Me not one to hog ey lady mon. "Redman laughed. Viper gently moved Kim to the side, seeing the tension in his brother's body, T-Mac approached his side. "Come in Redman. It's a party here but no talk of business, cool?"

Redman stared into Viper's eyes. "No bizness now jus' fun mon."

None of yo' crew jus' you aight?"

The disgust was in Redman's eyes, but he agreed. "We have fun now but- "He said as he grabbed a bottle of Rose'. "Bizness lata." Redman smiled his evil smile. "Cool?"

G.T. entered the V.I.P section to a lot of cheers. He smiled, as he continued to wipe the sweat from his face with his white towel. Viper approached him and placed his arm around his shoulder. "Nigga that's what I'm stressin' right there! "He screamed drunkenly. Viper was on his second bottle of Ace of Spade. "T-Mac whut chaa tink?" His words were slurring badly.

He ready. The boy put them otha niggas to shame. T-Mac held up a glass and tipped it toward G.T. "To you boy." Viper held up his bottle. 'Get my man a bottle so we can have a toast. "He looked down at G.T. who was a lot smaller then him. "Whut cha dr-i-inkin' baby?"

"Bring me some Hypnotic. "G.T. responded. Chip walked to the bar and came back with the bottle. "Here ya go big homie. "Then he held up his glass.

Viper looked around the room to make sure everyone's glass or bottle was ready. Redman's actions made him narrow his eyes. He was forcefully holding Kim's wrist and her beautiful face was showing she wasn't liking it one bit. Silently, Viper cussed to himself. He removed his arm from around his protégé and approached Redman from behind. His thoughts told him to blindside the man, but the environment was to smooth to ruin it like that. Instead he calmed himself and spoke. "Redman let her go baby. "Viper faked a laugh. "It's time fo' you to bounce. "His voice as gentle as a summer breeze.

Redman released Kim and quietly turned to face Viper, who was his exact size "fuck chu say mon? "The words came out slurred. Chip, Doug, and T-Mac begin to move closer, but Viper sensed their motion and waved them off. He took a swallow from his bottle and begin to talk. "Leave nigga, fo' shit get funky an' don't worry bout me callin'. I can do business elsewhere. "he sipped his drink again,
"Chu don't understand." His smile appeared, then he took a hit of the cigarillo in his hand. He exhaled the smoke in Viper's face before finishing his statement.
"Chu leave when I say mon...not chu."
Viper switched the bottle of Ace of Spade to his right hand. This nigga gotta be insane! He thought while rubbing his chin with his left hand. Redman continued to talk when Viper gave no response. "Chu could lose eva'ting mon. I mean eva'ting! "He started to laugh uncontrollably.

At the mention of something happening to his family, Viper reacted as quick as the deadly snake he was nicknamed after. The bottle he was holding became a weapon and it crashed against Redman's head. Glass shattered and before anyone could move, he landed a hard-left hook, that dropped the man unconsciously to the floor. "Get this trash out of here now! Viper yelled. "An get them deadheaded bitches out this club! "Doug and Chip pulled their Dessert Eagle 44's out and headed for the door. G.T. walked with them, not knowing exactly what he was going to do but sure he was going to do something. "Naw! G.T.   go wit' Kim an' my bro!" Viper turned toward the little lady, who now was holding a compact 9mm Glock. "We got this, get them out of here!"

"Can do boss. Let's go out the back fellows."
Kim lead them off, leave Viper to think. He stood over the man and looked. There was going to be trouble after tonight. Slowly, he grabbed another bottle of Ace of Spade and headed for the door. Viper removed his cellphone and called the front.
"Clean up in V.I.P."

Chapter Six

Tracy stood with his eyes pressed against the microscope. He used his finger nail to adjust the lens, that held the small drop of bacteria aboard it. It was Monday morning and his first period class, which was Biology, required the brain to process data at a time it was not normally ready. After all the drama experienced through the weekend, he was welcoming this calm school atmosphere. "Mr. McDavis, what do you see "Mr. Fruiten, a slim white man, said. He was slightly to the side of the overhead light looking at the lenses. Tracy smacked his lips and focused harder. Damn I hate this class! This was his worst subject and it was the one he most. "Give me a few mo' seconds to look. This really don't look like nothin' Wait! I see some movement. "He finally said."

Mr. Fruiten moved closer, talking to the rest of the class, who was in attendance. "class bacteria are a living cell. Matter of fact, it's any of single-celled microorganisms including some that cause disease and others that are valued especially for their chemical effects as fermentation. "He pushed his glasses up against his face and touched Tracy's shoulder. Once he had his attention, Mr. Fruiten continued with his lecture. "You see ladies and gentlemen, the life in bacteria can be formed by simple allowing milk to spoil. The chemical reaction begins the process. "He nodded calmly as he finished his speech. "Are there any questions? "Mr. Fruiten was now standing at the chalkboard looking at several hands raised. Ignoring them, he called on Tracy. "So, what did you see Mr. McDavis?"

He rubbed his chin thinking. This was a habit he'd developed from his brother. His reply was direct and on point. "I saw somethin' that was alive but dyin' because there was nothin' to help the survival process. "Mr. Fruiten nodded his agreement. The first period bell rang and the students in the classroom begin to gather their belongings for exit. "Students. "Mr. Fruiten held up his hand to get their attention. "Exams are in three weeks, so we'll be going over a lot of bioprocess and biological control. So, study, study, study...now you may leave."

Tracy walked into the hallway. His high school status was very well known so students of both genders patted him on his back as they walked pass. He adjusted his backpack on the shoulder of his Jump man shirt. There were two more classes before lunch. Then he would try again to talk to Ja'Zarri. She was still angry about him leaving her to keep his mother company. Tracy laughed as he made his way into his second class, where she would be. No matter the situation, he knew she would get over it. His eyes locked on her and her freshly braided hair. She focused on her purse trying hard to maintain her composer. Tracy took his seat and spoke. "Hey Zarri!" She said nothing. He said nothing more. Oh well! It was time to focus on Governmental History. She'd get over it sooner or later. Hopefully sooner than later.

After three periods of using his thinking powers, it was time to relax his body with some physical exercise. G.T. was nowhere to be found but the reason was understandable. Sometimes school was for everyone. His album was in its finishing stages, so he was spending more time at the studio. Tracy begin to do what he always did. A dunk here, a shot there, a low post moves one way, then back the other way. All this was done to put him in his zone. Nothing was around him, only thing that matter was making the important shot like Kobe Bryant. This is not between you! Jus' me an' the goal! He told his imaginary opponent before taking a hard right, then crossing fell into a fade away jump shot. Bucket!

Every move he did was master to the science. Slowly Tracy walked toward his daily resting spot on the bench. Not seeing his girlfriend sitting there opened his sympathy factor up. He hated when they did this but there was no come-between, when dealing with his brother. His eyes rested on her Apple Bottom jeans complemented by a Baby Phat shirt, tied to the back. Her white and pink Air Max gave her a street but classy look. Something he loved to see. Tracy smiled once he noticed the sly glances, followed by a smirk on her face. He shook his head. She a mess! His thoughts were disturbed by a man's voice. "T-Mac!" The voice shouted. "That's yo' name, right?"

Tracy looked over his shoulder into the eyes of a man about his height and weight. The man was a lot darker then him and wore a goatee. His attire was red windbreaker suit with matching red shoes. Seeing Tracy return to his book bag, the guy spoke again. I'm Shun. I just' transferred here from Crenshaw High in Cali. I here you the star shootin' guard homie? "Tracy looked at the papers in the brown envelope, then nodded his head. Placing them on the bench next to him, he begins speaking. "I am, what does it matta'?" He responded.

Shun laughed as he walked closer. He reached down and grabbed the basketball from between the bench area. "You see" His 6'6 frame moved with agility as he begin dribbling through his legs backwards. "Where I'm from, in order to be the best, you gotta bet the best homie. "Out of nowhere, shun took a step toward the goal and two hand windmills dunked the ball. "So, win ya ready. I'll be waitin' homie. "Then he ran his hand over his braided hair and turned to leave. Tracy stared at the back of the man's shirt. It read: Nothings Impossible. That was a true statement. Anotha' time! He told himself. Tracy grinned as he begins to read the papers his brother gave him. Challenges was something he wouldn't refuse but now was not the time.

"So, what was that all about?" Tracy heard from behind him. Ja'zarri was standing there staring through her Chanel shades. She had moved close enough to hear the conversation. "I hear he was a ballplayer, where he from. His mom moved him down here to Texas to get him away from that gang stuff."
"An' where'd you hear that?"
She giggled. "Girl stuff. We gossip. Besides some of my friends thinks he's cute". Ja'Zarri moved toward the bench to have a seat. She looked over his shoulder once she settled in behind him. "What you ain't mad no mo'? "Tracy asked after he turned the page he was reading over. "Yes an' what you readin'?' Go figure. These are contracts an' stuff my brotha want me to read an' understand. It deals wit' his bidness." Ja'Zarri said nothing for a moment. "boy you kno' I love you right?"
"Yep"

"Jus' wanted you to hear it again. "Tracy placed the papers down and turned to face Ja'Zarri. "I love you too Boo." Then he kissed her gently on the lips. "Now chill out so I can finish some more of these papers…aight?"

Chapter Seven

The importance of power is maintaining your respect and the importance of respect is maintaining enough power to uphold your respect. Whenever one is damaged, the other half suffers.

This thought bounced off every corner of Redman's head, as he sat in the dark of his 450,000 home. He inhaled the smoke, from the gigantic Chemdog weed filled pipe, that covered his whole hand. His eyes were lock on the two set of yellow eyes staring back at him fearlessly. Again, he took a drag from his pipe, then placed both hands on the Mossberg 12 gauge, that lay across his desk. More and more hate elevated inside him, every time his thoughts shifted to the 6-inch scar, that lined the left side of his face. Redman watched the two set of eyes, as intense as they watched him. He rubbed the newly accrued disfigurement to his handsome dark face and gritted his teeth. Slow Murder! Slow Murder! Silently he spoke these words until they formed a bitter taste in his mouth.

For one of the most powerful and respected drug suppliers in the Gulf Coast area just the smallest dent in his armor, could cause business associates to build false assumptions. This was a no-no, so a national warning had to be sent. At this moment, he was only sure about one thing and that was he personally wanted to be a part of Viper's death. Redman stood up, grabbed the Mossberg, and walked toward the two set of eyes watching him. Viper had opened a past demon that would rest at nothing, until this arrogant son of a bitch, was erased from the face of the earth. He stopped in front of the eyes. Hissing and pouring bein to sound, next came deep growls. Viper's face begins to formalize into a pair of the eyes just feet away from him.

"CHU WANT TO FUCK WIT' ME MON! CHU TINK CHU GOT WHUT IT TAKES"! Redman yelled into the darkness, as the eyes roared at the sudden outburst. "WELL CHU FUCK WIT' ME, CHU FUCK WIT DEATH"!

The darkness of the room became bright with the blast of the Mossberg 12 gauge. A pair of eyes flew backwards and made a heavy thumping sound against the wall. The second set became hysterical. Loud roars came while the frighten animal circled around in its cage. Redman said nothing, as he single-handedly held the gauge I his powerful fist. The room came alive when his voice commanded the computer to active, by saying: Lights. His eyes stared at one of his precious black panthers lying, with half its head destroyed. There were no emotions from him. He just looked at the 5,000-cat gone forever.

CHU MOS' DIE!

He finally said after a moment of complete silence.

"Intercom activate!" Redman yelled. Intercom activated. His home system responded. "Get in here now Rasta blood clot! Intercom off!" Minutes later the door behind him opened, after a soft knock. In came a tall thick built man. He stood just inside the door. His dreads pulled back in a ponytail. War scars could be seen from, the many knife fights encountered. This was Redman's leading soldier. Loyalty was unquestionable, when it came to Buju. Redman turned to face the quiet warrior. "I want chu to find out Eva 'ting bout Vipa. He mos' die. "He paused and looked back at the cat, still in a frenzy." An' get someone to clean dis up mon. "Buju nodded. Redman walked out the room holding the smoking Mossberg. There was planning to be done.

Redman came to a stop in his burgundy 2010 Rolls-Royce Phantom drop head coupe, which was sitting on 24-inch Asante rims. He sat at the stop sign adjusting his radio to the CD of his choice. His companion, a Ciara look alike but a thicker form, sat in the passenger seat observing her surroundings. Her one-piece Gucci dress sat high on her golden-brown skin, while her Gucci sunglasses, scanned the area quickly. Mercedes, Charger, BMW! Redman raised up and pulled away heading back toward 635. After placing a few miles between himself and Street Approved Records, he began talking. "Did chu see Eva 'ting Missy?"

Missy nodded. "I see three cars, not four as you mentioned. "She replied. "There is one missing. "Her accent was gone as she spoke but could appear at the blink of an eyes. Missy was from the heart of Kingston, Jamaica but was raised in the states since she was thirteen. Now at 27, she was one of Redman's deadliest weapons. She was smart and deceptive.

Missy Gola was a 5'8 145-pound woman, with a bachelor's degree in Behavior Science. Her current job description was a psychologist for the Dallas Police Department. She could blend in with some of the high-powered people in the city and keep a down to earth appeal about herself when dealing with someone of lesser intelligence. Redman only used her for very important jobs. To him, this was an important job. Nothing could be out of place when dealing with Viper. Redman knew the man was no fool and to play him as one, would be a bad business choice. He didn't welcome bad choices in his life because they were known to end everything a man worked for.

Before Redman continued his conversation, he pushed the button to cruise control and relaxed. "The weakest link iz de guy who drives de guy who drives de Dodge Ram. Hiz name iz Zachary Bell but goes by Chip. "He went quiet for a moment before resuming the conversation. "I need chu to get close to him an' let kno' dere' every move. "Missy examined her French manicured nails, while she listened. This was always easy money. Most men that she approached were easier to control then children. Their body language was always the same. I want to fuck! She spoke softly. "So how much will this information be worth?" Redman switched lanes, heading toward the exit of Skillman. He wasn't ready to leave the North just yet. "It will be worth 50,000. "Missy nodded her agreement.

Redman pulled into an apartment complex to a lot of onlookers. He pointed at a black Dodge Ram on 26's. "Chu need to figure out how chu gonna get close to him. "Dis iz hiz living area so da rest iz on chu my dear. "He rubbed his smooth hand along her soft cheek. Missy rolled her neck in response to his light touch. "can chu handle de job?" Missy smiled at the question, showing her perfect teeth. "Tell me how much time I have an' She giggled. "You'll receive your monies worth." Redman nodded and bagged out the apartments. He drove toward downtown Dallas. "den me precious butterfly," Redman spoke. "We have reservations fo' Dinna... we then have dessert at home. Missy laughed sexually. "If my brother only knew you were fucking his baby sister, he'd have your balls."
Redman joined her laughing. "No, my precious butterfly, you'd be an only child."

They shared a small laugh at his sarcastisness. Missy knew Redman was only being himself because her brother was his supplier and the Kingpin of Kingston Jamaica. Only a fool would try to engage in war with him. Not even the police stood a chance. "It'z been a long time Missy. I've almost forgotten what it felt like. "Missy adjusted her legs. Then this should be more then fun" she teased. "Yes indeed." Redman responded as he caressed her thigh. They'd been secret lovers and business associates ever since she 21 and Redman was 25. "Let'z enjoy de' night." Redman said when he pulled in front of the Reunion Tower.

"Soon as I seen her/ told her I'd pay fo' it/ lil-moma the baddest thing around/ An' she already kno' it/ I pointed at the dunk/An' told her it 'pose to be yours..." (Plies)

Chapter Eight

There was a lot of activity going on at this car wash, off Illinois and Beckley. This Oak Cliff area was known for the hard hitters of the city. Most of the transactions were made here, while nieghberhood smokers hustled by washing cars and running errands, o the many fast-food restaurants along the street. The sun was shining brightly, giving the spot more push then it's standard settling. Women stopped by looking as though it was a Saturday with Maxwell on the stage. All of them had an Oscar award winning act going for themselves. With all the ballers out, it was a must they graced the scene with their presents.

T-Mac leaned up against the wall of one of the carwashes stalls. His tall frame was draped in Polo Black label, from head to toe. He watched the man that was attending to his car. In his hand was a plastic cup with Hennessy and coke. A few of his partners were out. Many of them heard of his possible entry into the NBA, after a year in college. It was a success story that everybody loved to hear, all he had to do was stay healthy. This made several people stop to speak. T-Mac had grown up in this area and kept in contact after moving to North Dallas, which was lower in crime rate.

Now he was waiting for his friend's brother to return. They'd become close after Donte was killed by an undercover officer, he'd tried to rob. "Damn baby my bad. This shit stay ringing" C'zar pointed at his phone. He was a dark-skinned heavy-set dude with diamonds across both pair of teeth. "Gotta' stack my chips so I can win in this poker game, feel me?" C'zar rubbed the pant leg of his Tommy Hilfiger jeans, searching for the Kush filled swisher sweet cigar. He was a dope boy. After he found what he was looking for, C'zar begin talking once more. "Man, that Challenger live! I started to get that bitch but" he laughed. "I wanted that. "His platinum covered hand waved in the direction of a steel gray Mercedes-Benz CL 65 on 22-inch Boyd rims. T-Mac smiled. "That bitch bitin'. You know my bro got this fo' me." C'zar fired up the sweet, while nodding, he supposed to come this way. I holla'd at him earlier. "T-Mac looked at his leather louis Vuitton watch. "I'm watin' now."

He looked around the spot. Even though he wasn't a dope boy, T-Mac understood the many do's and don'ts of this lifestyle. Of all his male friends, he was one of the only ones that didn't have to sell drugs to ride nice and live tight. This was thanks to his brother, a Dallas, Texas icon.
"Where Macfel an' pop at?" T-Mac asked sipping his drink.
"Man, C'zar took another pull from his sweet. "Them niggas might swang thru' but them boys' unpredictable baby. "He coughed. "I can't move on a maybe, ya feel me?" T-Mac nodded as he eyed the man walking toward him. "I'm done yungsta'." The man said while using the end of his shirt to wipe his face. It was hot outside and obvious for the eye to see, that his work had caused a bunch of discomfort. Thinking this way, T-Mac handed the man a $20.00 bill, He excepted it wit' a smile. That made things seem better just that fast. "I 'preciate cha'." Then he walked toward someone else for work. Today was just beginning.

C'zar looked toward freeway 35. Coming their way was a sky-blue dodge Viper. Two people occupied the vehicle, as it crawled through traffic at a moderate pace. "There that nigga is now. "T-Mac watched his brother and G.T. while they pulled in next to C'zar's car, in the back. Both men hopped out and looked around. Viper focused on the Mercedes as G.T. stared at a few women walking by. Viper rubbed his chin smiling. His muscular light brown chest shined, with the sun's rays, reflecting off the VVS diamonds, hanging from his chain. He started talking when T-Mac and C'zar got closer. "I'm feelin' you boy. G.T. you like this?"
G.T shook his head up and down indicating his answer. "It's on point but I'ma Jaguar nigga myself. "Viper looked at G.T., then to C'zar. "this nigga a cornball. Always on some mo' shit C'zar." He chuckled. "that's where we're comin' from at this moment. He wants that trash. "Again, Viper laughed.

Everyone joined in good naturally. T-Mac stood a few feet away from his brother, who was still looking at the car. "Whut you got planned?" T-Mac asked and looked at the Benz over also. It was a show stopper for sure. Still focused on the inside of the vehicle, which was covered with oak woodgrain, he spoke. "Jus' fuck wit' yo bro nigga. C'zar you did that boy. "Viper looked toward him." Yu kno' I'm gone clap back right?" C'zar smiled. "You betta'." He passed the sweet to him. Viper excepted it. "Come fuck wit' me on sum'em. "C'zar asked.

"T-Mac I'll be right back, then we gone. "Viper responded as he begins walking in the direction C'zar had gone." So, what's been up tall ass nigga?" G.T asked. He ran his hand over his braids making sure nothing was out of place. "waiting' on yo' album release party. I'm bumpin yo' shit right now." "That's what's up!" He smiled. G.T. was rocking a Negro League jersey from the Atlanta Black Crackers. "I jus' got my sign in bonus today. I checked out a condo an' a ride. That's where we were. It's 'bout to go down. "His diamonds shined hard as he smiled. T-Mac grinned in return. "I'm feelin ya baby." He continued. "Believe me, I'm feelin' ya... jus as soon as I hit this league, I'm a start wit shots, then pop bottles. "He sang the words to Birdman and Wayne's single.

G.T. laughed at the quote but said nothing. He was watching Viper, who was walking back toward them. Two ladies briefly stopped his stride, then allowed him room to continue his steps. "Bitches a trip Gee!" Viper said with a smirk. "Them hoes straight up told me they wanted to suck my dick... both of'em at da same time. "He laughed harder. "That's how it goes when yo' Gucci flats ain't got a scratch. You want this numba'?" Viper asked in his arrogant tone. Neither one of them expected the hand me-down number to the ground. "That's good. Neva trust a bitch when you could change da way, she lives fo'eva. Now let's ride! I got us somethin' waitin at da Hilton Hotel anyway."

Tracy McDavis pulled into his mother's driveway at 2:30a.m. He leaned his head against the steering wheel of his car. It was six hours before school. A rule he always stood firm to was, no matter how late he stayed out during a school day, be in first period on time. T-Mac exhaled as he drug himself out his ride. Kicking it with his brother, always throw time to another part of the world. If he hadn't snuck out the room, there's no telling what time he'd pulled up. Smiling to himself, T-Mac placed his key in the door and stepped inside the house. Momma should be sleep! He reminded himself. His mind begins to reminisce on the fun he had with G.T. and his brother. There was a set of black twins, a set of Puerto Rican twins, and a set of German twins. How Viper pulled that off, T-Mac was still wondering. So much to drink and smoke with witch ever set of women you wanted. He shook his head at the thought. He did that! "Tracy!!"

T-Mac looked in the direction of the voice, that had brought him back to reality. His mother was sitting in the Livingroom, in the dark. "Tracy!" she called again. "Yes ma'am. "He answered.

"Boy you got too much goin' fo' you to be out in them streets." "I was wit' Vince momma" He protested, like it made a difference. "I'm still goin' to beat the bell tomorrow." T-Mac knew his mother only wanted the best for him and he wanted nothing more than to make her proud. T-Mac also knew his mother understood the bond between him and his brother. "I'm not goin' to lecture you because you've heard these same words befo'." She raised up and walked toward her room. "I jus' wanted to make sure my baby boy got in safe. Now get you some rest so you can handle that hang over. "His mother teased him as she walked by to go sleep herself. "Momma don't worry, I'm gonna' be fine ... not fo' me but fo' us. Then an' only then will everything be good." They hugged, then went their separate ways. He had to get a couple of hours of sleep. His graduation was nearing, and he wanted to make sure he was there.

Chapter Nine

Extreme surveillance had been put into play to keep a tight observation on Zachary "Chip" Bell, their number one prospect. It was a must that every move, dealing with him, be known always. For the last week, 50,000 was given to foot soldiers, in regard to following Chip and Viper. Redman wanted to know their every move. Viper and his street urban style had made things difficult but not so with Chip. His daily routine was logged in like a college campus schedule. All activities were checked and rechecked again. Missy sat diagonal from Street Approved Records in a window seat of Wendy's restaurant, off Forest Lane in North Dallas.

She was impressed by the action she'd witnessed in this short time. Viper had his business priorities together so well, that showed no signs of illegal activities involved. It would be a very hard case to build, without an inside informant. Missy glanced at her watch. It was 12 o'clock. In a few minutes her secret would be leaving to make his rounds and stop at his favorite eating gala. She wanted their encounter to be by coincidence, so it was best to get moving now. Papa John's was about 15 minutes away, but she didn't want her 745 BMW to be seen. Missy scanned the lot one more time before collecting her things. There was another car she'd missed. A new model emerald green colored BMW 535. She admired the smaller BMW. I haven't seen that yet! Missy thought as she strolled toward her car. A must do! She concluded.

Doug and Chip sat in front of Viper's desk counting some of the cash retrieved from one of his many weed houses. The money counting machine was sealing 10 thousand stacks at a time. Chip was working the machine and passing the fund across to Viper. "Doug." Viper said as he stacked the money side by side. "What you think 'bout da BMW baby?"
"That bitch hoggin' but I'm 745. What It cost?"
Viper looked toward Chip. "You hear this nigga?" Chip smiled but said nothing. He knew his boss was about to be himself. BIG MONEY MAN!

Viper continued. "You kno' what they say, if you gotta ask a price then you can't afford it" He begin rolling some of his mind relaxing Kali Mist, inside a strawberry blunt wrap.

Doug laughed. "Shid you can say that but nigga I gotta kno' what I'm payin'." Chip nodded his agreement, as he finished the last stack of bills.

Viper looked at Chip, then his Presidential Rolex. "Doug you full of shit." He picked up the phone and called the front. After several rings, he begins talking. "Kim where G.T. at?"

He listened, then spoke again. "Well when da nigga calls back, tell him to call me. I'm rollin' aight'?"

Viper hung up and resumed his conversation with Doug, his right-hand man.

"Tell me sum'em I need to kno' Douglas." He used his government name for seriousness.

"Well I got 50 mo' foot soldiers on standby, "Doug paused to gather his thoughts.

"An' I received da dough from two of da houses. That's what we got here, 250 stacks. "He pointed toward the desk.

"Getting' ready fo' da close up. We got about 50 pounds left."

"An' I'm on my way to check da other spots "Chip chimed in.

"Aight then, meet back here. Doug come roll wit' me. "Viper rose to his feet and headed toward the door with both men in tow.

They stepped into the parking lot of Street Approved Records. Viper's attention was caught by a pinkish BMW, exiting Wendy's across the street. Had he not recently purchased one himself, this probably would've went unnoticed. That mus' be a bitch in that pink ass car!" Chip when you gone get sum'em else? That truck old news baby. "Viper teased his worker while opening the passenger side door to his new BMW. "Doug drive." Chip opened his door as he responds to the question. "I might hit you up wit' sum'em later this year. This... "He patted the roof of his Dodge Ram. "This boy gone stand up unda pressure. "Chip showed his rose gold bottom teeth with a smile. His dark complexion always tilted the light toward his mouth. Viper waved him off and got inside the vehicle. He started talking to Doug, who begin maneuvering his way into traffic. "Man, I don't like Chip. Why he still here, I can't figure it out to save my life."

Chill Vipa. I told you I got'em."

"You betta nigga!" Viper fired up the strawberry flavored blunt. "Your betta!"

It took Zachary Bell about 30 minutes to ride around and do his daily house checks. He did this with no emotion what so ever. It was always easier to clear his mind when alone. Chip made it his business to always get a little me time. A man finds out who he really is, when he sits in solitude. Even though Papa John's wasn't exactly solitude, it was close enough and the food was great. This was the place of choice when he wanted to collect his thoughts. Chip stepped out and looked around the small shopping area the restaurant sat in. Everything was its normal self. He was casually draped in an Oxford White Dress shirt and black tie, black pants and shades by Shipley & Haloes, which set off his eel skin loafers. Clean wasn't a good enough word to do him justice.

Chip raised his arms over his head to stretch. Today wasn't bad so far but that could change with one phone call from his baby's mother, Keisha was using his daughter's as a weapon against him, in order to force him back into a relationship with her. Through all the drama, it was a short dating world for him. He smiled as he replayed Kanye West words...*You kno' what yo'/you a bitch/you should have a travel agent/ cuz you a trip!*

His attention was grabbed by a light brown complexion woman strutting his direction. Her features were close, if not relentlessly better looking, then the singer Ciara. The walk with importance attached to every stride she took. Her hair was pulled back in a ponytail, exposing her soft neck line and full breast. Every portion of her body was enhanced through the Armani white strapless dress, she wore. Chip watched her as she held a conversation on her cellphone. Their eyes locked and neither of them turned away. As she neared, her phone was folded and placed in the big Coach bag, hanging from her shoulder. Chip was no fool, this woman had class to the highest degree.

Never releasing his glare, she smiled. "You know it's not nice to stare?" Her voice was soothing with a slight accent. Chip continued to look into her olive shaped brown eyes. They were so entrapping. He watched her just a few feet away from him. "Let's try this differently. My name is Missy and do this handsome gentleman have a name?" Chip thought about the question. It wasn't the question that disturbed him but the way to answer it. This wasn't a woman he thought he should give a street handle to. Something as small as that could ruin his chances at containing her attention. "I'm sorry. Your jus' so beautiful. I was lost of words to say. Zachary…Zachary Bell. "He held out his hand to her. She expected it. Missy smiled good heartedly. He was a lot smoother and nice looking then she'd expected. "In that case- Missy said removing her hand from his. "Missy Galo."

"Are you here to meet somebody? Chip asked. Missy shook her head. "No just wanted to eat something different. And you?"

Chip noticed the confidence in her speech. That drew him closer like a magnetic pull. "Not at all. Would you like to join me? Maybe I can turn my boring life into excitement."

"The feelings mutual. "Missy smiled her award-winning smile. Works Every time!

Viper kept glancing at his wall clock, then to Doug, who wisely made no eye contact. He walked back and forward in his office. His steps were soft but held overbearing authority. Everybody he'd learned to trust was present. All except one person. The one who had fail to return phone calls or respond to any texts, sent by Doug. Viper came to a complete stop in front of his number one man. "Whut's up wit' this bitch ass nigga?" He asked arrogantly. "You said he was on you, then I alt to kill you, huh?" Viper pulled his chrome .40 caliber pistol from his holster and held it in his hand. Kim nor G.T. made a move to intervene. They both knew Viper was a dangerous man once rubbed the wrong way. "Where he at Doug? It's past 5 o'clock!" He yelled. "An' he got my money!"

Doug nodded his understanding. He held up his hand, trying to calm the situation a bit. "It won't happen again. Let's see what he has to say. I jus' got a text, sayin he on his way an' he'll explain everything."

It betta be good too! Still angry, Viper holstered his gun and returned to his huge leather recliner, behind his desk. "G.T. what da fuck you went an' bought? That bitch nice." He asked the question with more aggression then intended. He knew G.T. was on his side. G.T. stretched his legs and arms to loosen up before speaking.

"You kno' I like them cats. That's a Jaguar XJ wit' custom 20's in da front an '22's in da back. "He adjusted his jewelry on his wrist. "Da color two toned powdered whit ova raspberry red."

Viper smiled. "What it got inside?"

"The hook up nigga! "G.T. yelled. "Six Kenwood 12's, surround by sound, two 18-inch fold down flat screens, white leather, cherry oak woodgrain. I dropped sixty on da bitch, so I'm on. "His diamonds glistened as he beamed from his brief inventory of his car. Viper nodded his approval. Before he could continue their conversation, a buzz from his intercom sounded. He looked to Doug, who's face showed frustration. "Kim go let this broad nigga in!"

Kim's petite body sashayed out the room and moments later returned with Chip. In his hand was a duffle bag. Viper motioned for her to grab it from him. As soon as she removed the bag, Doug sprung like a hungry wolf. Chip reacted to the sudden movement but was unable to avoid the attack. Doug's blow knocked him to the floor and in the blink of an eye, drew his pistol. I put myself out there fo' you an' you act like this. "His words were filled with emotion. "Nigga this bidness, everything gotta be like clockwork."

Chip held up his hand in protest. "Let me explain Doug!" He knew he had to lie. On his way over, he frantically put together something that would give him a lead way. Chip knew that in no form or fashion, could he indicate, he'd simply lost track of time with a woman, he'd just met. Thinking back to their conversation and how smooth it went, was almost unnatural. It was like everything was a dead lock. He cleared his mind and spoke as though this was the truth. "Man, my baby's momma called an' said my dauhta' sick. I took rere to Parkland an' got caught up. She caught some kind of virus. You kno' how long that take? All the money was safe. Ain't no slick shit man. "Chip rambled.

Doug still angry, soften up a bit with the news, looked toward Viper. He nodded. Then and only then, did Doug replace his weapon. He stepped back, giving Chip some room to return to his feet. "It ain't nothin' like you thinkin' Vipa. "Chip explained once again.

"Man, I'm not heartless but why you ain't answer no texts. "Viper asked, excepting a drink from Kim. She was trying to calm him down.

"I, I, I- '

Viper waved him off. "Save it nigga. Let this be da last fuck up or you gone receive a dishonorable discharge. Only reason you ain't gone now..." He pointed toward Doug. "So, you betta thank him."

Sipping his drink, Viper spoke to Kim. "Now run da numbas back at me because I need to know how everything is connecting again. "Kim was not only the manager of Street Approved Records and secret lover, but she also was his business accountant. Everything that was something, she was involved in. Her actions were strictly legal. Viper liked her because she wasn't naïve to the game and would get her hands dirty when it was necessary.

"Well Vince." She walked behind his desk to stand next to him. "All the records and merchandise sales are collaborating wit' where your trying to go legally'" She continued to give the ends and outs of his process. It was almost time to walk away from the negative side of the game and become straight legit.

"Gee it's all 'bout you baby." Viper smiled. "When yo' shit drop its ova! He said excitingly." G.T. only grinned. This was a dream come true, everything he'd worked for was coming to life and all he had to was enjoy the fruit of his labor.

Chapter Ten

School was nearing an end and Tracy was going through the dilemma of choosing which college he would attend. There was two weeks left until he'd give his mother the smile and excitement, she so dearly anted. Her only wish was to see him graduate. Three universities were waiting on his decision. One of the recruiters, Tracy gave no thought to being a down south patriot, the University of Connecticut was automatically eliminated. Sitting slightly about about OKC, was Rick Barnes from the University of Texas. He'd already flew Tracy out to their campus and gave him a tour of the school's grounds. A full scholarship was offered, and he had to do was seal the deal with an agreement.

At 6'7 230 pounds, Tracy had generated a nice buzz around himself since his freshman year. He was following in LeBron James shoes with having his high school games broadcasted on televisions. Tracy had become more dominate through youth development leagues as the calendars turned. The more he played the better he got. Rick Barnes was excited to have the attention of one of the most anticipated players on the recruit list. The one-year stoppage on the NBA's requirements, made this possible. Tracy was a sure NBA draft. He was a person that could come to a team and lead both mentally and physically. Tracy drove toward Hillcrest High school judging around his decision. University of Texas! He finally said out loud. His thoughts were put on hold when the sound of police sirens grabbed his attention. At a school known for good behavior, the DPD (Dallas Police Department), were escorting two young men and two young women away in handcuffs. This was uncommon. No violence was tolerated, and examples were made of those who did violate.

Tracy shook his head, while making a right, into the school's parking lot. Today was starting off strangely. He found an empty space and killed the ignition to his car. Staring over the school grounds, Tracy had to admit, he was blessed to attend this school. He drove a car that many of the teachers couldn't afford plus had three major colleges sweating over his decision. He wanted for nothing and had the heart of one of tha baddest chicks in the area. Sometimes he had to pinch himself to understand it all was truly happening. He gathered his leather Gucci travel bag, which was stuffed with his books and exited his vehicle. Most of the day would be spent in study hall and that would be used to tighten' up on his weak points for testing. For the seniors, this was their mental preparation stage to generate success, while transitioning to the working society. Tracy strolled towards the cafeteria with the morning sun beaming on him like highlights in a woman hair. Close, but not yet! He coached himself, on his way into the student filled eating area.

Ja'Zarri walked toward T-Mac as he sat on the bleachers tying his shoes. She looked beautiful, a splitting image of Selita Eubanks on the model runway. Her wraparound Chanel Dress hugged her body and displayed every curve visual to man's eye. "I ain't gone ask. "She said, sitting next to him. Tracy laughed and begin doing high knee kicks to warm his body up for his everyday practice. "It's good you finally get da picture. "He spoke between movements. Ja'Zarri rolled her eyes but didn't respond. Again T-Mac laughed. The tempo of his movements begins to speed up. Slowly he transformed into the person his name came from. Several women, hoping to be a mistress of some sort, migrated toward the basketball court. Often his practices generated numerous spectators but today there was more observers than any other time. What's the surprise! T-Mac asked himself.

A few minutes into his shoot around, T-Mac understood why so many people had come to watch him loose himself in his game. Shun the 6'6 guard, that transferred from Cali, was bending his arms back, trying to loosen up. Shit! T-Mac mumbled as he took a shot and missed. He glided toward the ball with four long strides, only to come face to face with his opponent. Both men locked eyes, for what seemed like eons, before words passed.

"Let me get that ball playa? "T-Mac asked. Not bothering to reply, shun started talking.

"I hear you on yo' way out da door so…He grinned. "Pass da torch da right way homie or let me take it." Shun motioned toward the court.

"It's jus' me an' you. "He sung the words to the Tony, Toni, Tone song.

T-Mac started into the dark-skinned man's eyes. He could feel the supernatural energy coming from both, him and this man. Tension was filling the area, as the onlookers held their breath, waiting to see what could transpire. In one motion, T-Mac snatched the ball and walked away. "Get yo' on fire. That's how I got mine. His mood was messed up, so he sat next to Ja'Zarri and begin untying his shoes. Ja'Zarri asked. "What was that about Tee? "T-Mac replied emotionless. "Nothin'. "He looked up at the man standing about eight feet away from him. "I feel like ya overrated T-Mac an' straight up homie, I got 1,000 say ya can't stand unda this. "Shun patted his chest. The low whispers and growls made him more powerful. T-Mac gritted his teeth and spoke. "Yo' money is punk money. Gone keep it because fuckin' wit' me, ya jus' given it away." Again, the crowd edged them on with louder sounds. They wanted this battle to go down.

Shun smiled. His face showed the enjoyment of this small exchange of words, that was being passed between the two. "Is that so?" Shun asked nonchalantly. "Well I got a drop top 64 Impala wit' switches an' Dayton's. Put that Challenger up an' I'll throw in anotha' 20 stacks. Is that enough to say, I'm da truth?" Damn! T-Mac thought. He studied Shun's face and the seriousness was there. The money wasn't the exciting part but the challenge itself, had T-Mac's blood boiling. Raising to his feet, he stepped back toward the court, where his destiny stood. "Tracy!" Ja'Zarri yelled after him. He waved her off and continued walking "How do I kno' you'll pay?"

Shun laughed. "There's mo' to me then meets da eyes. I brought da car an' da title today, if ya game?" T-Mac nodded, shun continued talking. CHOOSE someone to hold da winnin's an' we'll see what happens. Far as you, I kno' ya good. I've done my research well….an' yo' family live."

"Aight because I don't have da title to my ride, this is kinda unexpected, but my word is like gold. You win, it's yours. Warm up an' let's go!" Shun smiled. "Now that's what's up!"

T-Mac waved toward one of his teammates, who'd overheard the arrangements. He reached inside his pockets and pulled his keys free.

"Here hold these, your responsible fo' da winning's. He's gonna hand you sum'em too, aight?"

The man shook his head. When T-Mac turned around, his girlfriend was in his face. "Tracy don't do this. What do you have to prove?" She grabbed his hand tightly.

"You right, there's nothin' to prove but there's sum'em I wanna prove. That's the difference." Ja'Zarri smacked her lips and stared into his eyes. She snatched off her earrings and held them in her hand. "Then let's go win us anotha' car." Her precious smiled appeared.

"That's what I'm talkin' bout. "T-Mac kissed her lips, then headed on the court.

Shun met him in the center of the court, holding his ball. "Same rules as da playground. Call yo' foul, respect da call an' good ball dawg. Jus' because it's money on da line don't mean blood has to shed dawg. That's a deal?"

T-Mac thought for a second. "One mo' thing."

"What's that?"

"Quit callin' me dawg nigga"

Laughing, shun replied. "I'll try. Shoot fo' ball."

"Then it's my ball. "T-Mac pulled up a nailed the shot.

"This all to be interestin'." Shun grabbed the ball and walked to the top of key.

The crowd had thickened. It would be any minute before the school's staff came to investigate the sudden gathering. Even when they came, it would be too late. Nothing but the Jaws of life would be able to separate these two from each other. Everyone stood around watching. Their faces showed the excitement that was now brewing. One man would pull up for a long shot, nailing it, as though it was a free-throw. While the other man would drive to the rack like Kobe Bryant, making score look much easier than it was. Basket for basket, dunk for dunk, both men sweated their hearts out, knowing one mistake could cost them the game. T-Mac held the ball in his hand repeating his saying. (It's not between you! Jus' me an' da goal!) "12 to 13 T-Mac. "Shun said after a few shallow breathes. "You up one an' we goin' to 15." He inhaled some more. "Yo' move!"

Using his left hand to hold the basketball out parallel of the bleachers, he once sat. T-Mac faked that direction and came back right. Taking three quick steps, he raised up, elbows pointing toward the goal and shot. SWOOSH! T-Mac looked at shun, who shook his head in disbelief. "One mo' nigga an' ya dead! "T-Mac yelled. His fist pounded his chest like a drum. Several of T-Mac's friends begin to cheer. The recreation yard grew loud, causing attention to the area. It would be hard to ignore is by anyone's standards. Soon teachers would come looking. Sure enough, Coach Henry came. The students separated to allow him room to step through. He stood there looking. T-Mac and Shun stared each other in the eyes. "What's goin' on here?" Coach Henry sternly asked. His common sense and basic intellect answered the question before anyone else. "What's goin' on here McDavis?" He addressed Tracy by his given name but was met with the same silence. Looking at both men, he realized something deeper was going on and it was going on and it was beyond what the eyes could see. Coach Henry thought better of interfering, being this way something that every man in the world has to learn to battle, pride. The coach stood there and watched like everyone else in the crowd.

"Nigga what I tell you!" T-Mac yelled back. He chest passed the ball.

"Fuck what you stressin' dawg!" Shun retaliated in frustration. He walked right up on T-Mac. "One-point dawg an' you win homie.

Let's go!" He handed the ball over. T-Mac smiled and tried the same move but was met with a different outcome. He went through his legs hard left but Shun reached just as quick, jarring the ball loose. Scooping it up, shun raced toward the goal to tie the game. T-Mac moved to defend the basket just as quickly as Shun had attacked it. Both men took to the air at the same time. It looked like a scene out of the old Kunfu flicks. The sight left everyone present with their mouths gapped. Silent stares erupted into cheers as T-Mac penned the ball to the back bored.

Then like a spring, bounced back up and slammed it through, for a 15 to 13 finish. The yard went wild again. T-Mac never heard a sound, he was too busy yelling and screaming the words of Muhammad Ali. "Ima bad man… I'm da greatest…I told you, can't nobody stop me! "Ja'Zarri rushed to his side holding the keys and title to the car he'd just won. "You did it baby!" She laughed and hugged him tightly. T-Mac focused on Shun, who was now sitting on the steps near the school building. His head was in his hands. The bell rung causing a disturbance in the crowd of students. People move toward the building. A few people showed their condolence, with pat and slaps across the back as they passed. T-Mac pulled himself together. His point had been proven and his mark would forever be stamped between these walls. He kissed Ja'Zarri and grabbed the keys plus title from her hand. "Stay here aight!" she nodded. Shun looked up briefly when he saw T-Mac approaching. He was in no mood for small talk. His anger was to the max. It had taken him months on months to hustle for that Impala and just like that, it was gone. Nothing in life was guaranteed except death and today that fact had stayed true. "Yo' Shun!" T-Mac called out.

"What's up dawg?" Shun responded without looking up. Tracy laughed at the comment.

"Hey hommie, you still on that shit?" He rubbed his chin, wiping away the dried sweat. "Sometimes you find what ya lookin' fo'. If you did yo' homework like you said, then you'd kno' I don't need yo' ride or money. "T-Mac stared at Shun, the anger wasn't gone but he was a bit calmer. T-Mac picked up where he'd left off. "I play to get my family away. My brotha want it this way. He sacrificed himself, so I'd have this chance nigga, you feel me? Ain't nothin' weak 'bout me. I eat, sleep, an' shit this game. "T-Mac handed him his keys, title, and money back." All I want is yo' friendship. "He extended his hand.

Shun looked at him before taking a tight grip of his hand. "If that's all you want, then you'll always have a friend in me."

"That's good to kno'. T-Mac said. He left the man standing there. His girlfriend greeted him with a hug once he returned to her. "You good baby?"

"Yea, I couldn't be betta. Makin' a new friend always has its benefits." He smiled. "It's time to go eat. You ready boo?"

Ja'Zarri held his hand tightly. They walked toward the parking lot. Her answer was in every step she took.

"Niggas try me, but they come up short/ I feed off blood cuz I was raised wit' sharks/ I'm suckafree/ neva let ya eat off me/ respect da game that I learned/ cuz I was raised by g's... "Street Approved, off G. T's album was playing in Tracy's head as he left the crime scene. Somebody call 911 cuz I'm bad! He laughed.

Chapter Eleven

Viper sat behind the wheel, of his Chameleon painted 600 Mercedes-Benz, drumming his fingers impatiently. His mood was darkening by the second. For the last couple of weeks, it seemed as though he'd viewed several cars behind him. Viper looked through his rearview mirror investigating the cars behind him. Nothing so far looked out of place, but it was hard to search the faces located in the driver's side because of the hard rain coming down. The hot humid weather was strongly bringing spring in. Looking back forwards, he lightly pressed his foot on the gas acknowledging the fact, the traffic light was green. His mind was working overtime. Everything he'd placed into motion was starting to show some real growth. Secrets! Secrets! Secrets! He told himself.

He was no fool by far and by being this, a lot of years were saved on his still young life. Viper moved his right hand in the direction of his companion. Softly he caressed his side. His .40 caliber was snuggly in its hostler, under his arm. If anyone would keep quiet in stressed situations, it was this cool piece of steel. He knew trouble was brewing and the chief was a Jamaican asshole. Why Redman hadn't reacted yet was a mystery. Viper touch the bottom to his iPod. Racing through the first three CD's he came to a stop on his latest purchase. He hit volume and waited. Sade's gentle voice captivated the speakers and begin calming his unsettled nerves. Her classic sounded just as good as the first day it surfaced. "Smooth Operator" He lost himself in the song and continued driving down Ledbetter road, heading toward Duncanville, a suburb outside of Dallas, Texas. There was some real estate that needed to be checked upon before placing any investments into them.

I kno' I ain't Trippen'! Viper glanced in his rearview mirror again. A Ford Taurus was a couple of cars back and the same dark-skinned chick was behind the wheel. He studied the woman carefully, not fearing her witnessing him because he sat behind five percent tent. Viper shrugged his shoulders. Yes, this was the people and the car he'd seen days before. She was good at her tailing assigning but not good enough to fool him. "Redman!" he said out loud. "If this how you wanna' play, then I guess I'll let you kno' I'm not da ordinary nigga." At the next traffic light, Viper made a right and drove into a wooded area. It had houses spaced out along the way, but nobody lived in the vacant homes. Keeping his eyes locked on the vehicle, he made a quick U-turn and removed his best friend.

Viper eased on his brakes. He was cruising toward his victim. It was like a wildlife scene in the making. No matter what sex or breed, nothing or nobody, could be taken for granted. In order to be in this line of work, it was safe to say they had blood on their hands. The Ford Taurus turned the corner and surprise was written all over the woman's face. Her look of disbelief sat openly, at the royal blue Mercedes, driving her way. This mistake could become deadly. Viper smiled at the sudden shock the lady was going through. Glancing at the houses sitting remotely by their selves, on the corner, Viper snatched his steering wheel to the left causing a head on collision. She had no time to react, as the big 600 smashed into her car with the force of a canon. Her head flew backwards from the impact closing off the light in her view.

With the speed of a cheetah, Viper discharged fifteen shots out his window and into the driver's side of her windshield. Not caring if she was dead or not, he broke loose the frame of his car and sped away, Viper pulled his cellphone out and pressed (1) for speed dial. Shortly after a few rings, a soft voice answered. "What's up Vipa?" "Report da Benz stolen an' come get me, I'll be walkin' down Ledbetter. Hurry up, I gotta get out this area A-SAP. I'll explain mo' lata'"

Kim replied. "I'm on my way now. "Then the line died out. Viper did likewise. Kim was his first choice because she wasn't that far away and would look less suspicious running a couple of red lights. Looking around to make sure no one could see him, he took the butt of his gun and broke the two front windows and repeated the process with the back. Then he started walking. The insurance company would pay for the damages. There would probably be an investigation but that was the least of his worries. No gun, no crime! "Who this islander think I am?" He laughed at his own question. "Betta come harda!" He calmly walks in the rain.

Hours later, Viper sat in Kim's Livingroom rapidly speaking in the receiver of the phone. "Doug I'm tellin' ya, this nigga playin' me to mu'fuckin' close!" He pulled smoke from the cigarillo between his fingers, before continuing his conversation. "Where that nigga Chip at?" Doug paused for a moment. "Truthfully Vipa, I don't even kno'. He came by an' dropped some money off, then left." More silence. "Sum'um 'bout some bitch he was goin' to meet."

"How long ago was that?"

"Shidd that was earlier. Why what's up?" Doug questioned.

Viper rubbed his chin trying to gather his thoughts. Why wasn't following his intuition about Chip was beyond his understanding. Something about his characteristic's didn't fit. It was making him feel feeble minded. "no reason homeboy. Get a hold of that nigga an' both of ya'll fall ova Kim's house. I got some stuff to go ova."

Laughing slightly, Doug responded. "You still ain't told me what's up on that incident."

Viper looked toward Kim, who was sitting legs folded, in the couch, applying nail polish to her toes. He blew air from his lips. She looked so exotic with her silk booty shorts and matching sleeping shirt. The shirt sat right above her waistline. Her hair still wet, gave off a strikingly mysterious look about her, that made him come toward the table. There his glass of Hennessey rested. "Doug I kno' you got mo' sense than that, right?" Viper asked. "If not, nigga slap yo' self-cause I can't."

Doug took the verbal assault good naturally. He'd messed up. It would be a stupid move to discuss anything incriminating over the phone. "Yea." Doug said. "I should cause I slipped on my game."

Viper's attention was grabbed again by Kim pulling her hair over her shoulders. She was trying hard not to stare at his well tone body. Smiling at her discreetness, he ended his call. "Doug bring G.T. also aight'"

"That's what's up. Anything else?" Doug asked.

"Naw I'll be waitin'. Call when you on yo' way. "Viper placed the receiver in it cage and looked at Kim.

Feeling his eyes, she looked his direction. "Why you looking at me like that boy?" Kim slightly blushed and squirmed like a small child waiting for a second, "you sittin' there like this an' you askin me that."

"First this is my house," Kim smiled. "Second, you the one had me in the rain. I was like this before you called. She giggled.

"Well come here!" Viper order.

She shook her head and pointed toward his Calvin Klein boxer briefs, which was poking out because of his excitement. He smiled. "that's what's botherin' me shidd. "Viper exclaimed.

"Well your little friend is going to have to relax." Kim got up displaying more curves, then her small frame was supposed to contain. "It's that woman time in my life. Something you don't like."

Damn! Viper grumbled to himself and leaned back caressing his hard on. No matter how horny he was, there was no way he was going near any bloody pussy. It was a principle of the matter. "I guess I'll take a nap cause I need to get some of this energy off me".

"Well it seems like you are getting' soft in your demands."

Viper frowned. "What?"

"I still can relax you." Kim licked her lips and moved toward where he was sitting. She bent to her knees in front of him and begin kissing along his penis print. "Let's see if I can't give you some pleasure an' a nap before the fellows come." Her small hand removed his erect dick and placed it in her mouth, where her hot tongue begins the process.

Their understanding of one another was something that needed no explanation. They both knew that, if the choice of a life time companion had to be chosen, then they would stand hand and hand. At this point, the word's, "If it ain't broke, don't fix it" stood solid as a fortress wall. Kim was one of Viper's most loyal friends, lover, and business partner. Plus, she enjoyed her position. What more could a man ask for. Everyone sat around Kim's Livingroom amongst her fluffy bluish-gray cushion furniture. The curtains from her front window was pulled back, showing the misty early morning. A number of cars sat in and around her driveway, given' off the feeling of a car show. Stealing the show was a raspberry red, two tone powder white Jaguar. Next to it was a peach 745 BMW, giving the dimming sun something to smile for. The glow of these two cars alone, made the black Dodge Ram look more appealing.

Studying the middle class nieghberhood, Viper stood there wearing a white purple label Polo unit. Everything was ice cream down to his suede white Polo boots. He spoke, not bothering to look back. "I'm ready to close eva'thing down by next week. Da money is all comin' in as supposed to so... I need to start focusing all my attention on G.T." Pausing, he turned to face the room. "Now if anyone of you want those spots, go fo' it. I'll have nothin' to do wit'em tho' period." Viper stared at each individual in the room. His eyes rested on Kim. She wore a tight-fitting Baby Phat shirt, tight fitting Apple Bottom jeans, and no shoes.

"Kim tell me exactly what da schedule brings in da weeks to come. My brother's graduation is comin' in two weeks an' I want concerts set up from here to ATL" Kim nodded her understanding and begin shuffling through the stack of papers in front of her. Clearing her throat, by taking a sip of water, she started. "First promotions are in place as we speak. We have a couple of shows in Texas to kick things off. One in Houston, then another in San Antonio. From there we headed to Atlanta and if the games good on to the West Coast."

Kim paused to let everyone grab ahold of all the traveling coming in the near future. When she was sure all was stable, she added. "there will be a lot of traveling but the luxury Benz bus will make it a bit more comfortable." Kim pressed her lips together, giving her cherry lip gloss a wetter shine. She scanned her notes while gathering her thoughts. "As for the money coming in... Let's just say, we're on our way to some big things.

"Finish her sentence, Kim locked eyes with Viper. She tilted her head towards him. It was his stage now.

Viper stood before them rubbing his chin. G.T. you ready?"

G.T. smirked at the statement. "What kinda question is that?"

"It's a real question nigga?"

"Man." G.T begin. "I'm 100% real nigga put me in any spot, I come back drop." The other occupants of the room laughed. G.T continued. "If I don't give my all, then I ain't ready but I do see that baby."

Viper smiled. "The world waitin' an' you da Messiah. My bro' gone come wit' us on da road afta school done. You kno' he decided to fade U.T., huh?"

G.T. shook his head. "Naw I didn't but I'll be sure to get at him to show some love fo' big homie." Viper agreed. "Chip what's up wit' your daddy? Fo' da last week or so, you've been in a hurry to leave us. You kno' I had somebody tail you right?" he lied.

Chip's eyes showed his surprise. "It's nothing to hide Vipa." He was caution with his speaking. "I jus' got a chick name Missy that I'm feelin' is all. I'm tryna make sure I put it down, ya dig?" Pausing, he rubbed his hands together nervously. Viper smiled for the thousandth time. Doug sat quietly, observing the whole play. This nigga gone get us killed! Doug exhale hard from his frustration. On the third sound of his name, Doug came back to reality. Viper was talking to him. "Damn nigga give me da run on da cash an' get yo' mind right. You are acting fraud. I need ya like fish need water." Doug nodded but continued to think his own thoughts. His world was spending at this moment. I should have excluded this nigga, cause all this fall back on me! With those thoughts tap dancing on his brain, he begins to go over the information regarding the last 20 pounds of O.G Kush.

Chapter Twelve

After tonight's session, all the pieces would be together. Every move that Viper had planned would be in the palm of her hand. The game of kiss and tell was one of the deadliest flaws to human kind. People often wanted others to know how well they had it, rather it be sex or financially, they cap to talk about it. Missy smiled to herself as she stood at the foot of the bed. She'd convinced Chip to meet her again tonight but to his surprise, it was for casual sex. Her curvy figure pressed against the fabric of the purple Victoria's Secret lingerie, she wore. Missy stared at her prisoner. He was handcuffed and blindfolded to the bed. Submission sex was her expertise.

R. Kelly's voice sang over the bedroom system in his condo. *"There's something yo' eyes baby/tellin' me you want me girl/Tonight is yo' night/See you don't have to ask fo' nothin'/I'll give you everything you need/So girl don't be shy"* Honey Love covered the short husk breathes being taken by Chip. He was in a trance by all the touching and teasing. His heart raced, faster by the second, trying to anticipate her next move. She was good at this cat and mouse game. Chip inhaled slowly in his darken state of mind and continued to listen to R. Kelly sing." *......I got all the answers girl/to the questions in yo' head/An' I'm gonna be right there fo' you/ Give me that Honey Love."*

"Zachary ….do chu hear me Zachary?" Missy broke through the sound of the music with her, now visual, Jamaican accent.

Her body gleamed, from the reflection of the moon, shining through the open window curtains. Missy's full breast, small waist, and thick ass demanded attention. "Relax Zachary." She continued in her sexiest tone. "I promise not to hurt chu." It was hard to refute the fact that she loved to watch men, especially. Handsome men squirm under her control. Missy licked the bottom of his foot, making him jump from the tingling sensation of her touch. She softly kissed the inside of his leg, while crawling toward his erect penis. Her hair hung over her face giving her an Egyptian look about herself. Making her already exotic features stand out even more.

Missy sucked around his hip bone causing Chip to pull against the chains of his handcuffs "Missy take this blindfold off. Ahhh can't take it any mo'…I Ahh…have to see you!" Chip struggled to regain control of himself. "shhh! "Missy's voice was soft but stern. "I promise chu will neva forget tis night Zachary." She used her tongue to lick around his chest nipples. Her free hand messaged the tip of his dick head. She rotated her rhythm up and down, while moving her lips toward his lower stomach. Slowly she lifted her body over his penis and placed him inside her wet vagina. Both moaned from the act. Missy relaxed and placed both palms on his chest, positioning herself so he could suck her breast. Kissing his bottom lip again, she whispered her words. "Iz it nice Zachary? Iz it what chu wanted sweet Zachary?"

Missy contracted her pussywalls against Chip's penis, pulling tightly, she raised her ass cheeks to the top of his dick. She moved in a quick and easy rhythm, her juices leaving a shine along his eight-inch staff. "Ohhhh!" Missy moaned. "Chu so deep in me Zachary." Her eyes were shut, and she was in a different world, as she rode him harder and harder. Her walls tightened and loosen with every motion. The sweet smell of sex in the air. Nothing smelled better to Chip. He nibbled on her soft nipples causing her to gasp at the sudden pain. With Missy's body covered in a coat of perspiration, she raised up in the sitting position and begin rubbing her breast, build up the orgasm. "Cum wit' me Zachary!" She yelled "I'm cummin' Zachary…Oh' god cum wit' me!" Her accent was heavy, filled with her lustful state of mind.

Not being able to withstand the sound in her voice any longer, Chip's condom wrapped dick exploded at the same time Missy's pussy walls did. His voice was loud like hers. He pulled the cuffs and squeezed his toes. It hurt him with pleasure so much he screamed. "Stop! Please stop!"
Missy eased her movements. She was in full control. She slowly kissed him. This was her show and she was in full control. "Did you enjoy Zachary?" Missy unstraddled him and removed his condom.

"Yes, I did "He responded in a raspy voice. Missy untied the blindfold for the first time tonight. She looked in chip's misty eyes. He was a baby all over again. Next, she unlocked the handcuffs. "relax while I go get a soapy towel and clean us up. We'll talk some and... "She paused. "Maybe more. "Missy left the room toward the bathroom to dispose the condom and retrieve a warm towel. Laying with her head in Chip's breast plate, she twirled her legs inside of his. Missy caressed his ab's and talked. "What do you do to maintain this comfortable living you have?" Now there was no sign of her native tongue. It came and went when she desired. Chip ponder on how he should answer the question. He knew from their previous engagements that she was a psychologist, that worked for the Dallas Police Department. Thoughts of the FED's crept in his mind but were pushed away after their continuous dates. Like so many men, he let his guards down and allowed his feelings to get involved. "Well" he licked his lips nervously. Sensing his uneasiness, Missy spoke to calm the setting. "No need to be afraid. I'm only asking because I'd like to know what I'm getting into. That's if we travel down the relationship road. "Quietness filled the room. It was what he needed to get his mind right.

Chip looked out into the darkness outlined by the room. He liked this beautiful woman next to him and understood her need to know. Arranging his thoughts, he decided to come clean, hoping she accepted him for who he was. "First Missy, I'm only tellin'you this because I want us to continue to build on what we've started. "chip looked at her. Missy nodded. He spoke again. "There's nothin' permanent 'bout what I do. Nothin' last fo' eva so I'm builden' fo' an' exit. The dude I work fo' moves a lot of exotic an' high demand weed. Kush, Kali Mist, an' so forth?"
Missy smiled her answer but said nothing. She knew how the mind worked so she gave just enough to keep him talking. Seeing her head movement, Chip picked up his unfinished statement. "We're plannin' to close down afta' Monday, two weeks from now. Everyone's transitioning' to the legal life."

Missy raised up on her elbow and looked into his dark face. Her interest was sparked by his last statement. This might help! She thought. "Why Monday Zachary?"

Chip brushed the back of his hand along the side of her cheek line. (She's so gorgeous an' smart!) The words floated through his brain. "My boss brotha' graduate that day so everything gotta be done. It's going to be smooth. His artist Gangsta Tee is blowin' up da underground scenes. So, he on high demand. We'll be on tour fo' two months afta' that. "He looked at her reflection coming from the moonlight. He knew this was a woman he could be with for a long time, maybe his whole life. Missy's mind fast-forwarded. If Redman was going to strike, it would have to be now or that day. Viper would be in a relax state of mind. It was time to complete this meeting and get to Redman. Buju would have to step up his surveillance. She begins to kiss and lick his pubic area. Instantly his sex organ came alive. Sliding her tongue slowly down the side of his dick, she mentally thanked him. She continued the process, then took his whole penis into her mouth, not faze by the girth of him. Missy swallowed and returned to the top, "It's time for some more." She replied as her lips returned to its assigned oral job. (Thank you, Zachary)

The next day Missy Galo walked into the well-furnished Plano home, wearing a pink Prada coat and pants suit. Her freshly done Shirley temple curls, hung slightly over her face. Hiding the expression, she wore. She was here for business and nothing more. Missy studied the room as her Gucci open-toed high heels, pressed softly along the carpet. Briefly she thought about Chip. In such a short time, she admitted, that he was a fun and enjoyable person to spend time with. She eliminated the thought, heading toward Redman, who sat at the front of the diamond shaped table. He was smoking from a gigantic bung; it was filled with Island Sweet Skunk. Some of his favorite marijuana from the Vancouver Island. His hand stroked the skin of the eight feet long boa constrictor, that twirled around his body. Redman watched missy 5'8 model frame like stride, march his way. Her walk demands the attention of every man present in the room and that she received. Buju and two soldiers stood when she approached the table. She motioned for them to stay seated, but they ignored the request and stood statue form. It was more of a defense tactic, rather than respect, that's usually gave to women. Redman digested the smoke through his lungs and blew the waste in her direction. "Missy chu don't sit or whut?" He asked. This was early Saturday and a work day for her. "I can't stay long so please quit smoking until I leave, I have information that's wore its weight in gold. "Missy scratched the top of her head, waiting for him to do as she'd asked. Redman obliged, and she spoke.

"As I've said, I can't stay long. I must be in the office this morning." She glanced at her platinum watch. "If you're going to make a move. It must be soon. As soon as next Monday because he will beef up his security. His brother graduates that day and Viper is serious about going legit. All of his houses." She smiled mischievously. "Excuse me, you call them traps… they're being given away or closed down. He'll leave the city to go on tour with his artist. They will be gone at least two months. She paused letting them comprehend her words. "So, in my opinion, you should stack up your men and make a move soon. A suggestion, on his brother's graduation day. When happy the average person forgets to watch their surroundings. "Again, Missy glanced at her watch." I'd like to catch the bank before it gets too crowded. "She stared into his eyes…No smile.

Missy pushed her emotions out of her mind. What she was doing was strictly business, nothing personal. She understood that in another world and under different circumstances, Chip would be someone she could spend more time with. At this point, he was only a check. "Are chu sur 'bout tis bidness Missy?" I won't pay fo' info'mation dat'z wrong. Redman rubbed his scar on his face. He was disappointed that her schedule was preventing them from having some play time. Something he was much interested in. Missy exhale frustratingly.

"I have no time for games Richard an' I will not repeat a word of what I've said. I need my money, so I can leave, or I'll let my brother know about chu behavior. I'm sure he'd like our little secret." Her accent was chopping in and out do to her anger. Madness was taking over her state. Redman only smiled at the threat. He rose to his feet. The yellowish-green snake became erect causing a gasp from Missy. He laughed at her expense. "Don't be e'fraid Missy. Chu a'wayz have me fo' chu' po'tection...." Redman handed her a money bag filled with crisp bills. "Eva 'tings dere ... Count it on chu own time ...leave!" He commanded, with no response, she turned and exited the house. Redman watched her leave and then turned to face his head warrior, who was adding fire to the bung sitting on the table. "I wunt chu to have Vipa's eva move. Where he shits an' whuteva time it'z done. Chu an' chu men do dis personally."

Buju crossed his legs and smoked. He wanted his ears to do the talking. Redman added. "Vipa has fucked wit' de w'ong mu'fucka. Whoeva wit' him will go to hell an' open de door fo' me when I come. "His laugh sounded like pure evil." Gud girl Missy... gud girl." He massaged the tip of his snake head. Dallas, Texas was about to change forever, and he would be the cause of it.

"Mista mista Scarface went walkin' down da block/out jumps some fiends an' steals all his rocks/ Pulls out a gun an' shoots down all da fiends/An' mista mista Scarface went up da block again. Scarface.

Chapter Thirteen

It was Monday evening, Viper stood next to his BMW 535i, talking to his protégé, Gangsta Tee. Both men looked around the middle-class neighborhood, while conversating. "Ya sho' ya don't want me to roll wit' you an' momma?" G.T. asked Viper. He spoke of the CEO's mother as if it was his. "cause straight up it ain't shit. "He adjusted the Street Approved logo on his chain so that it lay flat over his wife beater. The San Diego Padres jersey he wore was open showing his customized blue crocodile belt along the ends of his yellow leather shorts. He wore no socks with his Air Max. The color matched that of his unit. G.T. rubbed a hand over his freshly done corn rolls. Viper placed his hand on his chin, something he did so often. Giving himself an opportunity to think. G.T. was like family but this was a night his mother needed to express herself. She'd waited all these years to see this and now it was about to happen, it was better to her be free of wonders and worries.

"Naw Homie." Viper looked at his watch, then back towards G.T. "Gone an' do you." We'll hook up afta' I drop momma off. We gonna hit da highway tomorrow so you need to have it on yo' mind' ya dig?"

G.T. agreed with a head gesture. "I'll hit da nigga up on text an' let him kno' I'm wit' him through ya'll… you sure though?"

Reaching his hand out, Viper answered. "Yeah I'm sure. Fuck wit' me lata." They shook and released each other's hand.

G.T. bagged out the driveway as Viper watched. He tossed the deuce in the air at the moving car, then entered his mother's house. That you Vince?" His mom asked from the back room.

Viper laughed softly. "You expectin' somebody else?" He responded.

"You an' yo' mouth." She complained. "I'm almos' ready an' I ain't gonna let you spoil my moment. "You jus' like yo' daddy." His mother yelled.

"I ain't an' stop sayin' that too!" Viper hated the comparison to a man he never knew. "An' hurry up, you gonna make us late. We gotta get goin' if you wanna stop by da mall an' get that stuff fo' Mac." It was his turn to blow off some steam her way. "I don't understand why you ain't already have it. "Women! At that moment his mother poked her head around the corner and rolled her eyes at Viper. He laughed. "Come on momma, fo'real!"

Buju sat across the street with two of his dread haired soldiers. The blinds were slightly closed so he could watch but not be seen. His two men were in the back-sprinkling gasoline on the floor of the house's basement. Inside the deep freezer was the owners of this resident. Buju and his team had invaded the older couple and killed them seven days prior. Now they were setting the stage to extinguish any evidence of their existence. He watched the Jaguar pull out and leave the nieghberhood. Buju dial a number into his phone. It was time to disappear before the family of the deceased came looking. He cared nothing about the death of these people, but they weren't his focus.

"Yes!'
The voice on the other end replied. Buju turned away from the window when Viper entered the front door.

"He's drivin' de emerald green BMW as chu said. I'll contact chu when we wit' him. "The line went dead and Buju replaced his phone. He looked at the two men walking his way. They held plastic containers. "It'z ready Buju. Now we wait." Buju leaned back against the chair he occupied. This was just the beginning.

Tracy McDavis walked around the auditorium holding hands with his girlfriend. They were stopping and talking to the other students set to graduate today. Both, him and her, made their rounds, then sat next to Ja'Zarri's parents. Tracy was acting like a child all over again, he kept glancing toward the door, looking for any sigh of his mother and brother. The sidekick he carried vibrated and Tracy pulled it loose immediately. It read: We're on our way! U kno' how momma is! Congratulations Bro! Broadly he smiled. The message was a good feeling. Ja'Zarri noticed his expression start to shine and rubbed his thigh. Her kiss came next. "Boy you know; they wouldn't miss this for the world. Relax, we've done the hard part." Then a second kiss came.

Minutes later his phone vibrated again. "What up nigga! I'm proud of you! G.T." Tracy smile and silently said thank you for some reason his stomach wouldn't stop dancing and that was making him uncomfortable. He excused himself to go outside. Right now, he needed some fresh air. Tracy stepped through the swing doors and looked out at the stars. His intuition was giving him a bad vibe. Placing his hands behind his head, he closed his eyes and took a deep breath. "God please guide me right!" Tracy turned and headed inside.

"Momma I told you to hurry up. Now we gone be late!" Viper was talking to his mother as they drove towards Foley's on the other side of North Dallas. His eyes kept scanning his rearview, making sure no one was following him. So far, he hadn't notice anyone.
"Vince, we're goin' to be late an' that's good..." She shook her head. "I don't want to hear all that borin' stuff no way. I jus' want to see my bey walk across the stage." His mother paused. "Something you should've done."
"Momma don't start." Viper said flatly. "I am what, I am"
"You what you wanna be. An' slow down."
Viper looked at his watch. They were going to be a little behind schedule, which wasn't all that bad. Exiting the freeway, Viper slow down a notch."
"Thank god"
His mother replied. Viper shook his head. Foley's was in sight. The lights were about a half a mile away. "An' don't take all day either." Viper protested before they got there. Ms. McDavis flicked her tongue out at her son playfully. Both started laughing. Today was special indeed.

Buju was riding solo in his brown Ford F-150. He made sure to keep a good distance, understanding the Viper's street sense. Redman had notified him that one of his smartest trackers was dead. There was no way he'd allow that to happen to him or his men. "I'm followin' him as we speak. Where chu?" Buju smiled.
"Ok" Buju said "I think he's head chu way. Are Chu ready?" He listened some more before closing his phone. His two men were making sure to stay as far behind him as possible. They drove separate cars and carried assault rifles. Both complete with hundred round drums. Buju retrieved his Mac-11 and chambered a bullet. Redman was five minutes away from the mall.

Redman came to a stop at the rear of the mall. Cautiously he looked over the parking lot, before getting out the 86'Mustang, he'd drove, 75 was alive as always and that made the noise level that much higher. This would be just right for someone with a speeding fetish. No police or security guards were visual. Redman walked into the stores entrance, his 9mm Smith & Wesson in his waistband. The navy blue Rockawear shirt concealed the gun perfectly. His jeans were loose, and his Air Jordan's were tied tight just for this occasion…running. Redman walked slow around the store replaying his plan in his head. He planned to kill both together in his car. He browsed around in the men's department, trying not to be seen. There was no telling who would enter this store. There were only two entrances to the store. The one he'd entered and the front parking area. The assault would have to be quick to enable him a chance to escape. Redman looked at his watch, 8:30pm. He looked up at the sound of the bell. A large smile crested his lips. An attractive older woman, wearing a sundress, a white belt, and white heels, hurried in his direction.

Viper studied the parking lot. Nothing seemed out of place, not even the Ford F-150 that pulled in a few spaces down from him. Three more cars did the same. The small Nissan's door opened, drawing his attention to a cute Hispanic woman getting out. He reached for the half-smoked cigarillo in his ash tray and added some fire to it. He closed his eyes and let the exotic plant mellow him out. With his eyes still closed, he unbuttoned his purple Versace shirt, giving him easier access to his pistol. His mother didn't like the smell of weed so this was the time to get to cloud nine before she returned.

When Viper opened his eyes, his heart sank and almost skipped a beat at what he saw. Instinctively he removed his gun and opened the door to his BMW. His mind begins to calculate a plan that would save his terrified mother from the hands of the enemy. Redman's arm was protectively around his mother's neck making a shot at him difficult. Viper took two steps toward his target but was sidetracked by the human silhouettes in his peripheral vision. A couple of men approached from the far side of the parking lot. They were armed with assault rifles. Fuck! He screamed to himself. Not giving his mind a chance to think, he moved in the direction of the small Nissan. Shock replaced the confusion in Viper's head, when a third man exited the ford F-150. He never thought to pay attention to the truck. The tented windows making it seem safer than it was. Seeing the long hair made him unconsciously think the driver was a female.

Viper's fake retreat served its purpose, causing the two men to raise their weapons and give chase. He spun around, falling to one knee, and fired a series of shots. The first attacker fell as both slugs slammed into the center of his chest. People started running when they heard the shots. Some froze in their shoes, not knowing how to respond to the chaos going on. Suddenly they seem to understand that if their feet stayed there so would their life. Buju opened his Mac-11, sending Viper diving to the ground by his car. War was in full gear and survival was at its highest peak.

Viper rose from behind the BMW at the same time his mother's head exploded "NOOOO!" He screamed at the horrific scene playing in slow motion in his enter-mind. His mother's body flew forward, then hit the ground hard. Redman's smile showed pure satisfaction. Viper replayed the scene repeatedly, within the few seconds it took place. "NOOOO!" His voice yelled another time. He took aim and fired nonstop. "I'ma kill, youuu mu'fu" The words were cut short by the piercing pain that sliced through the bottom of his side. Viper hit the ground, eliminating the feeling. In one quick motion, he ejected the clip and slammed another in its spot.

The Jamaican man with the AK-47 opened fire once more. The shots hit Viper in the leg and arm. He was balled up behind the car with his gun several feet away. Viper's breathing begins to shorten, when the car shook from impact of more gun fire. Viper closed his eyes and thought for the hundredth time, in the last minutes, about what happened to his mother. The thought was beating at him with every breath he took. No way could they live after that. Opening his eyes, he dove for his gun and focused on the man holding the assault rifle. He shot, the man fell. Viper turned but felt a blow that clouded his vision. The kick was so powerful, it knocked loose his gun. Then a stomp came, taking away this wind that filled his lungs. Buju kicked the gun out of reach. Another form appeared next to the big Jamaican. Redman pointed his gun and looked into Viper eyes for a long time, before speaking in broken English. "Chu neva fuck wit' me egin. Now go visit chu mutta...whereva she iz. "Viper never heard the sound from the gun.

G.T. rushed to get dressed. The news was rolling across the T.V screen and the reporter talked about a triple homicide, in far North Dallas. He listened slightly. After witnessing the emerald green BMW with bullet holes, he already knew what happened.... Witnesses say three men emerged with weapons and started firing. A dark man held the woman..." He never heard the rest. His feet were rushing to the door. Twenty minutes later, he stopped in front of hillcrest high school and ran full speed into the auditorium. G.T. scanned the faces looking his way until T-Mac left the stage jogging his way. "What's up giant?" The man asked anxiously.

G.T. locked hands with the taller man. "I have some fucked up news fo' you but I can't tell you here." Let's go!" G.T. commanded. They exited the school and headed to T*Mac's house.

Chapter Fourteen

Tracy sat in the dark of his mother's home, thinking about the tragedy that happened yesterday. On his graduation day, the most important day of his life, he'd lost not only his mother but his father figure, Vince McDavis. The pain was transparent with every tear traveling down his face. Tracy couldn't understand why God had cursed him, after all the good he'd done. Taking the only people, he cared about was gone and he wanted now to reunite with them. Grabbing the bottle of Grey Goose by the neck, Tracy took a deep swallow and placed it down on the table. He was a hard drinker, but this was the only thing keeping him from acting stupid. Someone murder his family and there was no trace. The police didn't have a clue where they'd went. Bullshit! He raged.

G. T's explanation of the confrontation that transpired was mind blowing. Tracy knew the man he talked about, was the same man his brother had hits with the bottle at G.T.'s release party. Everything came together like a puzzle. The man's name was Redman. He was mad about his brother trying to cut his illegal contract and go legit. Stupid! Tracy admitted. The phone rang but he made no effort to answer it. Hearing his mother's voice brought more tears to his eyes. She seemed without a worry in the world.

"Tracy if your there, please pick up the phone. "It was Ja'Zarri. This was her tenth time calling. Now wasn't the time, "Baby I love you and I want to be there with you. Please pick up...I have your diploma. "She begins to cry, then the line disconnected.

Tracy's understood what she wanted, and he loved her for caring, but this was a time he needed to gather himself. He was eighteen with a whole life ahead of him and now there was problems to sort out. The

thought of walking away without answers just didn't sit right with him. He knew this life could corrupt a person of his caliber. He reached for the Grey Goose once again and took it to the head. He was drunk off the liquor but didn't care. This was his counseling. The voice of his mother sounded again. Tracy's attention was drawn like a magnet when the woman begins to talk.

"Tracy this Kim… I called you at your brother's house, but I didn't get an answer there… So, I'm trying you at your mom's. I know it's hard because it's hard for me too… He'll never know I'm pregnant." She shortly cried over the phone for a short time.

"Sorry…Vince told me you have a blueprint of everything. We'll discuss that later though. You're a smart man and I know you can handle yourself but I'm here if you need help…" Kim gathered herself, then finished her statement…" wit' the burial arrangements."

Tracy was standing at the answering machine, he needed someone that understood, he could talk to. Hurrily he grabbed the receiver. "Kim you still there!" Tracy yelled harder than intended. The liquor clouding his thinking. He was a child in so many ways. "Kim" He asked again.

"I'm here Tracy." Sniffles could be heard through the phone. "Are you alright? Do you want me to come over? It's no problem…I promise." It took him a minute to gather himself. "Kim…don't kno'…what to do…How to handle this. I need to bury my family, well you help me?"

"Sit down and relax. Give me 30 minutes and I'll go over everything when I get there." Kim took a deep breath. It was time for her to be strong. The person she so deeply loved was dead and his brother needed help. "We'll make it through this."

"Thank you." Tracy hung up, then him and his bottle reunited.

Tracy was awaken by banging, followed with screams and shouts. A male voice yelled "T-Mac! T-Mac! Open up!" A women's voice hollered the same thing. Both people took turns. Finally, he rose to his feet and walked toward the door. The banging begins as he walked.

"Hold on!" Tracy yelled. "I'm coming!" His head was pounding. It felt like a gorilla was using his skull for a bass drum. Opening the door, Tracy stood to the side and allowed time to enter. Kim, Doug, and G.T. frowned at the foul smell of liquor in the air. This was too much for him to tackle by his lonesome.

"You aight fam?" G.T. asked. He stood still searching for a light switch.

"I guess as good as I can be. "T-Mac watched Kim and Doug open up windows. The house wasn't dirty, but they chose to clean up anyway. Kim grabbed the empty Grey Goose bottle from the floor and carried it to the trash can in the kitchen.

Doug sat down in the loveseat and waited. He was loyal to Viper. Helping his dead friend was at the top of the chart. There was a lot to be done so T-Mac would have to choose his path immediately. Kim returned to the den and lowered her small frame down next to T-Mac. "Tracy you have a lot on your plate." Kim stared at him. "More than you really know." She looked over him as he rubbed his chin. He was so much like his brother. His smallest movements reminded her of Viper. Kim shook her head and massaged her temple. She spoke. "We're here to help you in any way possible. These... "Kim motioned with her hand." ...are his true friends. After the funeral, you have to focus on the business part of this life. Either you sell this operation or there's work to be done."

Tracy said nothing. Kim was going to be his silent leader. Nothing in his mind was saying sell what his brother sacrificed his life for. He knew it would be hard to give up his dream, in order to save his brother's. There could be no mistakes. Bagging out was not an option. That's why he needed help. "My brotha talked nicely of you Kim. "Tracy looked at her beautiful face. She was a smaller painting of Maliah. "He trusted you wit' his life." Tracy watched the bright beam shine on her face. He pushed forward to scared to stop talking. "Doug, I don't kno' you but if my brotha trusted you, then I do too."

Doug nodded but stayed quiet. Tracy took a deep breath. "G.T" I need you. Are you in?"

"I'm in like a baby in a pregnant hoe. "G.T. said flatly "You can guess da time, don't guess on me."

Tracy forced a smile. "My family was murdered an' I want da son of a bitch that did it. I don't kno' a lot but I will avenge my family wit' or without ya'll. People I don't kno', I don't want around me. I'm goin' to get those I'm comfortable wit'. That's it! Kim tell me about G.T.'s concert dates."

Kim paused only a brief second, then told him what she was planning to tell him anyway. "They've already been postponed...two weeks or we'll breach our contracts."

Tracy frowned. "Two weeks." He repeated. "Well we need to bury my family because I have a lot to learn in that time."

Kim watched Tracy. Already he was showing what bloodline he was from. Within the last hour, so many of Viper's traits were revealing themselves. This would be easier than she thought." T-Mac was already setting the stage to his management style.

Doug grinned. "I think I'm goin' to like you younsta... yeah I think so."

"Yeah it's going to be easy for you to adjust." Kim gave him a motherly smile.

"Your brother had some major stuff cookin'. I'm sure you've heard about some of it."

Tracy rubbed his chin for the thousandth time. His head was hurting from the constant drinking. "You're his legal assistant huh Kim?" She agreed, and Tracy moved on. "We'll I need to make sure all that matters are dealt wit' correctly. I'm goin' to get rid of one of these houses an'…where's my brothas Benz?"

"It's in da shop getting repaired." Doug said. "He had an accident wit one of Redman's goons. You weren't told 'bout it cause yo' brotha didn't want you worrying 'bout what was goin' on wit' him."

Tracy licked his lips. His body felt dehydrated from so much drinking. He walked to the kitchen and retrieved a glass of water. Tracy started talking as soon as he entered the room again. "Tell me what you kno' 'bout this nigga Redman." He locked eyes with Doug.

Doug shifted his weight in the loveseat, trying to get comfortable. He then started speaking. The matter was touchy, but it had to be spoke on. Swallowing a sip of water his words flowed. "Redman is a major figure in da underground exotic weed trade. He had some of da best killa comin' out of Jamaica. Which not to mention, is where I think he ran too." Doug reached in his pocket and removed a pack of blueberry blunt wraps and a half of ounce of Kali Mist. "Do you mine?" Doug asked.

Tracy shook his head disgustedly. "Come on nigga. Is this some of da weed here?

"Is this what my family died behind?"

"Not exactly. Vipa liked this to smoke personally…but he sold O.G. Kush." Doug quickly rolled a blunt, lit it and place it in rotation. The first person to grab it was Tracy. "Go on!" Tracy commanded.

Doug nodded. "This islander was mad that yo brotha didn't need him no mo'. Yo' brotha was to big fo' him an' that was fuckin' wit him. You undastand yo' brotha was on some major paper. He was Redman's top buyer." Doug continued to tell Tracy about he could never fully understand in one day. Tracy was a student in school and his ears was wide open. He knew he had to pay close attention. This choice could change his life forever. He cared nothing about himself at this moment. All he wanted was to find the person who'd killed his family.

"One mo' question Doug." Tracy looked at the room. These were the people in his corner as of right now. He prayed these individuals would give him the same loyalty, they gave his brother. "how did they get that close to my brotha an' he didn't see them?"

Doug rubbed his eyes, then inhaled smoke from the blunt. "I really don't kno' but we'll find out." Doug looked at the man's face. There was something there he had missed, and it was the look of revenge. Doug held his breath. This was going to be serious.

"G.T. that's a promise. T-Mac that's a promise. Kim that's a promise. Whatever it takes. I'm wit' you." Tracy allowed a tear to fall. That would be his last.

Chapter Fifteen

Missy Gola looked at the papers scattered across her desk. She was disgusted with herself, for the lack of focused she was giving while at work. Her frustration was evident in everything she did. The more she tried to concentrate, the more the pain bubbled in her head. News station all around the city was targeting the murders that took place, only three days ago. Every channel was flashing a picture of Buju and Redman, in in hopes of finding out which area they were hiding. Using her index fingers, Missy massaged both sides of her forehead. The migraines were starting to appear at odd times. Times she'd rather loose herself in work. On the front cover of the Dallas Morning News were briefings about the owner of Street Approved Records, Vince McDavis. It talked about the success as a music CEO and the dominate style the underground label had brought to the scene.

She exhaled, when her mind replayed the number of Samantha, his mother. The media showed the graphic scene numerous of times, drilling the assassination into the heads of anyone, who watched. Missy knew what kind of work she was into but never had she helped Redman get close to anyone outside of their lifestyle for good reasons. Samantha McDavis was a committed YMCA youth assistant, that had more friends than anyone she could think of. This wasn't sitting right with Missy. She slammed her fist on the desk angerly and stood up. Every time she turned on the television, it was a program directed toward the murders. Missy stood and looked out her window, sitting over downtown Dallas and thought. One of the most dangerous men of the states was still lurking....and she knew where he was.

Police had no trace of his whereabouts. Missy turned and walked back to her seat. Redman was using the strength of her brother to hide in the hills of Kingston, Jamaica. No officer from coast to coast dared go into this challenge, for fear of an all-out massacre. They lived and died by their own savage rules. Some of the most heartless men of that island and others, choose to call these, highlands, their home. She picked up the phone and dialed. While waiting, her mind tossed around some of the stories floating concerning Viper. He was set to become major after the release of his artist G.T. album. The survivor of the family was an eighteen-year-old, with several colleges breathing down his neck. They were trying to persuade him to join what they said was the right program.

"Hello." A male voice answered. Missy smiled as she heard the smooth baritone sound. It was nice to hear from him again. "Zachary!" How are you?" She forced excitement in her voice.

"I'm fine. I've been tryna reach you, but our schedule hasn't been able to coincide wit' each other. "Chip paused for what seemed like hours. "You have seen the news, right?"

Missy gasped slightly. This wasn't the way she wanted the conversation to go.

"Yes…was that your boss?' She already knew the answer to the question.

"Yeah an' even tho' he was hell to deal wit', I hate it happened." Chip was silent before speaking again. "Can we meet Missy? I'd like to see you."

Missy wasn't sure why she'd called. She knew their short-lived relationship couldn't go further than where it was but for some reason, she couldn't bring herself to say no. "When would you like to meet?"

Chip laughed. "as soon as possible. How does tonight sound?"

"That sounds fine." Missy needed to see him one last time. One question she wanted to ask. It was beating at her head. "How's Viper's brother doing in this…" She thought carefully about how to finish the sentence. "hardship?"

"T-Mac aight, he got a hell of a team in his corna. Everything his brotha' done, is still movin' on track. Afta da funeral, he gonna jump behind da wheel of da label an' take off."

"Well." Missy responded.

"So what time can I pick you up?"

"9 o'clock fine?" she asked

"9 o'clock it is." Chip hung up leaving Missy in deep thought.

Chip and Missy sat quiet, gathering their thoughts. Both tried to concentrate on anything besides each other. For some reason this dinner was very uncomfortable to them. It had been several weeks' sense either of them seen one another.

Missy looked out the window of Reunion Tower. Its slow rotation moved showing downtown Dallas from different direction of the restaurant. She grabbed her glasses of wine, sipped, and then spoke. "So, what's been keeping you from me Zach?"

Chip looked at her. She had such an exotic glow about herself and the way her voice seemed to sing his name. He like her so much. Chip adjusted his shirt, so he could relax in his chair, before he answered the question. "I told you our last meetin', which by da way was somethin' to rememba. Missy blushed. Chip smiled. He continued. "I had to close down some of da spots we had. I decided to keep one for some extra money...An' what's yo' excuse beautiful?"

Missy rolled her neck, moving her hair to the left side of her face. The move reminded Chip of a swimsuit picture shoot. The only thing that was missing was cameras and flashes. The right side of her neck exposed a small rose lining her ear. She raised her head up letting her hair fall along her back before answering. She knew men were easily distracted by women's feminine gestures. "Well." Her smile brightened. "A few of my cases were at the ending stages. I had no time to slow down but I'll admit...I should've called. Again, she smiled. Her eyes took in every movement he made. His tension was easing up. (This isn't hard at all!) She told herself. "Now that we're here, let's enjoy."

A white male waiter approached their table. "Would you like to order now?" He asked politely.

"Yes." Chip answered. "What would you like Missy?"

She glanced over the menu quickly. "I'd like the roasted crab and shrimp, with lemon and buttering flavor...a Ceaser salad with ranch dressing."

"Will that be all, or would you like some dessert? Our lemon and cherry cheesecake are spectacular! "The waiter said with emotion attached to the statement. Missy bit her lip, then touched the tip of her French manicured nails to teeth.

"I'll see what the rest of the night brings. What will you have Zachary?"

"Bring me da baby back ribs wit' a baked potato wit' da works. An' yes bring two slices of your spectacular cheesecake." He said teasingly.

The man smiled in return to the joke. "Is that all sir?"

"Yes an' thank you." When the waiter was safely away from the table, Chip resumed their conversation." How about that guy?"

Missy giggled. "This is his job Zachary and you should toy around wit' him like that." She giggled some more, then added. "Even though it was funny seeing his face go from pale to red in a matter of seconds."

They continued the small talk. She now understood why she excepted this date. He was the key to her being able to keep a close eye on Viper's brother, the young infamous boy, that was going to try and fill his brother's shoes. It was the most she stayed in reach of the boy. Plus, there was no reason to end this friendship with benefits. Chip was fun to be around and since Redman's disappearance, there was no harm to be done.

Chapter Sixteen

A young boy stood at the front of the alter singing. His voice guided family and friends through the church doors like musical angels. Both son and mother were being put to rest. Pastor Williams of the Church of Christ was the presiding preacher. *"This song dedicated to my homies in that gangsta lean/why'd you have to go so soon/it seems like yesterday we were hanging/ 'round the hood/now I'm gonna keep your memories alive/like a homie should..."* For the first time, the church was excepting R&B to be sung in between their walls. The boy's small voice was captivating. It took so much of the sadness out the day and allowed the beautiful purplish tulips to distract people from the horrible moment at hand. Tracy leaned his tall frame down and whispered in Kim's ear. "That was my brother's favorite song. He always liked to relax to it. Said it helped him rememba who he lost."

Kim squeezed his hand but released no words. She didn't trust her voice now.

The both of them had put every thought that came to mind into the funeral arrangements. The marble black and silver caskets sat side by side, opened. Water filled eyes smiled even more as they walked toward the front to view the passing people. Tracy shook hands with several people given' their regards. Today he was being the man both parents had made of him. He wore a white tuxedo with a black tie. It gave his lean structure a professional look. *"God my God/could you pass on this message foe me/tell'em put down the dice for a second Lord/and listen to his homie/would you tell him I'll neva let go of his memories/his son will know /you don't have to cry no more/cause God got his back..."* The young boy sung until Pastor Williams approached the pew. Everyone focused his way. Tracy along with his crew members sat next to each other, while Kim and Tracy's family sat just behind them.

"Sometimes the lord brings us togetha fo' different reasons.

He begins. "Sometimes it's something as tragic as sayin' good bye to someone you love. "Pastor Williams paused. "Yes, it's hard to say good bye but it's easier when you kno' where their goin'" He looked over the crowd before resuming. "But the good book says he does things fo' a reason. What reason is good enough to take a loved one away. "His voice rose. "Maybe it's to help you find yo' way back home because we've all sinned and came short of the glory of god." Hands begin to clap, and heads started to nod. His electrifying speech was showing people the way. It was touching the souls of everyone present. Even the woman at the back standing out of sight. Her golden-brown complexion couldn't be seen from where she stood. She exited before the service ended. Pastor Williams words was traveling behind her as though they were trying to contain her. "So, smile because these two precious angels have gone home."

After the final piece of dirt was placed on top of the two caskets, Tracy left. He sat in his brother's office staring at the gold containers in front of him. They held dirt from grave sites. These were his reminders. Tracy drummed his fingers on top of the desk. He hated the confusion going on in his life. In a blink of an eye everything that meant anything, was takin. Feeling his emotions raising, he inhaled air. Pastor Williams is right! Tracy rose, grabbed a container, and walked toward the one-way mirror. Everyone was loyal friends to his brother was still here. They busied themselves around the label. He notices Chip stayed firm to his word, saying his good-byes and leaving. Tracy ponder over that thought briefly. If he was disconnected that much, then he didn't need to be here.
Yeah! Chip must go! He concluded.

Next week was a very busy week. All was riding on G.T. and his album. No need to be sued for breach of contract. That was one more problem he didn't need with the present ones. Turning from the glasses, Tracy went back to his seat behind the desk. He placed the container, down and open the desk drawer to retrieve some business files. The files were arranged by Kim for his approval. Grabbing the files, his eyes locked on the butt of a gun." What's this!" Tracy moved the weapon, so he could see it better. It had a specialized hostler with his brother's name engraved in it. Viper...The Venomous Snake is what it read. He sat the files down and placed the pistol next to them on the top of the desk. It was a seventeen shot .40 caliber semi-automatic gun. Tracy studied the weapon for a second. He recalled seeing his brother show casing it on many occasions. Cautiously he removed his jacket, adjusted the straps to the holster, and placed it on. His brother's presents controlled the air in the room. Viper was strongly here in spirit, body, and strength. Nothing would stop him from avenging what happened to his family. That was something Tracy knew and that was fact. "Married 'til Death!

Kim knocked on the door and entered without waiting on a response. She gasped at what she saw. "T-Mac there's ..." Her words trailed off. Tracy looked up and frowned. "What's up Kim?" Her eyes were locked on him. He looked so much like his brother Viper, it was hard to believe it wasn't. Everything about Viper appeared to be in this man. "I, I, I," She fell silent once more. Kim pushed the door closed and stepped forward. Watching her, Tracy leaned back and rubbed his chin. Kim said nothing as she reached for the phone. With the receiver to her ear, she spoke. "Doug tell that guy to wait and come here for a second." She listened. "No, No, tell him to keep working. "Kim replaced the receiver and waited.

A few minutes later, Doug walked inside the room, giving the same look of puzzlement at Kim. Tracy laughed. "Why y'all lookin' like that?" He'd forgotten about the holster, holding the weapon, that was around his shoulders. When no one answered, he asked. "Well?" Doug grinned. "You look comfortable wit' that. "He pointed a finger toward him.

"Yo brotha loved that holster. It's ostrich skin. He had two of them."
"Yeah, you look so much like Viper, it's scary. "Kim chimed in. "And the guy out front wants to see you. He says he knows you."

Tracy nodded. "Well no need to be surprised, this is me an' I'm goin' to find da mu'fucka that killed my family. "He sat back in his chair and let his long frame stretch out. "An' while I. I mean we do.... we're gonna take ova this rap game at full speed. Tracy looked at them. "Are y'all wit' it? "He put his fist out, they touched it.
Doug said. "Til da end lil-bro!"
Kim smiled. "Yeah til the end. "Tracy removed his hand and rubbed his eyes. (I won't let you down!) His words were directed to his brother. "Now who is this guy? He rose to his feet and placed his hands in his pockets. Then he put the jacket on to conceal the gun. "By da way Doug, I don't want Chip aroun' here aight'?" Doug laughed. Tracy left the room. Doug looked at Kim. "He's so much like his brotha an' he doesn't even kno' it. He'll do just fine wit' this job ahead of him."
Kim said nothing but quietly she could do nothing, except agree.

Shun stood there wearing a Nike sports shirt, guess shorts, and a pair of 92' Jordan shoes. He watched as T-Mac strolled towards him, accompanied by a smaller man. "Shun what' sup baby? You good or what?" He stuck out his hand to the man. "This G.T. da heart of da label. "Both men exchanged fist pounds. T-Mac continued. "What brings you this way?"
"What it's a crime to spend some money at this spot?" Shun joked. "Really." He pushed on. "I wanted to show my condolence about your family. You know' it's been all on da news, feel me?" Shun looked around before continuing his statement. "I told you, if you need me, I'm here fo' ya. I don't kno' a lot but I kno' da streets an' from experience out there, there da same, no matter da state. "He stuffed his hands in his pockets to take his mind off his nervousness. G.T. looked toward T-mac. "I don't kno' bout you but I'm feelin' him." T-Mac agreed and G.T. resumed talking. "Is this one you hooped against?" T-Mac grinned. "Yeah he tried me an' found out its nothing happenin'"
'o' you still on that shit." Shun smiled. I still want action back nigga."
"Anytime baby but as of now, I'm gonna hire you. An' fill you in on what's bout to go down. That way if you wanna step back, then you can do so an' there's no hard feelin's. "T-Mac said.

Shun gave a small grunt. "I'm in, I hate what happened to yo' family an' whateva is whateva." He slowly raised his shirt to reveal his Dessert Eagle 44. "This ain't new to me Mac." G.T. looked at Doug and Kim, who was approaching them, before speaking. "He ready T-Mac say you in, then welcome aboard."

"Doug, Kim. "T-mac said." This Shun. He part of da family now. So, let's get him caught up on shit."

G.T. rocked his head back and forward to the beat in his headphones. He was building himself up by waving his hand from side to side. It was recording time, so his mind was locked on delivering his words hard as possible. *"I'm block bleedin'/mos' niggas they ain't eatin'/ my hustle strong/catch me broke, I get my muscle on/Death I'm facin'/but money, cars, an' hoes is what I'm chasin'/erasin'.... any sucka that's in my way/ 16 wit' one in da head is how I stay huh"* T-Mac was memorized at his new acquired artist. He'd never seen firsthand what G.T. was like in the booth. Everything was said with the emotions of someone who'd seen and heard it all. At a young age, the streets had raised him. Doug, also the labels hired producer, tapped buttons and adjustments with the sound trying to come up with the perfect beat. The whole room was bobbing to the sound. G.T. made love to the microphone in front of him, like a naked woman in his bed. In his mind this was a crowd full of people that he had to move, or it was over. T-Mac had to admit, he was overtaken by the sight of the man in the booth. He was like a real fan, instead of the CEO. This was going to be fun. *"Niggas die fo' they earns/bitches ain't born faithful, that's some shit that's learned/stay in da dirt like grub worm/snatch da hair out yo' head, wit' this heat like a bad perm/ugh yeah, you live an' ya learn/cause that's what makes da world turn! NIGGAS!"*

G.T. wiped the sweat from his forehead with his towel. The finishing touch was done to his last song called Live and Learn. Taking the headset off, he headed to the main recording area. "What ya'll think?"

Doug spoke first. "You killed that bitch boy. Give me some!" They bumped fist. G.T. looked at T-Mac standing against the wall. "You like it baby?"

"Nigga that's a crazy question. You ready. "T-Mac fired up the cigarillo filled with Kali Mist, took drags, and passed it to G.T." We gone hurt 'em wit' that one"

Shun was all smiles at the vibe happening. "Ya'll get down?" He removed a small zip lock bag filled wit' pills. They all were different colors and different symbols were on the front of each. T-Mac study them for a second before asking. "What's those?"

Doug answered. "Those my dear friend is what you call ecstasy. An' hand me a triple stack blue dolphin."

"They live?" T-Mac asked.

Shun shook his head. "Man, I see why you beat me. You square as hell."

Everyone started laughing. T-Mac reached his hand out. "Well break my virginity?" He laughed. "I'm havin' what Doug's havin'."

His family was hours in the ground and he was making a transformation into what his brother had shield him from. This life was like quicksand. Any man with no sense of direction was bound to fail. Hurt was still in his heart but in order to drive this ship, all feelings had to be pushed to the side. Any weak link would be swallowed up and destroyed completely. T-Mac knew he needed these people. They were his foundation. The rest of his family wouldn't be loyal to his decision. All of them would say let it go and focus on his life. That was nice, but it wasn't something he was willing to do. At this point, he needed people to support his choice and not question it. These people felt as he did.

T-Mac smiled. Tomorrow he would get his brother's Mercedes out the shop. That would be his personal car from here on. His mind calculated all the things had inherited. It was more than enough to settle down with. "What's up on da night?"

He asked.

"Whateva wit'me? G.T. said.

"Me too. "Shun added.

"I'm in youngsta's an' I got da perfect place. "Doug smile. "It's da Dallas Gentlemen off Northwest Highway. "Everyone knew about the strip clubs in North Dallas. "An bring a lot of ones an' fives cause we gone pop bottles an' make it rain"

T*Mac looked himself over. "Yeah, I need to have some fun an' get my wig blew back. We meet up in an hour, that'll give all of us some time to get ready. I'm out. Make sure ya'll ready to cause I'm 'bout to explode in da game."

Chapter Seventeen

Deep in the rocky, dirty, and shrubbed terrain of Jamaica, where the jaguars and wild dogs howled toward the full moon, sat chaos. Where the clear blue water reflected its Caribbean beauty, giving the island a sense of diversion. In this highland sat Redman. He squatted with his back against a tall tree and looked out over the ocean. His gigantic weed pipe filled the warm air with a grapefruit and cinnamon smell. NYC Diesel was his choice of relaxing medication. This beautiful but dangerous setting was what he called home for now. It was far from where he'd just lived but the most important part was, he still possessed his freedom. Redman allowed the warm 75-degree temperature to relax his mind while he focused on his plans for the future.

He took a hard pull from his pipe, then released the smoke in the air. His smooth face now wore a beard and his once well-maintained ball fade, was several inches in length. He was disgusted with the raggedy clothes on his muscular body. Standing up, placing his sandals on his feet, Redman quickly moved down the base of the trees, making sure to stay in hiding. Not because he was worried about being captured. That was unknown in these highlands. He did this because it was better to move like he lived, and this was a long way from what made him comfortable. The only electrical appliance at hand was his cellphone. He used it often in order to keep in contact with the states.

After the murders, Redman was forced to flee faster than wanted, leaving behind a lot of valuables. Most of his things were in different names and most of his money was in off-shore accounts so the worry of losing anything wasn't in his mind. The only person outside himself that knew, was Missy Galo. Stopping close to a small village, Redman took another drag from his pipe and thought back to the killings. His mind replayed every move Viper made and the look on the woman's face. The fear could be smelled through her pores. If only he'd had more time, things may have been even funnier. He laughed, *Dat would've been icing on de cake!* Redman thought. *To fuck Vipa's mutta!* To this, his smile largened.

A piece of twig broke causing him to spend around and draw his weapon. Slowly, Redman scanned the dark wooded valley. "It iz I Redmon, me an' Buju have been followin'chu." The voice yelled into the air. "Redmon put chu gun up!" It was an order. Redman knew the voice well but under the circumstances refused to follow the instructions. Seeing no one was scaring him. "Show chu self an' I'll put me gun eway." He screamed back into the night. The voice laughed good heartedly and stepped from the woods about 20 feet away. Behind him and over to the side, stood several dreadheaded weather face men, all armed with AR-15 assault rifles. "Put chu gun eway now!" Kim ordered. He was the kingpin of this Kingston city. "It'z nice to have chu back. I received ey call from me sesta. I kno' de deal... let us talk." Now seeing his superior's face, Redman obeyed.

Kimdiki wore his long dreads pulled to the back in a ponytail. They were neatly kept. His clothes resembled that of a terrorist. He was more than the kingpin of Kingston, Jamaica. Everything about him showed power. "Chu been here an' no contact me." He waved his finger disapprovingly. "Tisk, Tisk.... chu like shit."

"I kno', I was tryna get me mind right befo' callin' chu." Redman relit his pipe. "Chu was quite out dere." He motioned with a waving hand. "I see chu still seasoned."

Kimdiki laughed. "The wild iz me life. Come now we must talk." Redman started toward the village he called home but was stopped short by a call. "No, I have ey yacht out to sea. We take de small motorboats out." He turned and walked into the darkness with his men close behind. Buju, a loyal soldier to Redman, allowed his boss to catch up, before resuming his steps. "He had a beam on chu fo' sometime." Buju informed Redman. "I also had no chance. "He laughed. "He knows dez parts. "Redman thought about it but said nothing. This was a very dangerous man and rubbed the wrong way could mean death. They walked across the sandy ground and entered the watercrafts. Tonight, would be very interesting.

Kimdiki's home sat on a cliff overlooking the ocean front. His castle put your mind in the times of the 1500's. Large concrete walls lined the outer house. The large manually opened gates were opened and closed by two armed guards. A small docking area sat behind the house, allowing entrance from the Caribbean Sea. His grass was well managed, giving the white ten feet wide road, an extreme glow over the land front. Redman looked out the upstairs guestroom window. He dried his naked body and smelled the saltwater coming through the balcony from the ocean waves.

Redman watched a few dolphins swimming by a small boat playing chicken to pass they're time. He stepped from the Balcony wiping his face. Throwing on a Tropical colored button-down shirt, some thin docker shorts, and a pair of tan sandals, Redman walked to the kitchen where Kimdiki, was already present. When he entered, the kingpin was present. In front of him was many sliced fruits. Strawberries, cantaloupe, cherries, kiwi, bananas, and many more specialties were covered in whip cream and nuts. The other half of the table had honey roasted turkey sausage, scrambled eggs, thick biscuits, and white gray. Kimdiki looked at Redman and smiled. He waved him toward the table, where he sat. "Today iz ey special day fo' us Redman. We have a lot to talk about. I need to kno' everything dat has happened wit chu. Chu had been ey frien' to me family ewhile an' I'll neva turn me back on chu..." he paused as Redman sat on the left side of his at the table. Kimdiki added. "Unless chu endanga me family but I have faith dat chu no do dat."
Redman nodded in agreement.
"In dat case chu will be welcomed at me palace as long as chu need. Kimdiki pointed toward the table. "Eat an' drink de best of what I have. Dere's no rush to talk but we mus' kno' what chu are into."
Redman noticed for the first time that nobody but two of them were present grabbing a freshly squeezed container of orange juice, he sipped.

Kimdiki curled his lips. "It'z elot to kno' Redman. I see chu eyez but eyez are betta when dey see chu an' chu no see dem." He tapped his head. "Now letz enjoy, dere'z too much to waste." Redman begin filling his plate. He still needed to get a haircut but that would come with time. This would turn out better than he thought. He ate, using this time to think. This man was too powerful to cross. Anything from cocaine to exotic marijuana, Kimdiki had the resources to acquire for you. His inter and outer state connection was high quality. People from the government

were deep in debt to him. These agents kept him informed for many years. This cost him a nice amount, which was no problem to him of course. No one could stay relevant for too long without filling some of the enemy's pockets. Kimdiki understood the theory ages ago. He was a smart man indeed.

Hours later, they sat in heavily cushion patio chairs, looking out over the clear blue water. The morning temperature was already at a high of 83' degrees. It helped to give the island that look, which attracted the many people to this place and made everyone feel comfortable with life. "So chu are in ejam?" Kimdiki begin. He waved the smoke away from his face, after exhaling from the huge weed filled cigar in his hand. "I give chu whuteva chu want an' chu make gud of it. Whut iz de reason fo' dis I have heard ebout? Chu have many tings to lose so…it's confusin' as to whut has happened. But chu'll explain to me." Kimdiki rested against his chair. His shirt was opened exposing a beaded crystal necklace over hi old frame. He was in great shape for a man in his late 50's.

Redman thought carefully before speaking. It was better to get as much of the truth out before he heard elsewhere. "I had ey connection dat was bringin' me elot of money."

Kimdiki nodded to acknowledge the situation.

Redman continued. "He tries to cancel de deal we make an' go legit but no…" He shook his fist. "We mus' continue. He no egree, den he disrespects eva ting dat I stand fo'. Vipa try to complete wit' me power. Dis!" Redman traced the scar along his face with his finger tip. "Iz whut he do." He gritted his teeth. Frustration was cresting the center of his forehead.

Kimdiki look toward him and for the first time passed the cigar in his hand. "Relax me friend. Chu mus' always kno', nothin' in life iz fo' eva…nothin' Chu put ey price on chu head fo' something dat could've been replaced. An' whut ebout his brotha?"

Surprised, Redman looked up. Kimdiki smiled showing slightly perfect teeth Stopping their perfection was a small gap between his top front teeth. "I kno' mo' den chu tink. All last night I hear."

(Yes, chu did!) Redman thought. He spoke. "de boy iz no threat to me mon. He was neva of dis life. Only ey well known school kid."

Kimdiki laughed. He reached for the fruit bowl to grab a purple grape. "Den tell me why he no sell de company he'z brotha controlled?"

(Whut de fuck chu sayin!") I don't undastand Kimdiki."

Again, Kimdiki curled his lips. "De boy iz someone who could come afta chu but if he'z no threat den," he shrugged his shoulders. "It'z nothin' jus' gud to tink ehaed me friend."

"No he'z no threat mon."

"Yes, I hope chu right because ey small spot on ey rug could leave ey dirty stain in de house. "Kimdiki tapped his head. "Alwayz tink chu have not been tinkin' which iz why chu're in dez situation." He reached for another cigar and fired it up. But chu have time to relax now. Enjoy de comfort of me house." His smile tighen. Then Kimdiki raised and left Redman to himself.

Some of the things his mentor said made valuble sense. It had him questioning some of his actions. Maybe something so small had grew into a mountain, pushing him to think irrationally.... but there was more than he had shared. That more into the problem. The boy was of no concern to Redman. There was no way someone of his caliber would impose a threat toward him. Redman was death to the first degree and was afraid of nobody. He laughed to himself as he smoked his cigar. (Little kidz stay in de sandbox!)

Buju entered the area. "Wat'z up wit'... "He tilted his head toward the departing figure.

"Have a seat, "Redman commanded. "Dere'z something to discuss."

Chapter Eighteen

T-Mac sat in his newly acquired 600 Mercedes-Benz, talking on the phone. The hands-free device allowed him to concentrate on the road as he drove. His girlfriend of five years was complaining unstoppable about the lack of time spent with her lately. So far, the conversation was going one-sided. No matter what he said, it seemed to be the wrong words. "Look Zarri! I've been busy. If that's not a good enough answer, then I don't kno' what else to say." He took a breath before continuing. "Yeah I here ya but there's a lot of shit I have to take care of. This happened at a terrible time. "T-Mac pushed the gas pedal as traffic begin to move. He was leaving his house in Oak Cliff. His mother's home, he'd decide to sell. There was to many memories in that house. T-Mac was still in shock at the attention this car was bringing. It surprised him daily at how many people knew his brother. Many women waved at the passing car, even without receiving a reaction. It didn't matter to them if they put their bid in. "As soon as I get things situated, then I'll make time fo' you…. yeah, yeah, I kno'" He switched lanes. "But you gotta undastand what pressures on my shoulders now. "Shaking his head," T-Mac added. "Aight baby, I'll call you later when I'm done. Bye… I love you too."

Reaching up to his ear, T-Mac removed the devices and placed it in his pocket "Women!" He said to his passenger.

"I kno' that's why I don't have one. "Doug grinned. "Get ready to take a left, then a quick right at the first street. "T-Mac drove looking at the flatland. Coming into view was a bunch of barbed wire fencing around a lot of trees. "You neva told me what was important bro." It was nice to be able to call this man brother. In this world someone close was needed. "You see I got women problems." He joked.

"Yeah I see, "Doug pointed. "See that dirt road, follow it until you see a brick house."

"Where we at?"

"We're right outside Oak Cliff. The country parts." Doug leaned forward as the kennel of pit bulls came into sight. The dogs were sectioned off on a pie shape piece of the land. "This my uncle Jeff's farm. It's still Dallas county but deep out so they'll neva come unless we call 'em."

T-Mac braked the car behind a new Chevy pickup truck. An older man stepped out of the house and walked toward them. T-Mac questionably looked at Doug, who was already disengaging from the vehicle. "Come on." He commanded. "Unc' what's the deal old man?" Both men embraced. When they separated, his uncle asked. "this the boy you talkin' bout?"
Yeah this him."
"Well," Uncle Jeff said. "let's see what he's made of."
Doug laughed at the puzzled expression on T-Mac's face. "It's time to teach you how to use that piece you carryin'" He patted the shoulder of the younger man gently.

As they headed toward the back, a military style shooting range started to appear in front of them. It had life size targets set up in different areas around the yard. A barn, containing window targets, sat in an angle. It had close range shots, then long range shots. "See that?" Uncle Jeff pointed. "There was a long line from one side of the course to the other side of the field. A tiny target was attached to it. T-Mac nodded once he took it in. "We'll that's a bonus shot. It's to teach you how to hit a movin' target or person... close and far off. "Uncle Jeff wrinkled his forehead. "Yo' brotha loved this game. We'll see if your cut from the same cloth." He looked off in the distance.
"You knew my brotha?"
"Sure did. Taught him everything he knew about a gun." Jeffery Hicks was an ex-Navy Seal and at his age could still outlast many of the youngsters today. The old man looked at his nephew. "Doug you wanna give it a go befo' I take ova?"
Uncle Jeff hit a switch causing all the targets to dis appear.

Doug pulled out his pistol. "Yeah let me break shit in." He looked at T-Mac.
"You might as well get comfortable, we here fo' awhile."
"Oh Yeah youngsta, "Uncle Jeff begin. "There's motion detectors connected to paint balls guns... Put these on, "He added. "They'll shoot at you while your shooting at them. This helps you defend an' attack... keeps yo' enemy off track."

Uncle Jeff spit on the ground. "Let's go Douglas." Hearing that, he sprinted toward the first shot, aimed, and fired his dessert eagle 44. The motion made the machines shoot at the moving person. Easily Doug avoided the shots and fired at another target. The machines pace picked up, shooting faster causing him to dive on the ground for cover. He rolled and shot from behind his hiding spot, a ball of hay. Like a rabbit, Doug was up and running to the other side of, the half a mile course. More shots flew his way. He stopped alongside of an old car to gather himself. The target on the line was coming his way. Doug raised his gun and fired. The panel on the far side turned red. Uncle Jeff walked toward him. "Yeah boy you som'em else."

Wiping the sweat from his face, Doug looked at T*Mac. "It's on you now. That's the short course."

T-Mac looked at Uncle Jeff. "You said my brotha liked this shootin' game?" The old man agreed. T-Mac continued. "Then I should like it too." He lay his shirt down and removed the .40 caliber from his hostler. "On da count of three" He said as he chambered a shell inside the head of his weapon.

"Three!" Uncle Jeff yelled and pushed the switch that controlled the course. T-Mac's agility was as good now, as when he was dribbling a basketball and his aim was much better then Doug thought. He moved in the same direction and fired at the same targets that he'd witness Doug shoot at. Suddenly a barn door opened, catching him by surprise. The machine landed a shot that hit him in the leg. He had to drive to avoid a fatal shot. Without thinking, T-Mac raised and fired, taking the defender down. Moving at a moderate pace, he let off five more shots, only missing once. The red light appeared again. "Good job son!" Uncle Jeff yell from behind.

Finishing the course with no major paintball wound, T-Mac smiled. For the first time taking this challenge, he'd been shot two times and neither one of them were deadly. His eyes screened the grounds he'd just left. A few surprises caught him off guard but those only made him that much more anxious to run the course again. "Not bad fo' yo' first time, "Doug said. "You managed not to get yo self-killed."

Uncle Jeff nodded his agreement.

"There was some'em everywhere. It was hard fo' me to aim." T-Mac said.

"That's why the guns are attached to motion detectors." Uncle Jeff explained as he scratched his head. "You not bad, sure you ain't used one of those befo'."

"Neva."

"In that case," Uncle Jeff added. "You can't do nothing but get betta."

Doug shook his head. "You ready to try again youngsta?"

"Hell yeah!" T-Mac grabbed an extra clip from his and reloaded. Once finished, he looked toward Doug. "Small bet, I say I ace this fo' 10 stacks."

"Small huh." Doug laughed. "Yeah he cut from da same cloth. That's a bet but shit get a little more difficult."

"I'm wit' it." T-Mac adjusted his eyewear. This was another challenge and he excepted it.

Dallas Gentleman's, on the north side of town, was well populated for a Monday night. It seemed like the high rollers and week to week workers, were trying to relax in the present of the ladies. This club was known for having nothing less than a dime piece gracing their stages. They often had dancers from around the globe stepping along their floors. With liquor and money floating around that atmosphere, there was no telling what a drunk mind would do to impress a pretty face, flat stomach, and big ass. Still running off the adrenaline of earliers event, T-Mac sat next to his new crew. His tall, Slim Thug resembling frame, was engulfed in big expensive jewelry and stylish cashmere Versace jumpsuit. Doug, Shun, and G.T. sat counter clock wise, forming a semi-circle around him. Each man knew it was their job to protect T-Mac because he was still in growing process. Even though he was handling it well, this was a new position he was in.

T-Mac slammed shot after shot of Ace of Spade, his brother's favorite drink. His mouth was moving rapidly, not giving any thought to the words that came out or what was being said. "Doug...square bidness, I think ya'll fucked me ova." Another shot. "I didn't see that shit pop up out da ground." He rubbed his chin thinking about the screen. "Cleva tho'."

The rest of the clique were smiling. Long ago both men had given different but accurate side of the story. It was funny to hear T-Mac keep pointing things out. The more he talked, the more he sounded like his brother Viper. T-Mac hated to fall at anything he did.

"I wanted you it was going to get harder." Doug grabbed his glass filled with Crown Royal and ice. "I thought you had me 'til that dummy pop up on ya…. 10 stacks, shid I'm glad." He sipped some of his drink.

Shun entered the conversation. "That was the bet? Boy I wanna try that, fo' real" The excitement was written all over his face.

T-Mac reached in his pocket searching for his lighter. He kept looking across the room. The face of one of the men was familiar to him. Instead of pulling his lighter free, T-Mac held a stack of bills folded in half. "Here nigga! We straight." He tossed the money on the table of Doug. "Now, T-Mac added while watching him gather the cash up. "Drinks on you."

Four women were around the table. They were making it their business to be seen. People stopped by asking for G. T's autograph. With his CD ready to drop, people around Triple D was standing behind this hometown trophy to shine. G.T. watched the mixed breed woman giving him a lap dance. She was seductive as a snake charmer and with every move, she drew him in more. There was something about strip clubs he loved. T-Mac stood up and poured some of his drink down the small of the lady's back. G.T laughed. "Nigga you fucked up my pants." He said playfully.

"Fuck….it baby…. buy you some mo'. "T-Mac slurred. At 6'7, he towered over body present. Finally, his mind registered who the person he was looking at.

The group of men were seated across the dimely light club. They were slightly in people then his crew. This in itself made him mad. The reason being, people often got courage in numbers. No one around him was paying attention to the staring and whisper, except him. "G.T. you gotta hata in da mix."

"Always do." G.T. moved the woman aside. Doug and Shun frowned, not exactly what was going on. "Doug," T-Mac made no attempt to look away. "Rose' is what I'm sippin' on."

Doug grunted. "I got cha but what's up?"

T*Mac placed his hands on the table to steady himself. He was drunk as hell.

"It's da nigga G.T. hit fo' some cash wit' them crooks at school." His words came jumbling out his mouth.

Shun and Doug shook their head laughing.

"Where?" G.T. asked.

T-Mac pointed directly, not trying to hide his acknowledgement of the clique. At first sight G.T. didn't notice the other three men until the darker man got struck by some light G.T. begin talking. "Dat's da Rally brotha's. Big love, Pistol, an' Smooth. Smooth's da oldest an' da mos' rational of them all."

T-Mac sat down. He was confused. "Explain?" Was his only word. G.T. ran his hand over his Allen Iverson style braids. He didn't know where to begin. "Dem boys hard hittas out da Oak Cliff area. They move a lot of work out there. Big love da heavy-set nigga fuckin' wit' dem hoes..." He paused, allowing a brief survey. "He da muscle, no questions asked, he gone move. Pistol da nigga wit' his hands behind his head. Da nigga ain't got no fight in him but he gone bust that iron asap. Smooth da brains like I said earlier. All of'em is said to have a few bodies unda they belt. "G.T. stopped again but only long enough to take a sip from his drink. "Ken you already kno' bout. He really from da Cliff, feel me?" T-Mac shook his head. He really wasn't in the mood for drama. "He might feel mo' froggy wit' backup."

"Fuck it, I'm game." G.T. took a swig and washed it around in his mouth before gulping the rest.

Doug held up his hands. "Money an' drama don't mix. If they bring it, then we meet it. Until then, fuck'em." All of them agreed. It was the best way to go about the situation.

Nothing happened for the most part of the night. Trouble seemed to appear an hour before closing time. T-Mac rubbed his arm casually against his weapon stationed underneath his shirt. He figured if his money got him entry with a gun, there was a slight chance some else had too. He watched the group advance toward their table. Noticing their movement, everyone around T-Mac stood to meet the group. Everyone except T-Mac that is. He playfully kissed the hand of one of the two women hanging on his shoulders. T-Mac was becoming more like his brother in many ways.

Smooth held up a bottle of Cîroc. He raised his diamond hand. "What's up playas?" His voice was low and gentle. "We ain't here on no drama shit. That's fo' da birds but I got some news you can use."

Big Love, who was 6'4 300 and built like a defense of lineman, stood hard faced, waiting for action. T-Mac took this in. "Whut you talkin' bout...Smooth right?" Smooth nodded. "I gotta lot of love fo' yo' brotha Vipa. Do y'all gotta nigga name Chip down wit' y'all?" He asked.

"Use to, "Doug replied. "But spill yo' words an' stop speakin' in tongues. We got shit to do."

"I thought so," Smooth looked at his crew. Big Love, Pistol, Ken, and Jip, one of his newest recruits. No one looked nervous and that was good. These was some heavy boys and their reputation alone could shake a tree. "Da nigga ain't right. I hear shit an' I feel like da nigga on some hoe shit, feel me?" I fucked wit' Vipa an' from what I kno', a hoe nigga neva get a fair shake. It's da law of da land. Chip," he paused. "Scored some work from me da otha day. He says he finna do him, watch him because I think he soft like a wet napkin." Smooth's eyes were locked directly on T-Mac.

Seeing the content of the conversation, Doug and the others sat down. For a long moment nothing was said. Then the silence was broke by the hard thump of a bottle. "Here!" Smooth said. "This fo' you G.T."

Confusion crossed G.T.'s face. "What's up?"

"Ken gave me da run down. Leave that kid shit in da yard. We getting' money in da city...too much fo' bullshit like that."

"I'm feelin' that." G.T. put his fist out for a pound.

"Rememba' what I say Mac. Watch everybody like yo' brotha did. If not, you a sitting duck baby. "Smooth and his crew turned and walked out the club. Shun, dressed in an all red Roca wear suit, spoke. "T-Mac, looks like yo' bro got a lot of love dawg."

"You ain't seen nothin' yet youngsta." Doug said in reply to the man's comment.

"What was you sayin' Mac? Doug added.

Still in thought over the statement Smooth left on him, T-Mac answered. "All it ain't shit. I'm thinkin' bout coppin me a Lambo or a Ferri but that's anotha' discussion." He grinned. "Let's shake da spot. It's a long day tomorrow."

Each man joined in on the laughing. They stood and walked for the exit. In their arms were the ladies that were their company for the night. It was time for them to earn their money. Money an' da Power!

Chapter Nineteen

The word of Zachary "Chip" Bell kept pounding at her head. She sat staring at her computer screen. It was 3 o'clock in the morning and Missy Galo was unable to erase the deep intuition she was receiving. Typing in more words, she massaged her forehead to relax her sleepy eyes. For some uncertain reason, Chip's theory was dancing loosely in her head. Continues weeks, Missy sat behind her computer, hacking into Redman's personal syaytem but was having no success. She'd come to believe the cause of death for the notorious CEO Viper and his mother came from her information. After hearing the details that involved the working crew inside Street Approved Records, she wasn't so sure. Her facial muscles tighten as she looked at the screen, again she was refused entry. It was time to go another route. Missy tapped in some more words, waited, then repeated the process moments later she grinned. Her computer was flashing, and the downloader was activated. Smiling she grabbed a piece of paper and read.

Military tracking device. State of the art system. Can be installed in less than 30 seconds and contains a
Range of up to 40miles. For an additional 20 miles,
Must be installed directly into the vehicle motor
System....

Missy thought about what she'd read for a moment. Maybe I was used as a decoy, but why! The more she digged into this, the she wanted to understand. Maybe Chips on to something! There was only one-person Missy knew that could get this type of device, but he wouldn't do it for personal benefits. The price was marked at $75,000. That was very expensive and not many would consider it. It had to be more than meets the eyes. Missy was sure her instincts were right and long ago she learned it was better to follow them. Her eyes were hurting. Every time she tried to focus on the screen, it felt like she was suffering from a bad case of dyslexia. It was time to quit. She shut the computer off and headed for bed.

Chip came to a stop in his newly purchased convertible Chevy Camaro. He watched the reflection on the glass of the corner store. Smoke gray candy paint job with chrome flakes, glistened in the sun, bring out the 22-inch Dayton wire rims. Chip tapped the gas making the 426-house powered engine roar. His thick frame relaxed in the leather bucket seats as he cruised toward his destination. Both sides of the street were equipped with high quality houses. This was expected for the Farmers Branch area. It sat in the inside the Dallas County line but was often looked at as an outskirt. One of the reasons, the small community was patrolled by its own law enforcement.

With the mention of police, Chip shook his head disapprovingly. The fact still stood, if you were black and in an expensive car in this area, you were a suspect. They figured you were a dope dealer, thief, or a robber. That was all they needed to stop you. Never once was you an educated business man. Chip grinned and patted the steering wheel gently. Even it was a stereo-type, he admitted they partially had him right. The last house was approaching, he studied the figure in the yard. Her thick booty and thighs strained against the denim shorts parted on her. The shirt she wore was pulled back and read: STOP LOOKIN'. It brought a lot of attention to her full breast. She was calmly walking bare feet in the forest green grass, playing with her German Shepard.

Both her and the dog watched him as he pulled into her driveway. Chip got out wearing a salesman smile. "How ya doin' Pochahonis?" He teased. "It's a lovely day huh?" Chip looked around the neighborhood. It was nice indeed.

"Yes, it is Zachary and I see you've wasted more money. "Missy wrinkled her nose. "It's nice though and come here! You act like you don't miss me... I have good news too."

She pressed her lips together. It was hard not to like this man. Being around him was a lot of fun. Missy thought about the information and how much she wanted to tell him. His suspicion was the line that helped her develop a nice string of data. Missy felt if she brought this to the light, there would be question she wasn't ready to answer. She embraced him, letting her nose travel to paradise. Her favorite cologne, Dolce & Gabana Sportswear. Missy held him for a moment enjoying his smell. "I'm so glad you came by. You've been on my mind." More Than You Think!

"Is that so?" Chip smiled, allowing the sun to brighten the rose gold teeth in his mouth.

"Yes, that's so Zachary. I've decided to take my vacation early. I've been distracted and think it's for me to relax for a few weeks." She released him and stepped back. Purple and black Roca wear shirt and pants with matching Air Max shoes. His neck held a diamond chain, no logo. That brought attention to his pinky ring and diamond watch. (He's dope boy fresh!) Missy giggled out loud.

"An' what's so funny Ms. Sexy?" Chip asked. He was still looking at the houses. He would have to see if anything was for sell out here.

"Nothing boy. You wouldn't understand. Let's go inside, the sun in starting to heat up." She grabbed his hand and walked to her door.

Chip was impressed at how nice her home was. He closed the door behind him, let his eyes adjust, and inspected the inside thoroughly. Missy left with her dog at her hip. "Make yourself comfortable. I'll be a minute."

Chip didn't bother to answer. He was still taken aback by this house. Gold plate mirrors covered the walls from corner, giving the spectator a 180-degree view of her Livingroom. The furniture was just as amazing. Her couch was cherry oak wood with thick pillows. The couch was one long attachment that served as a loveseat also. Chip noticed she had it facing her fireplace. Her carpet was several inches thick and the color of black coal. It accommodated the white furniture.

Her financial state begins to enter his mind. Being a psychologist brought about $60,000 a year, which was good money but highly unlikely enough to cover a 745 BMW and this home. Chip frowned (I've seen that car from somewhere!) His thoughts were disturbed by a soft voice. "You like my house Zachary?" Not many are privileged to step through those doors. You on the other hand …" Missy held a long tulip glass as she strolled his way. Her hair was pulled back revealing her elegant facial structure. Missy begin talking after he grabbed the glass from her hand. She needed more information from him. "I know that look in your eyes. It happens so much when visitors come by." She waived her hands dismissively. "But I assure you I'm able to afford this and more. My family roots are very deep. Some stories are better left buried. "Chip nodded his understanding. She stood only inches away from him smelling like a fresh picked rose. Her beauty outshined everything in the room.

Missy sipped and looked into his eyes. She was really starting to enjoy his company more than she was willing to admit. That was the wrong thing to do. Missy kissed his lips. "You're a very handsome man and I enjoy your company, which is why you're here now. I'm sure you understand that?" She pressed her lips trying to phrase her next question correctly. "How is Tracy doing? Missy pushed on, because he's been on my mind."

Chip studied her briefly. "I don't kno'. I've been doin' me but fo' you I'll swing through there an' check on him. I'm pretty sure he straight tho'"

"Thank you very much." Missy passion was shown through her kiss. "Now... let's find a way to relax." Her clothes hit the floor.

Chapter Twenty

T-Mac sat behind his desk talking to Kim. In his hands was a cigarillo and some legal paper. He paid close attention to what she was saying. Being new to the music business, T-Mac made sure Kim was there on every move he made concerning the promotion of G. T's album. "Two days we need, I repeat need, to be in Houston for the upcoming concert. This," Kim pointed to the papers he was holding." Are the places in Texas? Which is easy to maintain because we're in the state but once we get to traveling, it will get more difficult cause of the locations." She licked her lips to add moisture and shine to them. "What we bring in is 25 grand a show and we're just starting so we good." T-Mac smiled at the numbers. Five shows would bring $150,000 and that wasn't counting the mixtapes and clothing sold. He was starting to like this business more as the days passed.

It was Wednesday or what some liked to call hump day, so the label was getting a lot of activity. Kim looked at T-Mac. Seeing the concern in his eyes, she asked. "What's on your mind?"

"Well I was thinking', I'm not gone go wit' ya'll." He rubbed his chin with his right hand, revealing the platinum watch on his wrist. "I don't wanna shut down da studio…Look what it's doin' now?" T-Mac tilted his head toward the one-way mirror. He put the cigarillo to his lips and pulled hard, giving the tip a red cherry topping. "What you think?" He exhaled.

Kim moved away from him and looked through the glass. People were moving around purchasing different items. They were getting a lot of business.

"So, who you want to go on this trip and can you handle this place for about a month? Your still wet behind the ears." She winked playfully.

T-Mac showed his even white teeth. Before speaking, he smooths out his White Versace shirt. "You kno' I want you to handle da business stuff on da road. You're really all I have right now an' I trust yo' judgement but I figure this will help me get use to runnin' this place. "T-Mac stood up and stretched his arms, then dusted the wrinkles out his pants. "Take Shun an' Doug wit' you on da road."

Kim said nothing for a long while. Her mind was calculating everything just spoken. There was things T-Mac didn't know about Doug and it was beating at her to explain the whole situation to him. Being on the road with him would take all her strength since Viper was gone. Seeing the distant gaze in her eyes, T-Mac stepped to her side.

"What's on yo' mind lil-mama?" He placed his hand on the small of her back to get her attention. T-Mac scanned her petite but stacked figure. She wore a Babyphat cotton jumpsuit with a pair of open toes Chanel stiletto boots. He understood why his brother was so captivated by this woman. Kim was smart, beautiful, and trustworthy. That was hard to find in many women today. Even his longtime girlfriend was on a bookshelf when in comparison. "Oh, Kim exhaled hard. "I'll talk to you later but consider that other request done."

T-Mac frowned. It was something deeper then what she'd let on. He noticed the change of mood when Doug's name was mentioned. Before he could push farther, a man T-Mac wasn't looking forward to seeing entered the label's front door. He bit his lip, rubbed his shoulder where the .40 caliber sat, and spoke. "Scuse me Kim, let me talk to this nigga. Can you call an' check on that BMW? See if it's ready fo' pick up. "His back was to her as he exited the room. When T-Mac approached the man, he ignored his outstretched hand. "What you want here nigga?" His face was tighten in a ball.

Chip held his hands up in protest. "Wait a second homie?" He looked around, making sure not to seem threating. He didn't want this brief encounter to turn deadly. "I kno' you got some bad blood in yo' veins fo' me but I jus' dropped by to check on ya." Chip stared in the younger man's eyes. "Honestly I don't kno' how you got these ill feelin's but it ain't nothin' like that. Check game, I cut fo' Vipa ...even tho' he was mean as a rattle snake." He laughed slightly trying to kill the edge. "There's some shit you gotta find out to understand. Jus' kno' it ain't me. I'm movin' on cause I'm tryna build me some'em. You can feel that huh?"

T-Mac relaxed a little bit. What the man was saying had some substance to it, "Come inside." He said and turned back toward the office door. T-Mac sat down on the long leather couch, leaving the desk occupied by Kim. Chip nodded her way, then took a seat across from him. T-Mac poured himself a drink from the bar next to him. "Help yo 'self if you like but finish what you were saying. Chip refused to drink. "I'm cool. It's like this, somebody helped that island mu'fucka get da up on yo' brother because that's not an easy task. But… it was done. "He rose to his feet. "We kno' that much. Somebody got some nasty motives an' it's stanky to me. Watch everybody close to you. Some shit can't be concealed. "Chip looked at Kim, who averted her eye's. "Some people kno' more then they actin' like. You be safe. "He rose and exited with no other words.

Something was deeply wrong, and it was starting to bother T-Mac. He watched Kim. Suddenly, she was becoming antsy and that was unlike her. T-Mac grabbed his drink and walked to the desk. He studied her for a minute. "Kim what's going on that ya not tellin' me?"

Kim looked up at him. Her heart skipped a beat. Tracy looked so much like Vince, it was breathtaking. She relite the cigarillo in the ashtray. She took a few drags to claim her nerves before speaking. Once her heart rate slowed, she started talking. "Rememba' when I tell you this, you must continue to move around like you don't kno'. Understood?"

T-Mac tighten his eye's, then downed the remainder of his glass. Kim watched him shake his head in agreement. She continued. "I knew it was gonna come up. I just didn't think it would come up so soon. She paused.

"Where do I begin?"

Hours had passed since Kim and him talked. T-Mac was walking back and forward, shocked about the information received. Shun, the only outsider to the label, sat patiently waiting for his boss to reveal to him why, he'd called him. From the look on T-Mac's face, this was a serious matter. Coming to a sudden stop in front of the small bar, T-Mac begin talking. "Shun there's some real strange shit goin' on aroun' here. "He made himself a drink. This was starting to become a habit. Under the recently acquired stressful lifestyle, he found that drink and smoking was away to release much needed pressure. "You drinkin' my nigga?" Shun nodded. T-Mac made the drink and handed it over, then started talking. "I need you to be eyes aroun' here. You da only one I can truly say can't benefit from my brothas death. He exhales. That was still hard to deal with.

Deshaun King understood what was being asked of him. He'd been exposed to the streets at 11 yrs. Old and became a devoted Los Angela's blood gang at the age of 12 yrs. old. This became his everyday living. Loyalty helped him develop a long-lasting relationship with the O.G.'s of the block. That helped him to gain status and enabled him a chance to hustle from the cocaine trade going on. Shun thought back to these days. It was like a soldier in the army. A coach stepped in and grabbed a hold of his life, after seeing him play basketball at the recreation one day. He remembered Mr. Tubes words clearly, the day he talked to his mother. "Ms. King yo' son is very talented but I'm afraid if you don't get away from this environment, you'll lose him to the streets. "That next week his mother packed up and left for Texas.

Now Shun was staring at the man that befriend him, when it was clear to anyone, he'd challenged his status. Shun sipped his drink and

spoke. "Speak to me straight Mac. I don't understand da way you talkin' in riddles."

T-Mac downed his glass of Cîroc, letting the burning of the liquor to calm his anger. After refilling his glass, he started talking. "Look Shun, it's some kinda love triangle goin on but da specifics ain't all clear. "T-Mac walked to his desk and pulled the drawer back to retrieve the box of Kali Mist weed. "Here fire some'em up. "He handed the box to Shun and continued speaking. "Kim, Doug, chip and G.T. all in some Soap opera shit. All three of them made a play for her. She said they made a few comments about getting bigga then my brotha an' possibly pushin' him out da door were made. T-Mac waved his arms in frustration.

"Who said it?" Shun asked as he licked the paper sealed and added fire to it. "Mainly Doug and G.T. was jus' tryna fuck so she says. I really don't think he'd get down like that. My brotha grabbed him off da streets cause of my word. So that part I believe. "T-Mac continued. "But right now, everybody suspects. You da only one I'm trustin'" He grabbed the blunt from Shun. "Chip came through." T-Mac rubbed his eyes. This was getting to crazy.

"What?" Shun gave a questioning look. "Fo' what?"

T-Mac grinned. "That was my first response. The nigga made some good points but my gut tellin' me he ain't right. "He let out a small snur, then passed the cigarillo back. "I think everybody feel like I'm helpless so they waitin 'on me to crash.... but it ain't gonna happen."

T-Mac stepped over to the glass that looked out at the sales area just as a UPS worker walked through the front door. He watched Kim talk to the man. Whatever it was, he wasn't allowing her to sign for the package. "Scuse me my nigga"

He left the office in quick strides.

"There's a package for you Tracy." Kim frown at the man, before moving out the way.

"YOU Tracy McDavis?" The slim UPS worker asked.

T-Mac nodded. "Sorry fo' all this but I must verify that. This is certified mail." The man said. "Then sign here."

T-Mac complied with the request, got the package, and headed back to the office.

He said nothing to Shun as he hurriedly unwrapped the manila envelope. It read: Dear Friend, there's some things I'd like you to read. Hopefully it will help you get a grip on some problems around you. My deepest sympathy to you. If I find anything else of use, I'll contact you again.

(Military tracking devise. State of the art system

Can be installed in less than 30 seconds and
Contains a range of up to 40 miles. For an
Additional 20 miles, must installed
Directly into the vehicles system. For best
Results connect to the engines computer and
Set range to highest peak.)
.... Directions Below.............

T-Mac closed his eyes. *The BMW!* He looked at the envelope. No return addresses. That much was figured. "Come on Shun roll wit' me. "It was time to put some of these mysteries to rest by retrieving the main item... the BMW.

Chapter Twenty-One

T-Mac pulled his Benz into the three-car garage of his home. He got out just as Shun stopped the emerald green BMW, right behind him. T-Mac signaled for him to pop the hood. Doing as told, shun yelled out the window. "What's happening? I'll explain it to you. Come here though." T-Mac bent over, not really sure what he was searching for. He still inspected the engine. His intention was to see if anything noticeable stood out.

"Talk to me dawg." Shun demanded.

"Man, if someone put a trackin' device- "

Shun held up his hand. "Hold on!" he exclaimed. "A trackin' device. What da fuck you talkin' bout?"

T-Mac straighten up and faced his friends. Staring at Shun, he spoke. "I received this letta in da office an' some anonymous person shot me a memo fo' a trackin devise. What got my mind movin' was the way they said it had to be inserted, ya feel me?" T-Mac rubbed his chin while in thought. "My brotha was drivin' this." He motioned toward the car.

"You see anything?" Shun asked.

T-Mac laughed. "Man, I don't kno' shit bout a car. I'm gonna get someone to check it out. A needle in a haystack would be simpler to find then this fo' me."

Shun grinned at him. "So, all you kno' how to do is hoop?" His smirk turns into a full smile. "Watch out, this shit second nature to me. I been fuckin' aroun' since I was a child." Shun begin to study the motor slowly. He checked spots after spots, that could conceal some type of devise. "get some tools an' a towel. It's gonna get dirty." As T-Mac walked in the garage for a tool box, shun stuck his head under the hood to study. He asked himself questions to get his mind going. (If I'm hidin' some'em small, where do I put it! What's da best way to conceal some'em!) T-Mac spoke breaking Shun's thought pattern. "Here."

Shun grabbed the box and removed a socket wrench. After finding the right setup, he leaned against the radiator and begin disconnecting the governor. Shun rotated it in his hands, then smiled. He sat the piece of mental down, wiped his hands on the cloth, and started talking. "You might be on to some'em Mac. This- "Shun pointed. "Doesn't go on there an' my guess is, it don't go nowhere on da car. Have a look."

T-Mac grabbed another towel and picked up the governor, so no oil would damage his clothes. He took a screw driver and pushed against the half a dollar size device. There was no doubt in his mind this is what gave Redman the location of his brother's car. That and the help of somebody else. "Yeah this gotta be it." T-Mac wrapped the piece in the cloth and walked inside the house. He yelled to Shun over his shoulder. "Put that back togetha an' come in da crib. I got some calls to make."

Shortly after Shun entered the house. He was amazed at the design of it. Everything was of top quality, nothing generic sat anywhere in sight. Shun continued to look around. He followed the sound of T-Mac's voice to the back of the house. When he entered the room, his friend was just placing the receiver back into the cradle. T-Mac looked up. "You like this house?"

"Hell yeah! It's some'em to wake up to."

"I feel da same way. My brotha went through too much so I decided to keep it an' sell my mom's." T-Mac shrugged.

"I can't do nothin' wit two houses. Anyway, I need you to keep yo' eyes open fo' me. What I'm 'bout to tell you can't leave this room." He looked at the standing man. When no fear showed, T-Mac added. "I'm gettin' bugs planted in da record label. Anytime a nigga poot, I need to kno'. Somebody gone pay fo' playin' two-ends wit' my family. This happens tonight afta da shop shuts down."

Shun acknowledged him with a head gesture.

T-Mac stood up. "Now let me change an' let's hit da gym. You still want action?" "No doubt baby." Shun answered. Shun placed a hand on his shoulder as they left the office. "We gonna find 'em dawg an' I put my life on that."

Doug pulled up to Street Approved records and jumped out. He rushed inside carrying a bag. Testing the office door, he looked toward Kim, who was seated behind the desk. "Come open this door Kim!" Doug commanded.

"Even if I wanted to, which I don't, I couldn't. Tracy took the keys when he left and said no one is to be in there without him." She smiled. "It's one of his new rules."

Doug moved to the desk in three steps. "What da fuck this kid doin', my cellphone in that office."

"This his record label. You forgot that already?" She said sarcastically.

"I see you back on that bullshit." Doug stared at her angerly.

Kim tighten her lips. "Treachery in Vipa's eyes were small like a witch doctor.

Out of nowhere, Doug slapped her across the mouth causing her lip to start bleeding. He pulled back to hit her again, but his hand suddenly stopped. "Nigga what you trippen' on?" G.T. asked. He'd walked in on the incident surprising him. Before Doug spoke, he felt some cold metal pressed to his temple. "I have a good mind to blow yo' brains on the floor but niggas like you ain't worth the time in jail. G.T get back!" Kim yelled. "Leave before there's no other chance." Smiling Doug bagged away and exited the studio. G.T. looked at her but said nothing. She was softly crying, the gun still in her hand.

G.T. approached her. "What was that all about?"

Kim sat the gun down and looked around the label. It was good the situation occurred when there were no customers to witness it. A picture of anger was drawn on her face. "There's some strange shit jumpin' off around here and it's bothering me. T-Mac's my main concern." She dried her eyes and waved the problem away dismissively as though it was an imaginary fly. "We'll be on the road in a couple of days. I'm hiring some security. It'll be us and Shun. We got dates to make up." Kim was back in business mode.

G.T. bobbed his head up and down. This label was starting to get crazy, now that Viper was dead. He silently prayed T-Mac was able to right the ship. If he couldn't, then everyone riding was going to drown.

It was well after business hours when T-Mac pulled into the parking lot of Street Approved Records. Glancing at his watch, which showed 8:30 p.m., he was shocked to see two cars stationed in the personal parking spaces. The light was off in the front half of the building, but a dim glow could be seen towards the back part. (What da Fuck is up!) His mind was racing with questions. T-Mac unlocked the door and eased down the hallway, where the recording studio was. Music could be heard as he stood on the outside of the production area. T-Mac placed his ear to the door and listened. Music could be heard but nothing more. Slowly he turned the knob and entered the room.

Kim's back was to him. Her head was covered with large headphones. She rocked nonchalantly to the beat while her hands danced over some of the controls. T-Mac relaxed slightly, when he looked toward the soundproof booth. G.T., was hard at work putting finishing touches on several songs. T-Mac looked at his watch for the second time. 8:40p.m Special View, the observation company was scheduled to be here at 9:30p.m. There was still some time to let G.T. do what he does in the booth, before he'd have to get them out. He knew he was playing it a bit close but decided to chance it. Slowly T-Mac walked up to Kim. His cologne grabbed her attention before he was close to her. Unforgettable Sean Jean. It was something he'd splashed on after taking a shower.

Kim removed one side of the headset. She looked him over openly. He wore a white t-shirt, cotton shorts, and white Air Force Ones Nike shoes... Kim smiled approvingly. "That's my favorite men's fragrance."

"It explains where my brotha got it from." She nodded. "I bought the whole Sean jean Kit, soap, shaving cream, and so forth but it fits you too. "Kim turned back to G.T. "We're almost done just one more track."

Good! T-Mac thought. She continued. "Where's Shun?"

T-Mac rubbed his left hand over his chin, like his brother did so many times. The move displayed a diamond and a platinum ring and watch. This was really becoming him. "I dropped him off. We been shootin' ball all day at da gym. So, he wanted to go to da house and get some rest."

Kim looked at him once more. "That explains your dress code." T-Mac shook his head, then picked up the extra pair of headphones.

G. T's voice came back to him as he listens to the man below out the words to his chorus. *"Nigga what cha talkin about/frownin' yo face cause I'm runnin' da South/Nigga what cha talkin about/stackin my chips an' I'm holdin' it down/Nigga what cha talkin about/ if you ain't ready betta shut yo' mouth/Nigga whut cha talkin' about/ Street Approved wit' out a doubt."* T-Mac smiled, this was one of his favorite songs off the upcoming album.

"I'm breed hard, you niggas is stillborn/no need to talk about it/you niggas is still boren/I'ma mack truck, you suckas straight lack bucks/It's time to move da game/so I packed you/erased ya bank account, then joked you up...." G.T. rapped like this was his last chance. It reminded you of Nas with the song, 1 Mic. When he was through, T-Mac flicked on the light and spoke though the speakers inside the booth. "That's what's up! Come on and let me treat ya'll to some food" His watch showed 9:10pm. G.T wiped his forehead with his towel as he approached. He'd worked himself up a sweat. "So, what's up?"

"Nigga what you talkin about?" T-Mac sang the words to G.T. song. This got everyone to laughing.

"Come on I'm hungry too." Kim exclaimed. She hit the switch to the electricity. The room went black. Both men were already walking to the front door, so she quickens her pace to catch them before they reached the parking lot. There was no need to get left behind.

When Shun was sure the last car was gone, he pulled in, followed by the people from Special View. Quickly he unlocked the door and shut off the alarm. In a few hours there would be no privacy in Street Approved Records. No conversation would go unheard. The more Shun thought about the murders of T-Mac's family, the more he wanted to be a part of the team that found them. Killing wasn't a thing to him. He'd done that before in California and now he was willing to do it again. He fired up a cigarillo and stood clear while the company did their job. Time would push that snake out the grass and when it stuck it's head out, that would be it's last.

Chapter Twenty-Two

If things weren't already eccentric, this morning was a surprise for Tracy McDavis. It was barely business hours and T-Mac's mouth sat wide open. He was in shock, by the four 2011 dark widowed Ford Explorers, that were paling in the parking lot of Street Approved Records. Him and his team stared as the agents exited their vehicles. Know how the deceased Viper built this company, made each member uncertain about the severity of this ordeal. Times like this shook the trees in the back of their minds. They watched quietly while men entered the label and positioned themselves, quietly, in different areas, facing the entrance. These men had the look of weather patrol officers but the posture of Secret Service guys. Seconds later, the Mayor of Dallas Dave Kinney and the Chief of Police Marcus Romeo entered.

Kim said nothing when she stepped closer to T-Mac. Observing for a moment, she whispered. "Let me do all the talking until we understand what's going on." Her words were stern. More agents were entering the label behind their superior T-Mac's heart was beating so fast it could win a Kentucky Derby. Bulging wasn't a good enough word for his eyes. He silently thanked Allah for Kim being at his side. When she saw no warrants being presented, Kim stepped forward. "Who do we owe the thanks for this privilege this morning?" Kim reached her hand out. "I'm Attorney at Law and representative of this label… Kimberly Jones."

Mayor Kinney excepted her hand. "Nice to meet you Ms. Jones. I know our timing is out of sync, but we've been meaning to stop by sooner, rather than later. This is Chief Marcus Romeo. "Both people greeted, then the mayor continued. "I'm here to talk to Mr. McDavis. That's if your attorney permits it. "The mayor looked at Kim.

T-Mac did the same and waited until she approved. "Yes…sir…ah, that's fine sir." He answered.

"Well like I said previously, this conversation is well overdue. "Mayor Kinney paused. "Sorry for not attending the funeral service but some places aren't where reporters need to be. There was enough because of your brother."

T-Mac's face tighten in confusion. The debt of his brother was becoming overwhelming. "Sir do you mind, explaining da relationship wit' you an' my brotha?" Mayor Kinney smiled. He knew the news would bring a stranger feeling to the situation. "We're closer than you think son…but your brother was part of my campaign funding team. He helped me raise money for my second term and another youth program. "The slim tall President Obama reflecting black man smiled at his achievements. He brushed some lint, off his double breast suit, away.

Chief Romeo took this time to speak. "He was very active in the community." He looked around, then added. "Which brings us to this. The murders in question of your family are our top priority. We've placed a lot of men on this case. Right now, there's no direction…'

Mayor Kinney interrupted him briefly. "Our Special Homicide Division are on it night and day." Frowning he continued. "Son you just focus on your future and leave the rest to us."

"Sir how do you kno' so much- "

Mayor Kinney raised his hand. "There's more to this then you think. Don't take matters into your own hands. I promise to get this solved."

(Betta do it befo' me!) I understand sir." T-Mac replied.

Mayor Kinney reached his hand out to the younger man. He patted his shoulder. Sincerity was visual in his eyes as he spoke. "I'll be in touch. Here this should clear up some question in your mind. We should've done this a long time ago but Vipa wanted to do it his way." A smile crested his lips.

"Contact me at the number at the bottom. "Mayor Kinney handed a sealed envelope over and turned to exit the label. When the last agent was clear, everyone begins to breathe again. All of them had a probation sentence coming at the least, with the weapon in the company and nobody legally able to have it. Doug broke the silent morning with a speak.

"I told you Shun, this nigga was doin' things niggas didn't think he was doin'. Da nigga big!" Doug added. "I jus' came to get my damn phone. You locked it in da office yesterday." He headed in that direction. Kim turned to T*Mac "You want me to look over that?"

"No, if I got any question, I'll holla. Make sure everything ready fo' da road. Me and Shun need to talk." T-Mac looked at G.T "It's on you now nigga."

G.T. showed his diamond incrusted teeth. "I'm ready too." T-Mac and Shun walked to the office just as Doug was coming out. His phone was to his ear. "I'll get at you lata Mac." T-Mac nodded, then shut and locked the door.

He sat behind his desk and placed his feet on top of it. "take me through what I'm dealin' wit' so I'll have da correct undastandin'." "look on da floor where your sittin'." Shun waited. "yeah that small cavity on da floor panel…pull that up. "he commanded.

T-Mac did. Inside was several electronic recording devices. Shun walked up and leaned over the desk so he'd have a better view. "All these," he pointed at some machinery. "any part of da label can be monitored. Even da storage room so if you don't step outside, ya out of there. "Shun laughed. "Special view was da right choice." T-Mac joined in as he studied the devices. Shun picked up where he'd left off. "You said everybody was a suspect so look in that lower top drawer…yeah that box." Shun stood straight up and stretched. He was wearing a red and blue Texas Rangers jersey. It hung smoothly over his Rocawear jeans and brought out his classic red reebok. "That's a set-up to that nigga Doug's cellphone. It was here so I said fuck it. If he straight, then we'll jus' loose da phone an' let him get anotha."

"I knew I liked you fo' some reason. T-Mac grinned.

Shun smiled also "It cost a bit more but it's worth it. No one else shit was available, so they got lucky."

T-Mac looked at the envelope and begin to open it. After the first two lines, he looked away in surprise. Not believing what he saw, he read it again. This time T-Mac forced himself to complete the entire letter. I'll be damn!" Were the only words he could think of saying. Shun looked up in puzzlement.

"What's up?"

"You won't believe this." T-Mac's face was paralyzed in one spot.

Tracy spent the rest of the day unwinding. His new life was taking a toll on him and causing him to forget what was important in his life. Him and his long-time girlfriend sat by Whiterock lake, on a thick blanket. The picnic setting was her idea.

"Now," Ja'Zarri said. "Doesn't feel a lot better?" She asked, "Just me and you, doing what we do."

Tracy smiled. The environment was stress-free. "Yeah, I'll admit, this helps
Me get my priorities togetha."
Ja'Zarri reached her hand out. She was holding a chocolate dipped strawberry.
"Here…bite!"
He did.
"What's on your mind that's keeping you always from me?" We've always talked about everything but now it ain't like that. "Ja'Zarri put on a fake mask of anger. T-Mac exhaled. She could be so persistent sometimes. "You're my heart but," He paused trying to decide how much to tell her. "My brotha had more goin' on then I thought."
Ja'Zarri looked at him confusingly. She turned and grabbed some food from the basket next to her. "I know you don't want to let your brother's company go but is that going to interfere with your future? And what does his past have to do with you now?"
She jus' don't understand! T-Mac thought. If anyone was blind to this lifestyle, it was her. He calmed himself and reached in his back pocket to retrieve the letter from this morning. "This- "T-Mac waived the envelope toward her. "Is only da tip of da iceberg. Some people plotted my brotha's death. "He handed the letter too her. "Read this… an' I'm gone find out who's involved."
Ja'Zarri read over the letter quickly. After she completed it, she looked up at him. "You mean…" Her words stumbled out. "I thought." She fell silent. T-Mac nodded his head. "That's why I need you to bear wit' me. I'm messin' wit' some strange shit boo." T-Mac laughed to hide his true feelings. It wasn't good to let her see he was as scared as they came but at least he wasn't alone in this fight this time.

Chapter Twenty-Three

Kim stepped down from the Mercedes-Benz travel coach bus. Her wrap-around skirt and open toe sandals brought out the newly done micro braids, that hung down her back. "I know it's a lot of time on the road, but the money makes it that much better. "Kim's phone rested against her ear as she talked. She studied the parking lot of Street Approved Records. The companies hired workers were the only people visual G.T.., the one person she was looking for, was nowhere in sight. Kim continued to conversate. "I hired some boys for the ride like I told you I would. It's better this way so my focus is nothing but business." She listened and busted into laughter. "No! No! It's never like that bro. Your all that's left. Either you except the job as father and uncle or I'll sue for every dime I can. "Kim was enjoying herself teasing T-Mac. With this baby we're hooked for life...well get here so I can say good bye. We leave in a little while...alright Love ya."

"What T-Mac talkin' 'bout?" A deep voice asked from behind.

Turning toward the sound, Kim pulled her hair in a ponytail. "He just wanted to know what's going on. Him and Zarri at the house." She shook her head. "That girl scared to let him go."

"We almos' ready, huh?" G.T. removed his Versace shades from his head and placed them over his eyes. The morning sun was sticking it's neck out to show who was the boss of the day. "What up wit' them boys? Are they certified head bangas?" Summertime was officially in season. Kim removed her wide frame Chanel glasses from the side of her dress. After adjusting them on her face, she looked toward the people in question. "Tre, the 6'0 light skinned nigga leaning on the bumper of the bus. He was a pick-up man for Vipa and Monsta, that's my cousin. He won't let nothing happen to us no matter the situation. The nigga used to fight in the UFC stuff. "Kim watched G.T., who was just barely inches taller than she was. "Vipa was good at picking people out. He made a few mistakes but for the most part he was on point." She let her words sink in.

"G.T. made an agreeing head gesture. "Yeah I feel that ma."

"So, I'm sticking close to his blueprint." Kim added.

"No need to explain anything else, it's understood." G.T. responded.

With that statement, he started walking toward the men, so they could get acquainted. This allowed Kim the opportunity she needed to go into the label and finish some last-minute paperwork. Her phone begins to vibrate, turning the quiet lobby into the sound of a laundry mat. She made it to the desk, grabbed it, and looked at the screen. On the face was a picture of her dad. Kim sat down. They hadn't talked in some time. This would be a good conversation to have and the timing could have been better. She answered "ustedes llevan cuanto tiemp aqui?"

(How long have you been here!)

Her father laughed in response to the question. "I see your Spanish is better. I've only stopped in to see you and your brother. He's here again for some reason."

"We'll we need to meet now because I have some business to tend to later. "Kim bit her nail. She needed very much to see her father in order to tell him the new about her being pregnant.

Her father spoke. "Han comido ya? Have you already eatin? His thick Columbian accent carried through the phone.

Kim giggled. She loved to hear from him and loved the way he sounded. "No, I haven't. Would you like to take me out now or later? Lunch sounds great!"

"Your brother hasn't called back yet so where would you like to meet?"

She thought for a moment. "Meet me at Chili's on Buckner. Do you know where it is, or do you need help, 12:30"

"Si princess. I'll see you then." Her father replied. "I love you."

"I love you too papi." Kim hung up. She'd just have to wait until they were together to tell him the news. Her face was shining from the short conversation with her dad. One question in her head was disturbing her. It had her mind speeding. (What was Joe back in the states for!) Kim exhaled gently. Work still had to be completed. That would have to wait to be answered. She glanced at the clock on her phone, then got comfortable at her desk. (Better get started!) Yes, it would be good to see her dad before hitting the road. There was so much to catch up on between the two.

Alfonso Joseph DeMatio, was one of four siblings, on her father's side of the family. He was full Columbian and the youngest of three. Joe, which everyone nicknamed him, was 29. He was the closes to her age range 28. That enabled them the opportunity to build a bond between them. On many trips to Columbia, Joe would be the only person there. The others were doing their daily stride for success and they had no time to stop for long periods of time.

Through the years their separation caused them to lose contact with each other. Phone conversations became shorter with every passing month. Soon there was no contact at all. Both went to different colleges, grabbing life by the head and hustling for success. Joe's special talent for making a computer laugh, when it was crying became his way of life. He was one of the top underground hackers and a hired hand for many different organizations. Even though the money came fast and easy, his name started surfacing and the FBI soon was hot on his trail. After catching wind, he fled the United States, leaving behind nothing that would tie him to anything dealing with the bank accounts he'd delt with. He completely erased everything and took millions.

This was a year ago. Since then there was no word or connection. Joe DeMatio had vanished. Now he was back but for what reason. Kim asked herself this question while rearranging the papers in her hands. He surely didn't need any money, she was sure of that and why hadn't he called. It was a long time since they'd spent time together. Kim picked up the desk phone and dialed. A couple of rings later, a woman answered. "Hello!" she called out.

"Hi momma. I missed you." Kim said.

Her mother's smile could be felt through the phone. "I'm glad to hear that. Now what you gonna do bought this sister of yours?" She was speaking of her sixteen-year-old spoiled sister Katoya. Kim giggled. Both women were just alike. "Nothing you had her. I talked to my dad."

"Please come get this child … an' how is he gettin' along."

"He's fine, I guess. I'm about to meet him for lunch."

"Tell him hello for me an'- "The conversation was interrupted by her sister.

"Kim why you won't let me go?" She asked referring to the trips out of town. Toya continued. "You kno' I'ma fan of G.T.'s with his cute self."

"Get yo' fast self-off the phone. "Her mother ordered playfully.

"That's why you can't go. You too hot as it is." Kim shook her head. "An' I told you the clubs are going to have too much liquor. No minors allowed. No matter how grown you think you are, until you can show ID, you're out of there." Toya smacked her lips loud over the receiver.

"Well momma I have to go, I love y'all" she added.

"Love you too baby an' be careful."

"You know you wrong, but I still love you tho'" Toya said.

"Bye Toya." Kim hung up and headed toward the door.

When she exited Street Approved Records, the now owner and CEO of the label was leaning into a sky-blue Dodge Viper. Kim stood there watching. It seemed like yesterday when she last saw Vipa driving that car recklessly around the city. It was hard to believe that he was killed two months ago. T-Mac stood up and looked around. His body was covered in a G-Unit muscle, 87 jeans from Young Jeezy's clothing line and, a pair of pattern leather 95' Jordan's. After putting fire to the cigarillo in his hand, he reached back inside the car to put the interior lighter away. Kim only smiled. She liked the way he adapted to his new position. The men grinned her way as she approached. "What's up" she asked.

"We chillin'. You wanna hit this?" T-Mac asked. Kim declined. "I'm on my way to meet my papi. I don't want to smell like weed." That was understanding. "How long befo' you get back?" G.T. asked. "I need to get at some'em, feel me?" The rest of the men laughed. Kim smirked. "Well make sure your back by 3 o'clock. That's when we hit the road. I'd prefer you be back ahead of that or just relax. You'll have plenty of time for that." She shook her head and strolled to her car. She knew they were in a hurry to get back to their discussion. (Pussy, weed, an' alcohol was all men thought about!) Kim laughed as she closed her car door. It was the way of the world.

Shun walked in and took a seat next to G.T. He nodded to the room before speaking. "I don't smell it. Where it's at?" His mind was on the O.G.

Kush. This got a laugh out of Doug. Everybody was sitting in the office talking. Even the new hired hands were present. "I don't want no gun on that bus. A pound should hold ya'll on da trip but take two because I'ma beginna." He winked at Shun. T-Mac continued to talk. "Make sure all business good through Kim an' be safe. She already got da route planned out…oh here, somebody roll some'em up. "He pulled back a leather box that revealed vanilla flavored blunt wraps. "This what you want? Do some work youngsta!" T-Mac pushed the box to the edge of the desk teasingly. "Nigga you ain't said nothin'!" Shun reached for the container. Doug shook his head. "Two babies callin' each otha' youngsta's." A smile crested his lips. He twirled the ice around in his glass of Grey Goose.

Both men looked at him, then one another. "Since when does age have anything to do wit' shit?" Shun asked. While waiting for an answer, he added fire to the freshly rolled blunt.

"It's about how you operate in this world, old man." T-Mac chimed in. "My brotha was da best teacher I had. What you kno', I probably been knowin'" The word been was strongly enforced in the sentence. Doug held up his hand. "No offense, jus' jokin baby boy. I like to see you do yo thang." The man nodded at G.T. "I'm a part of that success story. I put in work, night after night, tryna come up wit' da best beats. When he succeeds, I succeed. I help put this label on da map too." G.T spoke up in his defense. "He's been puttin' in work. I can agree to that." T-Mac looked at G.T. Things were close to evolving. "I didn't question that. All I'm sayin' is don't underestimate me while I'm drivin' this car. I got da wheel an' I got control of this. "He waived his hands around the room." Now let's talk about this travelin' shit. "The conversation had him frustrated.

Kim sat in the corner with her father eating. Chilli's was graced with a light crowd so the atmosphere was a lot calmer for the lunchtime attendance. She was in no hurry to leave because there were a few hours to spare before the team hit the road. "So enlight me on why you're here pappi?" I was thinkin' about movin' back to Dallas, but I don't think I'm

really into it anymore." Her father responded.

"I would love to see you more." Kim sipped her drink. "An' what's the deal wit' Joe?" She kept the conversation moving because if her father didn't want to do something, he wouldn't, and it was a lost cause to continue down the road. Her father leaned his head sideways and inspected his daughter. He loved the fact that intelligence over rode her beauty. She'd graduated at the top of her class and was consistently growing.

"Well you know how Joe is… he's always into something. I'm goin to meet with him later and possibly discuss my plans." Alexander DeMatio was a very strong man. At his age he carried his power well. He was nice looking and expensively dressed on every occasion and today was no exception.

"Dad!" Kim showed her snow-white teeth. "You remember Vince?" Her father nodded. She continued, "Well, me and him were dating… I kinda got pregnant in the process." Kim started giggling. "You going to be an abuelo."

He clapped his head and touched her face softly. Then Alex DeMatio repeated the word again. "Abuelo." He said. "Maybe I'll buy a house down here, so I can be closer to my grandchild…your first eh?"

Kim shook her head in agreement. "An'" why?"

"Joe's not ready. Mary, Joanna, and Sophia doesn't want to be like the everyday Hispanic family." He frowns at the thought.

"That's why you have to come back more." Kim said to him. "An' make sure to tell the rest of them. Oh, tell Joe to come see me. Now let's eat because it'll be some months before I can enjoy your company like this again." "Si, that sounds fine to me." Alexander DeMatio picked up a Buffalo chicken wing and took a small bite from it. "I'm so excited. He added. Abuelo, sounds good every time I say it." Kim only smiled.

Chapter Twenty-Four

Missy walked out her office carrying two manila folders. She opened her car door, got inside and placed them in the passenger seat. The files contained the background information of a couple of employees that worked at Street Approved Records. Her job at the Dallas Police Department made gathering the documents easier because the people in question all had criminal records. Missy glanced at her watch. (My vacation and I'm still working!) She had a meeting in 15 minutes with a man her brother knew. The man was the half-brother of Kim, the legal advisor of Street Approved Records and one of the undergrounds best hackers. It did her some good that the man was in debt to her brother for a few favors.

Navigating down Commerce St. into downtown, Missy drove her BMW in the direction of the West Inn area. She didn't understand why her interest in this matter was becoming so strong. Her part was done. For some reason her conscience kept telling her differently. So many questions pounded at her head. (What was the reason! Why use a tracking devise! What was really going on!) Everyday she told herself to leave it alone, but the itch just wouldn't go away.

Placing her Gucci shades over her eyes, Missy exited the car, paid the meter, and begin walking. The meeting point was only minutes ahead. As she approached the horse carriage rides, a man stood there holding a single rose. His smile broadens as Missy neared. "For you." He said handing the flower to her brother. "Joe DeMatio!"

He laughed. "Shocked I assume. "Joe Dematio was Columbian and one of Missy's past lovers.

"Would you like to take a ride wit' me or are you in a hurry?" He asked. "I have time Joe." She climbed into the carriage and waited. Things were becoming stranger as the days passed. This CEO Viper was bigger than she thought. Joe sat next to her, electing not to speak until the big horse were walking.

"I've missed you. Your brother told me you'd called." Missy looked away.

"How long have you been involved with my brother?" Joe grinned. He studied her for a second before speaking. "Probably as long as you've been involved wit' Richard." The mention of Richard Tingwa's name made her face him quickly. "How do you kno- "Her words were cut short by his hand raising. "There's a lot I know and Redman's whereabouts goes along wit' that." Joe smiled his perfect smile. He was dressed in cream Polo shirt and slacks. The only jewelry visual was the two diamond earrings in his ears. "All that's beside the point. What do you need from me?" "Well," she bit her French tip nails. "Here read this." Missy handed him the information downloaded from her computer. "Can you help me find out who ordered this device? My skills won't allow me to break through the government protection seal." "What's your interest in this?" Joe asked as he grabbed the paper from her hand.

Missy thought briefly about the question, then she answered. The truth in this matter would be more suitable in this manner to get the help required.

"Do you recall the murders that took place with the owner of Street Approved Records?" He nodded his head, folded the papers, and handed them back. Missy was sure he had, because the story was the biggest of this era. Most people living would have some knowledge of the incident.

"There's something going on that I don't like. Maybe I'm digging to deep, but I feel like the kid is in danger." She paused. "An it's on the inside of that label."

Joe DeMatio looked at her. His feelings for her was still there. She was such a beautiful woman. "Your still not tellin' me anything. Doin' what you're askin' could result in jail time, if I'm caught." He stared at her hard. "An frankly a piece of pussy ain't worth that." Missy looked at him through her shades. This was one of the reasons they'd parted. He was to blunt at times. It seemed he had no true feelings for anyone besides himself. Knowing how close he was to the, COO (Chief Operating Officer) made her bite her tongue, information was needed. "Somebody got me involved...the person doesn't matter. There's something going on and all the pieces ain't fitting." Missy held her stare on him.

"The boy is around a lot of stars and blood isn't the only thing their after. He needs to know this. My brother said it's of no concern of his, so he directed me to you. "She shrugged her shoulders.

"Maybe I've takin a big liking to the boy and want to help him out of this situation he's in."

The rest of the ride was rode in silence. Joe grabbed Missy's hand as they came to the stopping area. He caressed her knuckles softly. He knew a long time ago this day was coming, and this was going to be the day he paid his dues. Joe stood up. "I'll do this, but my debt is cleared. Get that understand wit' Kimidiki. After this, I will see ya'll no more. "He turned to leave, then stopped suddenly. "You're lucky I want the truth also. Whoever did this deserves whatever comes their way. My sister was pregnant, and the baby will never know his father." Walking off, Joe called over his shoulders. "In a couple of days, I'll have the information you requested." His father wanted to see him again.

Missy flinched at the venom his words carried. May she was digging to deep. Her mind was starting to understand why the press was constantly airing this coverage in hopes of getting a lead for the police department. There were some major people behind this man named Vince McDavis. The conversation with her brother opened her eyes to this. Kimdiki told her to think about everything in her view. Things were getting crazier with every stone turned and there still was more to be flipped.

Doug sat near the window of Pizza Hut, talking angrily into his cellphone. Things were starting to unravel, and he wanted to make sure his name wasn't included, when it did. "Man, you need to get yo' ass back here." He listened. "Fuck that! You had this bright idea, not me." Listening. "How the hell is that? Send yo' boy an' finish what you started." Doug put emphasis on the word you. "Somebody that know to much is in the mix." He listened some more. "Shid that's bullshit." Doug laughed to push away some of the hate he had for this man. Money had messed up his better judgement and now he was trying to get clear before the arrow pointed back to his involvement. "Check game! I'm gone say this." Doug practically yelled into the receiver. This got him many unappreciated looks. "We go down together so either get back here of fuck you. "He hung up and looked at the man sitting across from him.

"What you think we should do?" Chip asked. "This nigga playin' games an' all this heat startin' to surface." Doug picked up a slice of pizza and ate it. He needed to do something to get his mind off this problem. "I knew from da start not to fuck wit' this but da pay seemed so live. Now I ain't so sure. This nigga damn near as smart as his brotha. "The last statement was more to himself then to his companion.

"Who is this new nigga?" Shun I think his name."
Doug shook his head. "He ain't no dummy. I can say that. He's closes to T-Mac an' da nigga cut from da streets. Young but smart."
"How long they gone be gone?" Chip asked.

"One month, give or take some days." Doug sipped his strawberry drink, then added "When this sucka get here he gotta go. I know just how to force his hand. "He looked at Chip. "An' your da ace in da hole." Chip looked at him questionably. "Me.... what you talkin' bout?" Doug didn't comment. He just continued to eat. Chip had no idea how far in he was. He only knew the small part that Doug gave him. Money took away any questions chip could think about asking. This was a chess game and he was only a pawn in the game. He soon be excluded from the front line. Doug had to get to his uncle and make sure he'd covered his tracks. The cat was out the bag and now it was time to catch him.

Doug hated to be the clean-up man but there was no way he was going to get caught behind this. Whoever in his way was going to die and that included Tracy McDavis.

Chapter Twenty-Five

Doug's mind was racing with plans when he came to a stop in South Dallas off Pine and Colonial street. Immediately he exited and sat on the hood of his car. His head was hurting so he took this moment to massage his temple. The street was busy as usual. This heroin plagued neighborhood was stacked with people moving fast in both directions and the look on their face was one thing...dope! Things were heating up and it was time to extinguish the fire. Doug started walking toward the front door of this run-down house he'd parked at. Half way up the walk way the glass screen opened, and a dark-skinned man appeared. "What you want here boy?" The man yelled again. "Listen!" Doug stopped on the porch inches from the man's face. "I need to get in touch wit' Uncle Jeff. You kno' this how he said do it, Paul."

Paul was his cousin and wanted nothing out of life except getting high daily. The only reason this house was still manageable delt mainly with his uncle's regular visits. "I ain't in da mood to be fuckin' wit' you so move out my way." Doug said and pushed pass his cousin. He sat down on the old sofa and looked back at the man. "An' put that hoe ass shotgun up fo' I kick yo' ass!" "Dis my house Doug an' I can do what I want. "Paul strolled to the back room. Doug shook his head at the sight of his family member. Dirty shirt, raggedy jeans, and nappy hair. He hated coming to this place but when Uncle
Jeff was out and about this was the best way to get in contact with
him. Chip was on his way to fulfill his end. It surprised him at how deeply involved he was. There was a lot to be worked out but keeping him on the front line would help just in case he had to disappear.

Doug grabbed his phone from his waistband and hit speed dial to his uncle's mobile. He looked around and shook his head again. There was nothing of value anywhere in sight. It was 2011 and this man still had a black and white television sitting on a wooden coffee table. That was a sad thing. His mind snapped back to reality at the sound of a voice in his ear. "Douglas I'm on my way toward ya. There's a few loose ends I have to get right. "Uncle Jeff said.

"Did you get my text?"

"Come on now son. What the hell you think I'm talkin'' bout?"

Doug laughed lightly. His mind wasn't focusing on nothing now. "That's my fault. It seems like shit fallin' apart to quickly."

"Don't think like that. There's too much to lose. That sucka you hooked up wit' is our focus right now. We get him, then we free. "His uncle paused briefly.

"The boy still in da blind huh?" Uncle Jeff asked.

"Yeah.... I ain't gone speak to much on him. He still wet behind da ears. This ain't his lifestyle, feel me? Doug responded.

Uncle Jeff added. "I got my partner on da too. I won't let you down son. To late fo' slip ups...then you know what you'll have to do in order to stay walkin' this surface." Doug frowned and looked at the floor. He'd dug himself in a hole and it was looking like there was only one way out. "Yeah if it comes to that, then it's done but I'm not likin' it one bit."

"There's a lot of choices, we don't like but have to make. I'll holla more when I'm there. "Uncle Jeff hung up.

Doug closed his phone and replaced it on his waist. For the second time today, he massaged his temples. This situation was getting stressful by the moment. There was about to be a lot of bloodshed and he wasn't sure if he was up to it. Doug was hoping to spare Tracy and allow him a chance to move on with his life. That was his way of showing respect to Viper. Money was the root of all evil and now he really understood what that meant.

Chip lay in bed on his back looking at the ceiling. The phone was against his ear.

"Need to see you baby. I'm fo 'real." He needed to get her away from her house, so Doug could do his thing inside. A thought popped in his head causing him to raise to one elbow. (That dog!) "I your bust but," He stopped and listened.

"Well since you can't get away," Chip stopped and listened again, then smiled. "Aight, so later tonight you gone swing through." He laughed. "Sex is on my mind. So, have it on yours. Do what you do, that way, we can do what we do. I'm waitin'. Kisses girl."

Chip hung up and lay back on his back. He'd have to notify Doug about the dog. Knowing him, he'd jus kill the animal upon entrance. The fact that Missy was somewhat involved with this chaos, was hard to digest. Chip understood that Doug was withholding information, but he didn't care now. All that mattered was finishing this ordeal and moving forward. Chip stared at the wall. It would be great to spend some time with Missy, before shit started to sink. He couldn't deny the feelings gained for her but for the 75,000 he was set to receive for his small part was fine by him. It would do him good to think with his head and not his heart. This money added to the 200,000 already in his safe would assure away for him and his children to escape. Chip closed his eyes and rolled on his side. After all, that's what this was all about. (Money!)

Missy placed her phone down and continued to watch her computer. The screen was blinking rapidly. Suddenly a small sentence appeared in the middle. It read: Press code number 451 to receive. She did, then waited for the information to appear. Missy thanked Joe for providing the two applications in front of her. There was nothing left to the imagination. He showed the pages she'd found and added pages, showing her who ordered the special device. Missy continued to read.

Jonathan Saltwater Sgt. In the U.S Army and head of the supply and cargo area. With Sgt. Saltwater making the initial transaction, business went through unnoticed. Joe, being the computer shark that he was, picked up on the trail, when one item was readdressed. For anyone paying close attention, this was a dead giveaway but who would suspect anything. No warnings, no worries.

Joe DeMatio gave addresses, job occupation, and family members. Missy giggled. He was too good to be told that. Her eyes scanned the screen and out of nowhere, three words jumped out causing her to place both her hands across her chest. (Street Approved Records!) It listed Douglas Hicks as Head of production producers. She stared at the name for a moment before pressing download on her printer. Missy stood up, she would send this to Tracy McDavis asap. This information would open his eyes to the environment around him. After this, it would be up to him to put in this corruption. With these words on her mind. Missy went to take a shower for tonight engagement. (Douglas Hicks-Jefferey Hicks!) It was at that very moment she made the connection.

Chapter Twenty-Six

A couple of days passed, things seemed to be going well, at least the surface was so Tracy decided to check the record label's set-up. The electronic recording advice were working perfectly. The dates, times, and days of weeks were stated with every different recording session. Special view done a professional job and T-Mac was glad he'd chosen them. Pressing a button, he leaned against his leather chair and listened.

Wed. 6-28 2:05 p.m.

1st. "Hello this is Flores N Smiles."

2nd. "Can I speak to Mrs. Anthony?"

1st. "Mrs. Anthony speaking. How can I help you?

2nd. "This Mr. Williams and I'm calling about…you said pink Kim? Sorry, about that but I need a dozen pink rose arrangement sent to a Jazmine Rose at 3100 Park meadow #103"

1st. "That's no problem sir. How will you pay cash or charge?"

Remembering the situation, T-Mac smiled. G.T. sent his girlfriend a late birthday present and Kim helped him find the right shop, one she liked, to deliver them. T-Mac continued to surf the recordings. He stopped at Kim's voice in his ear.

Thursday 06-29 11:30 a.m.

1st. "Hello."

2nd. Hi momma. I know you're not sleep?"

1st. "No child, this damn Sista of yours getting' on my last nerves." T-Mac continued to listen until he was sure the conversation was innocent. Glad those two were staying one hundred, he disconnected and closed the floor panel. Reaching for the top drawer, T-Mac pushed the device connected to Doug's cellphone. He sat back in his chair and listened.

Wednesday 06-28 10:00 a.m.

1st. "Hey what's up?"

2nd. "Nothin' boy. You comin' by today. I need some." Giggles

1st. "That's what we both need."

T-Mac pushed fast-forward and continued until something caught his attention.

Wednesday 06-28 1:00 p.m.

1st. "Yo' who at me?"

2nd. "Nigga what happened on that issue?"

1st. "I got it baby."

T*Mac listen closer.

1st. "Well make sure ya at the spot. We need to talk."

2nd. "I got me. Make yo' part done."

T-Mac was sure he knew the voice. (Why was Doug talkin' to Chip!) This sent shock through his body. Doug knew not to mess with that nigga, but it was apparent he was. He let the recording play on. Now he was on full alert. The reason behind his action had to show up.

Saturday 07-02 2:45 p.m.

1st. "Man you need to get yo' ass back here!"

2nd. "Mon whut chu hurry. Iz ok tings are fine Douglas."

1st. "Fuck that, you had this bright idea, not me!"

2nd." Chu owe me mon. Chu still have tings to do."

T-mac looked toward the production room where Doug was working. The one person his brother trusted inside his circle, was a snake in the grass. With the growth so high in front of him, he'd made a home there. T-Mac stood up and walked to the one-way mirror. The conversation wasn't over, he'd just paused it in order to get himself under control. He was perspiring fiercely. After a few mind steadying breathes, T-Mac returned to the desk and resumed listening.

1st. "How the hell is that? Send yo' boy an' finish what you started. Somebody that kno' too much is in the mix!"

2nd. "Not on me part mon. I paid chu 400,000 to do chu part. An' $50,000 to Missy to make sure dis happened. Da device on da car was good but his brotha still has ownership. I want da label...everything of his, I want."

1st. "Shidd that's bullshit!"

2nd." Iz not good fo' me dere mon. So, do chu job, or else Doug!"

1st." Check game, I'm gone say this. We go down togetha. So eitha get back here or fuck you!" End of conversation. 5 ½ mins the electronic voice stated.

T-Mac was boiling hot. Tears were at the wells of his eyes, but he refused to let them fall. Doug would pay dearly for his actions. No man should be allowed to live under these circumstances. That was something T-Mac knew from being around his brother. There were some people from his past, he'd have to ask for a favor or if that wasn't good enough, money wasn't a thing like Jay-Z said. He sat on close 6.5 million dollars. All that was due to their insurance policy plus Viper had a lot of stocks and unaccounted for bonds.

How he was going to do it, T-Mac wasn't sure, but he knew that Doug would die to hands that had never killed before his. He ejected the mini cassette, replaced another, and headed out the office, with no sound. Doug was involved to deeply, so it was better not to be seen or heard leaving like this. There was no telling how things might turn out. When T-Mac stepped into the afternoon heat, his mind was playing the lyrics of Welcome to my Hood in his head. *"I know some niggas from my hood that will rob Noriega/ I'm talkin' Noriega/Nigga da real Noriega/If you not from da hood/then stop impersonatin' us…"* Plies.

The carwash, in Oak Cliff was its usual active self. People were standing around, while others walked and talked to some of the major figures in this area. It was 3 o'clock in the afternoon so the scene was filled with Daisy Dukes and tube shirts. Dope fiends and children shared the job of washing, drying and shining the slab for cash. T-Mac studied the area as he sat in the turning lane. The emerald green BMW on 22's was just another attraction for the spot. After finding the tracking device on his brother's car, he made a point to have every ride he owed sweep, to avoid the same situation. To make things even harder for the people involved, T-Mac never drove the same car. It was best to keep everyone off balance.

Cruising slowly toward the big ballers at the back, T-Mac maneuvered into an open spot next to a lemon colored Escalade on 26's. He got out and glanced inside the cracked door. Peanut Butter leather, woodgrain, flat screens, and a partially drunk cup of purple stuff. Laughing at the unsecured mud, T-Mac took the time to look around the scene. His Street Approved Record label chain was getting a few stares as it hung over his lean frame. Everyone knew he was now the owner of the label. "Yo' wh-at up nigga?" A deep voice asked from his blindside.

(Big Love!) "Chillin' Big playa. This you?" T-Mac tilted his head in the direction of the SUV. Big Love smiled showing a mouth full of diamond encrusted teeth. For a big dude, he was well dressed. A large Enyce shirt rested on his huge frame and his pants sat comfortably over some orange and yellow Air Max shoes. T-Mac had to give credit where it was do. The nigga was clean. "Where yo' brotha at?" T-Mac added. "Smooth."

"I don' know baby. Why?" Big Love looked grim and reached inside his car door to retrieve the Styrofoam cup. He sipped and waited for an answer. "Shit I'm just askin'. I'm really lookin' fo' Czar."

"Oh, that nigga ova there." Big Love strutted the words out as he pointed to a group of guys in the corner of the carwash.

T-Mac looked over there and in seconds spotted him. He started toward the small crowd. "I'll fuck wit' you late." He yelled to get Czar's attention as he approached. The plan was to isolate him, in order to talk to him alone. Everyone turned to the sound and stared. Many of the men he didn't know so he waved for Czar. In return, Czar smiled and headed his way. "What up baby? How you getting' by boy?" They embraced. "I've

Been aight but shit could be betta."

"So whut brings you back ova here? You gotta lot on yo' plate right now."

T-Mac agreed. "Yeah I do. That's why I'm here." He shut down to think of his next words. "I need to talk to you. Is there somewhere we can cop a seat, so I can spill this shit to ya? I'm fuckin' wit' some deep shit an' money ain't a thang, if da job is done."

Czar frowned a long while before responding. He knew it was some serious stuff for this man to come like this at this time in his life. This wasn't your everyday street person so before he made a decision it would be better to hear him out, if not fo him, then for his brother Viper. "Come on ova here to my ride I jus' got it too." He shows the invisible settings in his mouth with a grin. They stepped to a two door Buick. Everything was customized with purple and white, down to the paint. "Get in. Yo' ya like it?" T-Mac nodded as he did so. "Now what's up?"

Tracy McDavis spent the next 20 minutes reliving the past events of his life. He looked off in space as he told detail by detail, the things that were going on. Passion could be felt in every word. When the last word left his mouth, T-Mac fell silent. Czar took his time before speaking.

"So whut you tryna do Mac cause if this is what's up, then I'll help you in any way I can. Doug a bitch nigga an' I ain't feelin' that." He reached in his ashtray and removed a blunt. Czar needed something to relax him. T-Mac turned quickly in his seat when he smelled the Kush in the air. (That's it!)

"Where you get that from?"

"I still had a lot from the last time I copped from Vipa. Why?"

T-Mac rubbed his chin. "Have you eva did business wit' Doug?"

"Yeah, Vipa had me pick some'em from him this last time." Czar responded. "I think da nigga had somewhere to go or some'em cause he was in a hurry." T*Mac snapped his fingers and laughed. "When I tell you to. I need you to call an' score some'em else from him. Here his numba. You got some paper?"

"Yeah in da glove compartment. Whut's up nigga?"

T-Mac said nothing. He grabbed an old receipt and wrote down the number. He handed it to C'zar and told him what to do. "Can you handle it?"

"Come on that's easy!"

T-Mac held the man's stare. "But can I trust you to for fill da job?"

"Nigga you call it's done! Me an' my boys on it like flypaper."

"What's yo' price? No nigga work fo' me fo' free. I don't want any debts when I leave Dallas. "T-Mac said matter of fact. Czar inhaled the smoke from the blunt. He could understand where the young man was coming from. "That's a good motto. Befo' I tell you my price, let me ask you some'em, aight." C'zar gather his thoughts. "Where you goin from here?"

"To be my own man." T-Mac looked at the man. "I still wanna go play ball fo' Texas. It's jus' some shit that has to happen... fo' my family, ya feel me?"

"That's da real. Give me 45 stacks an we straight. That's fo' my boys. I'm not askin fo' shit. Me an' yo' brotha was tight. Plus, you like family. Fuckin' ova you, like fuckin' ova ova me." Czar reached his hand out and T-Mac cuffed it with the both of his.

"Preciate ya." T-Mac said. Then he exited the vehicle. Things was set in motion and now it was time to catch this fish. With all these hooks, he was bound to bite one and when he did, it would be the one that killed him. Viper was reincarnated. Czar started his engine and rolled down his window. "Say Money! Hold me down. I got some shit to take care of. "He retracted his window and pulled off.

Chapter Twenty-Seven

Upon T-Macs return to Street Approved Records, he was met by Doug sitting at the front receptionist desk of the company. Doug glanced at his watch. "How long you've been gone bro? I came out da studio about 2:30 an' you were AWOL." T-Mac forced his feelings aside and masked it with a smile. "It was about that time, ya feel me? Zarri needed to see me." He lied. "I didn't' think it would take that long but ya boy be puttin' in work. I didn't say shit cause I wanted you to finish them beats. I got this nigga call himself D-Boy da underground Prince. Da nigga nice an' I'm thinkin' bout signing' him." T-Mac looked at his watch 5:30 p.m. "Nigga you can leave if you wanna, I'm gone close early today… about an hour from now." He wanted to be alone, so he could continue to listen to the tape. After hearing the conspiracy, the first time, the thought never crossed his mind to finish the rest of the recordings. He just didn't want that small piece of audio to disappear. Doug spoke. "I got some'em to get into. You sure you don't need me aroun' here?"

"Nah we cool. Them beats through, right?"

"Yeah an' I'm on some Dr. Dre shit. I sampled some stuff off Rick James song Fire and Desire. But you too young to undastand. Check 'em out though. "Doug put a smirk on his face. He walked toward the door. T-Mac was only steps behind him.

T-Mac grabbed the open door and held it. "Yeah Doug this young nigga live. He said he talked to my brotha' befo'." Doug snapped his fingers. "I kno' da nigga. Real Street Approved material…da boy can ride a beat an' got many styles of flow, he a group his self. That's a good pick up too." T-Mac closed and locked the door as Doug walked to his car. (ALONE AT LAST!) Doug was a good actor, but he'd underestimated the new kid on the block. To survive in this world, a man is required three things: Common Sense, Street sense, and book sense. Every one of those complemented the other. A person could live off two but in order to dominate the scene, he must contain all three. Tracy Mc Davis knew he wasn't a street nigga but since he was young his brother made sure he wasn't blind to the actions in the hood. Knowing and understanding is two different things. I was like talking and not listening. To many people did one without the other!

T-Mac looked around his office. He couldn't figure out how this nigga would want to play two ends like that. Every time him and his brother would talk, all that came from Vipa's mouth was we, us, and all. That was plural in his mind. We bringin' this… We bout' to do this…WE, WE, WE, never singular. T-Mac wasn't trying to fool himself. 400,000 was a lot of money but Doug would've gotten that and more. Frustration made T-Mac pound his fist in his hand. He walked to his mini-bar and fixed a strong shot to gulp down. (To you bro!) He took it to the head. Not feeling the power of the liquor, he grabbed the whole bottle off the shelf. T-Mac took the bottle back to his desk, open the drawer, and reinserted the tape. He speeds up the tape to the spot he'd left off from.

Saturday 07-02 6:30 p.m.

1st. "Douglas I'm on my way toward ya. There's a few loose ends I have to get right."

2nd. "Did you get my text?"

1st. "Come on now. What the hell you think I'm talkin' bout?"

(Uncle Jeff!) T-Mac recognized his voice. (Damn, this a trip!) The same people that has been teaching him how to maintain in these streets or the same ones trying to steal his brothers label. (Was what's Mayor Kinney sayin' true!) It had to have some substance to it, but T-Mac found it hard to believe. (Da nigga was huge.)

1st. "That's my fault. It seems like shit fallin' apart."

2nd. "Don't think like that. There's too much to lose. That sucka you hooked up wit' is our main focus. We get him, then we free."

If there was any doubt, it was now erased. Doug was behind all this drama. Him and Redman were in this together. T-Mac turned the bottle up, allowing the liquor the chance to burn his throat and water his eyes. From the sound of things Doug was trying to clean up things. That wouldn't help his situation though. T-Mac's mind clicked. He had an idea that would serve well. He needs to calculate the problem. (Let Doug do all da dirty work. Sit back an' keep close tabs on him. When he thought things were good, make him pay for his mistake, treachery, and disloyalty!) T-Mac sat the bottle down. He was smiling. This was the kings move and it was a must he controlled the game…but be protected.

The buzzer sounded on the building. T-Mac looked at his watch. 6:00 p.m. (Who was here at this time of day!) He exited the office and walked to the front. A UPS man was standing there with a package. This was crazy because it was well after business hours. T-Mac opened the door.

"Ahhh I'm lookin' for a- "He looked at his clipboard. "Tracy McDavis." He left the clipboard and went to T-Mac's side. In avertedly T-Mac followed. The .40 Cal pistol was fully exposed. He'd took off his shirt and totally forgot about the gun when he'd gotten up to answer the door. Now he was standing here showcasing the weapon. "I, I'm sorry." He said drunkenly.

"Here's my I.D. Check to see who it's from if you don't mind."

The man gripped his ID, checked the list, and handed it back. "It doesn't say. It's certified so we had find you. This is the third time befo' I leave shift today."

"Well sorr-ry bout t-that." T-Mac slurred.

"No problem sir. It's part of the job." The man turned to his van.

T-Mac went back to his desk and open the package. He begins to read the best he could under his circumstances. Jefferey Hicks names were outlined in yellow highlighter. Again, there was a note with all these papers:

Dear Tracy, I've came to this conclusion. It's up to you to put the pieces together but there right before your eyes.

"Anonymous."

T-Mac picked up his mobile phone and begin dialing. He wanted this to be done by the time Kim and G.T. returned. That would enable him the opportunity to focus on the future of the label. If all went well, he walks away with a smudge of dirt on his shoulders.

"What up dawg?"

"Shun, I got some mo' shit to talk to ya about. Where ya at?" T-Mac asked.

"At T-Lady's crib."

"I'm on my way." He hung and hurry out the door.

Shun's bedroom was built from the garage. It was nicely fit because people could visit and not disturb his mother doing so. T-Mac entered the side door to the sound of Snoop Dog's music. *"I once had bitch name Annie May/use to be all in them guts like eva 'day/Da pussy was da bomb/had a nigga on sprung/I was in love like a mu'fucka/lickin' da pearl tongue..."*

T-Mac sat down and added fire to the cigarillo behind his ear. "I see you on that West Coast shit," He pulled hard until the head of the paper was cherry red. "That's ova wit' though. Betta' get down wit' this South."

"Yeah we need some hard hittas but I gotta stay firm. We on d rise." Shun laughed and pulled a chair up to the table next to him.

"Why you ain't got anotha car too?" T-Mac passed the O.G. Kush. "That little wheel shit ova. 24's or betta."

"I got my eyes on some'em but I'ma keep a low-low. I'm from da West dawg." Shun throw up a W with his hands. "I'm lookin' fo' a crib too." He started coughing. "Damn this some fire. Fuck that though, get to da real."

T-Mac started talking. He was still gone off the bottle of Ace of Spades. He was surprised he made it without getting pulled over. T-Mac declined the killa back and continued to tell what was going on. It took a few more minutes before he was finish with the story. T-Mac looked at Shun. "What you think?" "You got da tape?"

T-Mac nodded. Shun walked to his dresser and removed a mini-recorder... "I use this in school sometimes." He smiled. "Sometimes I'm on it. Let me listen." T-Mac handed the cassette over with no words and allowed him the chance to hear the conversation himself. Shun looked up in frustration. "This nigga crazy"

"Yeah he is but I'm on him like clothes. That's where he fucked up at. I'm gone let him play clean up man, then I got Czar waitin' in da cuts." T-Mac grinned drunkenly. "Ain't nothin' slicka then a can of oil. I learned from da best teacha...Vipa da poisoness snake."

"As sure as the Blood family red... I'm on yo'' team."

T-Mac laughed. "Just be ready when it's time."

Shun nodded again. Loyalty was a part of his bloodline.

Chapter Twenty-Eight

"Chip how's things going?" Doug sat with his cell phone against his ear in his BMW. "Baby still wit' you or did she bounce?" He was in a bitter mood because of the situation ahead of him.

"Nah she right here, why some'em happen?" Chip asked.

"I couldn't get there da otha night. I had a few mo' ends to tie up." Doug looked around the parking lot. He locked his eyes on a yellow chick with a small waistline. The woman was focused on the child clinging to her hand as they entered a woman's shoe store. "I'm on my way now, glad you got her there still." "It was really all her but same difference though. She wanted to stay the weekend." Chip's voice faded from the phone. Pieces of the conversation could be heard. Seconds later his voice was clear. "Yeah do ya' thang she'll be there to check on her dog lata'" He laughed.

"It's time to get his ball movin', make sure she gets there." Doug's tone was stern and serious.

"She'll be there jus' take care of the bidness." The line went dead.

Chip's unexpected appearance at the record label brought a lot of old news to the light. He'd spoke briefly to T-Mac and Kim was forced to come clean on some of the stuff that occurred behind the scene. She told all about the sex attempts that the man tried. Everyone at the label had went after her at some point or time. Her loyalty to Viper stood solid. Doug knew she hated him for much more then shooting between her legs. Three days after Viper scored his stock of Kush, she caught him stealing a few pounds out the storage room. Kim had appeared when no one was supposed to be there. He begged her to be quiet and it took a lot to convince her, he was in debt and didn't want to bother Viper for any money. Her question was firm," but why are you stealing?"

Against her better judgement, Kim agreed to be quiet but daily it could be seen that the notion was eating at her. She was devoted to Viper much deeper than people could understand. Now that Viper was dead, she often vented her anger and that was the reason he'd slapped her. A love quarrel was the rumor floating around the label. Doug laughed. He turned the ignition and pulled the lever in. M....... hadn't caught wind which was good. The less he knows, the better he was. Doug checked the bag in his passenger seat before putting his foot to the pedal. Everything he needed sat in the bag. He drove toward Farmer's Branch. It was time to force Redman back into the states.

Missy stepped into her house and immediately deactivated her alarm system. Tiny, her German Shepard, danced around her leg before running off in the direction of the living room. She smiled at the animal's excitement. It was only two days but from the way the dog was acting, it would seem like weeks. Missy stopped in her tracks when she heard a soft growl, followed by a whimper. "Tiny what's the matter boy?" When there was no response, she yelled again. "Come here boy!" no sound. Missy walked that way and stopped in her tracks. The large dog was in a pool of blood laying on his side. Scared, she started bagging up. The white Persian Rug enhanced the look of the blood pouring from the animal's body.

"Please don't do that!" A man said from the dark. Missy stopped and stood erect. She turned toward the sound. A white hockey mask stared back in her direction. His hand held a gun at her head.

He spoke again. "I don't wanna hurt you so please don't make me have to. Is that understood?" Missy shook her head yes. He continued to speak. "Keep yo' hands against yo' chest an' walk slowly to that chair in da middle of da room. "Missy went to the chair as commanded. Her eyes searched the room for anyone else present. Once she was sure there was no other occupants, she rested her eyes back on the man with the mask. She didn't look at the dead animal. "Drop yo' purse an' put yo' hands behind yo' back...slowly." Hear the stiffness in his voice, Missy knew better then to attempt any foolishness. Her martial arts class would get her killed. The man duck taped her hands and ankles together. Now if she wanted to escape there was a way unless she could disappear and nothing about her was saying X-Man figure.

The man walked around and stood in front of her. "Missy Gola, right?" He asked knowing the answer.

"Yes." Missy responded. "What are you here for? I'm allowed to ask?"

"Everything I kno', you know Missy. Like where is Redman, like who killed Vipa an' why he killed." The man laughed. "You jus' don't know why I'm here or who I am... but, you'll learn shortly."

Missy's heart beat rapidly. (Had someone found out about her on the computer!) If so, nothing good could come out of this encounter. Missy faked ignorant. "I have no idea what you're talking about."

A hand went across her face, making stars brighten the heavily darken room. "I have no time fo' games bitch." He squatted down inches from her face and removed his mask. "My name is Doug. I kno' every fuckin' thing that's goin on. Everything! I'm goin' to call Redman's phone in Jamaica." Doug smiled. "An' you're goin' to talk to him. Afta that I'm goin' to kill you while he listens." Missy closed her eyes. She prayed this wasn't the way her life would end.

Doug dialed into his phone. He stood with his back to back. "Douglas Hicks." Missy said aloud.

He turned to face her. She spoke some more. "Are you related to Jefferey Hicks?" "Yes. How do you kno'- "The conversation was interrupted with a voice over the line. "Doug chu call e'gain mon."

"I didn't call to play games. I have somebody you should speak to." Doug placed his phone to her ear. "Talk!" he commanded.

"Where is my brother? You have gotten me involved" Doug removed the phone and begin talkin. "You try to fuck ova me, I fuck ova you."

Redman spoke. "What da fuck chu tink chu doin'mon'? She has nothing to do wit' us. Chu getting' in ova chu head Doug. Let her go an' we talk."

Doug went hysterical with laughter. "I'm getting' in ova my head. Nah I don't think so. I've been in ova my head when I agreed to help you. The bitch ass diamonds ain't even there." Hs shook his head at no one around. "All this shit fo' nothin' bitch nigga. I think that was jus' yo' way of getting' me to bite da bait."

Silence was on both ends of the line. Redman promised 400,000 and ¼ of the 10.5 million dollars' worth of diamonds that were supposed to be stashed in the walls of the record label. "It's dere, Chu kno' nothin'"

Again, Doug started laughing. "I told you to get back here and finish what you started...now its ova."

"Let me talk to him please?" Missy asked. Doug said nothing, he simply placed the phone against her cheek. "Richard, I want to talk to my brother. I had no idea of none of this his speaking of. You said nothing of it to me. No… I'm here with tis' mon gettin' ready to kill me." Her accent began to thicken with her frustration.

"She's right about one thing, she gonna die." Doug said calmly.

"I'm comin' to get chu. Chu will suffer mon."

Missy screamed to Doug. "Call my brother! He's the king pen of Jamaica!"

"Redman I'm gonna call her brotha now. Maybe you'll understand him."

Silence covered the line. "Chu are gettin' in ova chu head." Redman sad just as calm as the first time he'd picked up the phone.

"That's nice to kno…Tell her brotha you got her killed. Fuck you an' da rest of them dread head mu'fuckas." A loud blast echoed through the house.

Doug disconnected the line and walked to the window. He looked out into the night, in order to make sure nobody was focused on the sound coming from this house. The night was still come. That was good. He could leave without having to kill everyone in sight. Now he was waiting on the dread headed son of a bitch to return to the states, so he could deal with them too. Doug's brain was doing cartwheels. Redman seemed sure that Viper had some diamonds. The question was where or who? The main reason for him going to the storage wasn't to steal any pounds of Kush but to find a spot concealed enough for someone to hide something like that. He searched the platform brick for brick but found nothing. Doug only used the drugs to hide his real motives. (Maybe there is some!) That was his last thought when he exited into the dark and rushed down the alley to his car few blocks over.

Chapter Twenty-Nine

T-Mac sat alone in the office of Street Approved Records. He slowly loaded hollow tip bullets in the clip of his .40 caliber pistol. Three things were fact after hearing the latest audio from Doug's cellphone. One was, Redman was on his way to the Dallas, Texas area. That was good because it meant the ball was rolling. Two was, this whole scenario was a plot to gain what was in his late brother's position. At this point nobody knew where to turn. The third made the most sense. There was truth regarding what was happening. In the letter the Mayor gave to him, explained that David Kinney was the power of attorney over 10.5 million dollars' worth of undisclosed merchandise. Up until now, T-Mac choose to overlook the information because his plate was so full. To get a clearer picture of why the Mayor of Dallas was involved, he'd have to connect him personally.

The more the days passed, the more things were coming to light. Viper was a guy that never let the right hand know what the left hands did. That explained why Kim, his personal attorney, didn't have a clue about any of this. (How did Viper get that much diamonds!) That was what the mayor controlled. Someone with major clout or influence could only move that much in stocks, bonds, or real estate. Reholstering his weapon, T-Mac placed on the V-Neck Polo purple label shirt and grabbed his phone. He removed the letter, then dialed the number listed. He organized the papers on his desk as he waited for the line to be picked up. Several rings later a man answered. "Hello, may I help you?"

"Ahh... Mayor Kinney...this is Tracy McDavis."

Mayor Kinney voice perked up. "Hey son ahh, I've been waitin' on your call. How are you? I mean, are you alright since our last engagement?"

"Yes sir, I'm callin' about that letter. I need to kno' what all this means. Upon my brother's death you were power-."

"Hold on son! Where are you an' what kind of phone are you on?" The mayor asked.

T-Mac thought for a second. "I'm at da label and I'm on my mobile."

"Just relax son, I'm on my way, that's if you're not too busy?" Mayor Kinney asked.

"You didn't read about the Mayor of Detroit…No talkin' on the phone. Relax I'm headed your way."

It took almost an hour, but Mayor Kinney came. They were inside the office. For the mayor it was hard to move unnoticed. "The car I'm in is my daughter's. She just returned from Spellman on vacation. My schedule is so tight, it's hard for me to do anything." He rubbed his curly salt and pepper hair. "Did Kim read this…she is your attorney right?"

"She is but I didn't let her read it. Forget that, let's get straight to the business Mayor- "

Mayor Kinney held up his hand. "Dave short for David an' let me see." He scratched his chest. He walked to the mini-bar. "You mine? My wife has been on me to slow down but hell we all die of some'em." Dave Kinney made himself a glass of Hennessy with ice, took a sip, and begin. "Please listen, Viper your brother was involved with an underground diamond smuggling' organization. They were Italian business men looking for a black street-smart person. Your brotha was at a congregational meeting when it came up. Business with their people wasn't goin' right."

T-Mac frowned. "Who was Vipa there wit'?"

The mayor smiled before answering. He sipped his drink. "Me…I was there to discuss donations an' some political help wit' my campaign was in high regard. I wasn't elected yet. Your brotha seen away fo' both of us to gain." He exhaled. "Turns out they were lookin' to short chain Whoeva they had in their puppet strings. Vipa strung them along until afta election. I won, then he kidnapped the head of the company and forced him to sign a certified document statin' they'd made a transaction equaling' 10.5 million dollars. It's not all diamonds… piece of land that was wit' it also."

Mayor Kinney sipped his drink. He wanted to make sure T-Mac was still with him before going forward. "Being this was to much money to trust wit' anyone outside his circle. Yo' brotha brought me in."

"Wait! Wait! How are you in his circle?" T-Mac asked.

The mayor studied Tracy for a moment. "Your deceased dad is my brotha. I'm your uncle an' my image ain't always been good. Me an' yo' father was together when he got killed."

T-Mac bolt straight up in his chair. "But, but, yo' name is Kinney, not McDavis."

"That's right son. We have different fathers. We carry their names."
Mayor Kinney again stared at his nephew. Vipa knew but he held it,
so you wouldn't be distracted. He wanted the best fo' you, your all
he talked about. He continued. "After the Italian business man
disappeared some people figured he'd taken their money an' jewels
with him. There was Jamaican an' Asian organizations involved up
to their necks. Understandin' what he was against if someone got on
his trail, yo' brotha left me in charge so nobody would look yo' way.
He wanted you nowhere in the picture." T-Mac shook his head. He
understood fully. "That's why he was at me to kno' what was up wit'
this business but kept at me to focus on my future also. He felt like
they would eventually come fo' him."
This time Mayor Kinney nodded.
"So where do you have everything at?" T-Mac asked.
The Mayer finished his drink and sat down his glass. "There safe.
Anytime you want the numbers, there yours. You're the last of my
bloodline an' that's more important than money. We put them in an
offshore Sweden bank account in Europe."

The two men continued to talk. Everything his nephew didn't
understand, the mayor cleared it up. Their discussion went from
business to family. T-Mac placed his forearms and elbows on the
desk. He leaned forward away from the leather chair, then asked.
Can you tell me what type of person he was?"
David Kinney pressed his lips together. "That's the same thing yo'
brotha said when we first came in contact. You see I've always been
close to ya'll. It was by request of your mother that I stayed my
distance. Samantha said once y'all were old enough, she'd you
choose if I were a part of y'all life. "He breathes in, then released." I
guess she was savin' her baby boy... anyway when we were young
your father had this ideal about getting rich. He wanted to open up a
parts shop fo' cars but we had no cars or money. One day we were
trying to get this white Corvette out these white folks' garage...
"David Kinney shut down, reliving the moment. "It was supposed to
bring us 35,000. The parts that is. Things were goin' smooth until
that night. Your father got killed inside the car. Their son was home
an' surprised us both. I took what we had an' ran off to college... I
was 20 years old at the time."

Both men said nothing for a few minutes. It seemed clear now. T-Mac understood what his mother had done. She wanted to erase the image completely out of their heads. In order to allow them a chance to be their own man and travel in their own way. A smile crested his lips when he replayed his mother's words. "Ya jus' like yo' father Vince!" Viper was a hustler.

"Well it's late son. I got a long day in the office tomorrow. I'd hate to see the paper in the morning, if somebody caught me comin' out of here this time of the night." David Kinney laughed and reach for his nephew's hand. "I'll use all my resources to find the mu'fucka behind this. You let me handle it alright. I see revenge between those eyes."

(To late fo' that uncle Dave!") I hear you an' thanks fo' clearing things up fo' me. It makes things easier. T-Mac said.

"No problem...don't be a stranger an' use that number. I'll let Kristy an' Erica kno' you'll be in contact." He hugged Tracy before leaving.

T-Mac stepped in house and head toward his bed. He stretched across the silk sheet and looked at the ceiling. This job was becoming tired some. Kim and G.T. left five days ago and more problems had surface. T-Mac sat the cassette on the night stand. It contained the conversation of him and the mayor. He had to make sure it didn't fall in the wrong hands. First thing sunrise, it would be placed in the fire place, no need to create any new problems. T-Mac wasn't sure why he hadn't showed his uncle the papers sent to him. Or he did know why, it was personal and no matter how much he hated to admit it, he wanted revenge for the disloyalty of his brother. If the police didn't know where to look, then that was they're fault. He clapped his hands causing the lights to turn on.

An idea was at the top of his head. T-Mac reached into the drawer, where the papers where sitting. He reread the papers again. (That's it!) Copies of this needed to be made. It would be hard to get a hold of everyone dealing with this so Mayor Kinney was in luck. Doug was going to pay no matter how. There was only one place he could hide that wouldn't be searched and that was six feet deep. He walks to the shower and got in. He needed to relax his mind. This game was far from over and T-Mac didn't want to lose. (King's Gable!)

Chapter Thirty

Five days later, a later yacht sailed to the edge of the Gulf of Mexico. It anchored, and two speed boats dis engaged into the water below. Eight dreaded hair wearing men sat inside and hurried toward the beach of Galveston, Tx. There were no signs of the Coast Guards so the chances where high that the men would make it to the sand port unnoticed. The drivers of the water crafts neared the area and killed the engines, allowing the speedboats to glide in the direction of the bank. "Get ready to go. T'ere will be no waitin' understood!" Redman spoke just above a whisper. He flicked his flash light and received a flash in return. The transport vehicles were in place. Everyone grabbed their duffle bags and strapped them over their shoulders, ready for the short jog on land. Seconds later, the boats hit sand. Nothing was said as they raced to the awaiting cars.
"Hurry we don't want to attract attention!" Redman glanced at the men on his side. They were tough and ready for war. The drivers of the boats raced back deep into the water, heading toward the yacht, deep in the dark part of the sea.

Kimdiki gave Redman four of his strongest warriors. He wanted everything taken care of. If this was true that the kingpin's sister was dead because of Redman's greedy desires, then everybody that was a part of Doug's family would die. It was Kimdiki's order and it was not a request but a demand. In Redman's bag was a list of all Douglas Hick's family members. Chu mus' succeed or chu die! The words kept bouncing around in his head while the driver traveled down the boardwalk toward the highway. "Buju, we have ey bunch of shit to do. As soon as we get to da house, we get ready to move. Chu are in charge of dat group. Tis' mus' be done quickly so I will take some men wit' me to get his uncle. Redman relaxed against the seat of the big Sedan." Be ca'ful goin' a'fta Doug. He a very skillful man." The driver switched lanes, making sure not to accede the speed limit. This wasn't a good time to come in contract with any State Troopers.

With two of America's Most Wanted criminals, stationed in these two cars, there was nothing good that would or could come out of this. Redman continued to speak as he kept a skillful eye on the passing traffic. "We mus' complete tis' job." Buju nodded to the eyes that were staring at him through the rearview mirror. This was one of his most important jobs. Both their lives depended on the outcome of this mission. Redman said no more. He closed his eyes and tried to relax. It was close to a four-hour drive to Dallas and he wanted to be well rested when they hit the Dallas city limits. The police department of the Dallas county could be crime pursuing monsters. Sometimes it seemed like they had a magnet that attracted people on the other side of the law. For this reason, Redman wanted to have all his energy. He reached up and turned the radio on a Classic Rock station. Then he shut his eyes again. "Tell me w'en we near de city limits. Sleep slowly crept over him. (I'm here Douglas!)

No words were being spoke. The radio played loudly. *"Same ol' shit/jus' a different/out here tryna get it/each an' everyway/ momma need a house/baby need some shoes/times are gettin' hard/guess what I'm gone do-Hustle, Hustle...hard!"*

Doug bobbed his head and sang the words to the latest Ace Hood song. "Closed mouth don't get fed on this boulevard!" In front of him was two Dessert eagle .44's and a Mac-90 with no clip inside. He tightens the bulletproof vest around his chest and placed one of the guns inside the holster. It was only a matter of time before he received a visit from his enemy, Redman. Ever since the incident, Doug hadn't slept a night. Every night was pressure on top of pressure. Him and his uncle waited patiently

for him to show his face. There was no doubt that he was coming. When he did come, there would be a surprise waiting. Since their last talk, Doug had removed everything that was of any value from his home. Instead of being the prey, his mind and instinct was pushing him to be the hunter. He was holed up in a motel off the freeway of Oak Cliff. Doug pulled his navy-blue shirt over his head and put on his sweatpants. He slides his feet in his black Nike running shoes.

Sitting down, Doug tied his laces and grabbed the Mac-90. He turned it over in his hand and observed the make. His uncle had filed down the stock, making the weapon, shorter and giving the fully automatic an easier handling angle. Doug inserted the 150 round drum clip, then flipped on the switch to the inferred beam. He pointed at the door. Feeling like everything was working properly, Doug put the gun away, in his leather carrying-bag. He stood up and walked to the door. His plan was to watch his house and shortstop whoever came after him. Redman was slippery as a fish and there was no doubt in his mind, the man would bring help. Doug dialed his uncle's number and waited. Moments later the phone came alive. "Unc I'm on my way to my spot. Keep me informed on what's happenin' wit 'you."

"I'm waitin'. Some of the dogs lose an' a camera on. If they get to me, it's gone be straight up an' that's what I want. The only other way, they'd have to drop in out a spaceship." Uncle Jeff laughed lightly.

Doug held the door knob. "Make sure you stay like that. I'll contact you lata." He hung up and left the room to the words of Wheezy F. Baby coming out the radio. *"My black card in my pocket/I'm ridin' round in dat Gotti/.40 Cal in my boxers/ain't got time to be boxin'..."*

Redman sat quietly at the table while he studied the paperwork in front of him. His mind was searching through the past couple of years he'd stayed in Dallas. Every part of the city he had some knowledge of, but Jeffery Hick's address wasn't familiarity. Redman knew the man's personal history. Mr. Hicks was an ex-Navy seal, that retired after his second back surgery. This came 20 years later. The injury limited his field service. Not wanting to remain behind a desk the remainder of his term, Jefferey Hicks resigned. His credential with a fire arm was top of the line. He was labeled a marksman. Even at his age, he was a very dangerous man. His years and experience in open field situation gave him the understanding to react better instantly. Redman looked at the address again. Still he couldn't place the whereabouts.

Drumming his fingers impatiently, Redman picked up his burner phone and dialed. A women's voice was on the line rings later. "Information can I help you?" Redman hesitated, thinking of the best way to faze the question. "S'cuse me, I'm Matthew Hicks an' I'm tryna find directions to 5130 South land St. I tink it'z Dallas County but I'm not sure. "His accent clouded the conversation.
"Sir can you tell me the zip code? That will help me faster."
"Yes," Redman flipped the pages. "It'z 75881."
The women typed rapidly, then begin speaking. "What you are requesting will be repeated twice. Thank you for your service. Redman listened then clicked his phone off.

"Chu kno' where Doug lives Buju?" It was more of a statement, rather than a question so Buju gave no response. "T' en chu an' two men go to hiz place." Redman paused and traced the scar on his face. "Me an' de othas will go a'fta Jeff." He looked around at the men amongst him. "I want him alive. I will torture hem' til he begs to be killed. T'en I will torture him some more. Redman evenly smiled, then slowly stood up. Each man reflected the other in every description. Their eyes showed no signs of fear, which he expected nothing less. Kimdiki had some of the lands most dangerous renegade rebels at his disposal. Any member of the kingpin's clique would put their lives on the line to assure that no harm was brought the man's way.

Kimdiki had called in a favor to assure no Coastal Guards was in the area once they came close to the drop off spot. He wants them safely on land and him, safely out the picture. Once Redman told him the whole story, it was surprising that the man showed no emotions. He simply stated. "Me Sista was involved of her own will. Chu mus' arrange her death or chu will die wit' her. It'z that simple Redman. Everyone mus' go, no relations shud live."
"We kill everyone. Redman said. "Start at da head, Douglas Hicks. T'en we find da diamonds Vipa stole." He added. "Tunite we go. Now let's get some rest an' food."

There was nothing else said. The line was crossed and there was no turning back. All this drama was at a head. It would look better with death of the Hicks family. Plus, the diamonds would finally be his. The murder of Missy would be at ease. At this point, that's all Redman could hope for... or die himself. Redman shook his head. His luck was truly fucked up. It was by pure coincidence he was doing a drug trade with the last person to be seen with Danilo Giordano, the Italian businessman. Understanding Viper's personality, Redman knew that the man didn't just disappear. Viper was involved to the core and now he was dead too. So where were the diamonds? Or was he trying to solve a mystery? Redman sat back down and recalled the first encounter with Doug. (Neva trust a traitor!)

Redman's dark complexion shined as he sat in the burgundy 2010 Rolls-Royce Phantom drop top coupe. He smoked on a six-inch cigar made of whole leaves, while watching the peach colored BMW just a couple of cars in front of him. Redman knew his car was too expensive to hide so he made no attempts to conceal the 250,000 cars. They cruised down Northwest Highway, when the BMW turned into a detail shop. Redman followed. He already knew where the man works and who his boss was. Street Approved Records and the CEO was no other than Viper. Redman rolled toward the man and touch a button, sending the top inside his trunk. Both men stared briefly trying to get a feel of one another. Their thoughts were loud (Hustle or Square!)

Doug smiled. "Nice slab. What it run you?" He was dressed in a purple Polo tennis shirt, Red monkey jeans and white Nike Air Max. Redman stepped out of his car still holding his cigar. "It'z about 250,000. Can you handle it?" He asked, looking into the shorter man's eyes.

Doug shook his head aggressively. "It's too steep fo' me baby."

Redman was equally as well dressed, with his cream Sean John jumpsuit and Gucci loafers. "Do chu have time to talk?"

'It depends on what. Da FEDS everywhere, in everything, an' watchin' everybody." Doug nodded towards the Rolls- Royce.

Redman laughed and took a pull from his cigar. "It'z gud to t'ink safe but not to worry mon. Chu can search me if chu like." He raised his hands over his head showing no resisting.

"Nah speak yo' mind. As long as you're talkin' I'm aight'. I kno' when to talk."

"Fo' sure," Redman begin to speak. "Chu work fo' Street Approved Records? CEO iz Vipa right?" He continued, already knowing the answer. "How would you like to make 400,000?"

Shock was all over Doug's face as his mouth sat wide open. "Four hundred stack, how you gone produce that kinda money? An' what I gotta do?"

"I want de label." Redman dropped the reminder of his cigar and mashed it. He stared in the man's eyes, no smile.

Redman had his full attention. He chooses to try for the gold medal. "Chu don't kno' but t'ere iz ey ting of importance in de label an' I'm willin' to pay fo' it...up front." Redman paused. "Take yo' time an' get at me. Here's me numba." Several days later, Doug contacted him and Redman told him what he needed. When the money was exchanged, Doug contacted his uncle to complete the deal. Now Doug wanted to renege but that would not happen. His soul was paid for and Redman planned to collect! A fast come always turns sideways, if not played correctly. Greed is the root of all evil.

Chapter Thirty-One

Even though things were starting to stir, T-Mac pushed himself on the business part of Street Approved Records. He stood in the production booth listening to his latest signee. G.T. was the only real success and was holding the label down. For the last year his fan base pushed him to the top. T-Mac smiled at that small gain. Without him, G.T. would've been just another diamond in the rough. Now he focused on D-Boy as he spit into the mic. His style was gutter, with a taste of charm. *"Ima game*
Spitta/listen close an' you'll hear/da streets of today/as I erase last year/ I'm da prince of da underground/who hoggin' da throne/invadin' ya home,, captivatin' ya dome/got ya mind on buzz/like ya listenin' to a dial tone/ I'ma Triple D reppa, Louis V steppa, dope fiend helpa/while I'm passin out them honey combs/ I'm on yo' block like a telephone/ so call me up, if ya hella on/an' keep yo' mouth shut nigga, this ain't a telethon/Violate da code, then you hella wrong..."

T-Mac held one earpiece to his ear as he pushed some of the keys in front of him. It was good Doug was a work horse in the production room because there were several unused tracks to play with. That gave him the time he needed to find some credential and quality that could fill his spot. "What you think about him?" T-Mac asked Shun who was in the open headsets next to him. After no response, T-Mac tapped the man on the shoulder to get his attention and asked again. "What you think about D-Boy?"
"Shidd listen to da nigga!" Shun replied. They turned back to the glass and let the ghetto poetry grab their ears"...(*Money on my mind/stay thinkin' bout franklin/like a rat chasin' that cheese/I'm stackin my safe an'/(ugh) keepin' my eyes on da prize/turn yo' back, they like bears/tryna steal yo' bee hive/ It be why/my honey stay guarded/if you die on da spot/it means I couldn't avoid it."* T-Mac sat his headset down and Shun did the same before speaking. "See da nigga right there wit' G.T. If both of these niggas on, Street Approved Records gone shit on this nigga." Gleam showed in his eyes as he spoke.

"I feel that too." T-Mac said with little emotion. He walked around and stopped at the soundproof booth. D-Boy was a picture of Tyrese with a sprinkle of salt. He wore the everyday hustler's gear, white Tee, Dickies, and a pair of Gangsta Nikes. The one necklace he wore was VVS cut and held a crown at the end. That was his way of showing that he was the underground prince. The man was worth money, but it was hard to see it in his attire. Shun walked up and stood next to T-Mac. "What's on yo' mind dawg?"

"You bet not let D-Boy hear ya wit' that shit." T-Mac laughed playfully. D-Boy was from South Dallas and a member of the 357 Crips off Dixon." I jus' got some shit troublin' me right now."

"Dixon," Shun put a smirk on his face. "I'm from Compton, you Texas niggas ain't ready on that tip."

"That's what you thought when you got on that court." A smile crested T-Mac's lip. "An' you two down now." He held up his hands and shrugged his shoulders. "I feel you stuntin' on me. You gone though. It's all about me next year. Shun shook his head at the thought. He was behind a grade and make up courses were required. Shun wanted the extra year to per-fect his game more. "Fuck that Mac, talk to me on da real." He demanded.

T-Mac rubbed his chin, something he inherited from his brother. His words were undecided, so he paused longer than he intended. "I don't think I'm gone take that scholarship."

"What!" Shun yelled. "Nigga we give our time an' dedication to get to that point I kno' you don't need da money but- "He looked at the man coming out the recording booth. D-Boy was finished. "Look at Romeo. He went to school fo' him." T-Mac didn't respond. What was being said was drop, uncut, and the truth but it wasn't what was pumping in his heart. He wanted to take Street Approved Records to the next level and his intelligence was telling him he could. "D-Boy you what's up gangsta." T-Mac said as the man neared him.

"Mac there a lot on my plate. I do this fo' my brotha on lock. I didn't hold him down. That's why I scream Crazy J at da end of my songs. That nigga my motivation."

I feel that big homie an' that's deepa then ya' kno'" T-Mac put his fist out for a pound.

"I'm finna bounce. I got some shit to take off. I'll be there tomorrow to finish da rest of them songs... I'm glad you signed me cuzz." D-Boy said. He looked at Shun who was wearing an all red Jordan unit, when he said the word. "You niggas on some more shit but I'm glad you here too. T-Mac shook his head. "I'll fuck wit' you. Shun stay up cuzz." D-Boy exited the room laughing.

When they were alone again, shun brought the topic back up. "Now what's that shit you spitten'?"

T-Mac exhaled. "I just don't kno' what I want no more baby. Afta' this ova wit', I might do something else. Like Drake said everybody dies nut not everybody lives. Maybe I need to except what's in front of me."

Shun walked up and placed both hands on T-Mac shoulders. They looked into one another's face. The respect was mutual. Shun removed his hands and looked away. It was hard not to show emotions in a situation like this. In a short time, they had become like brothers. Seeing T-Mac continue to move forward with all the tribes and tribulations on his back was amazing. Shun spoke. "When this is ova, you need to focus on your future. It's easy to let Kim control this label. You have so much ahead of you an' to give it up, is crazy. He pressed his lips together, then pushed forward with the conversation. "Man, I look up to you, don't get caught up in da lime light now...rememba you can always come back to this." T-Mac nodded. What the man was saying was true but what was in his mind was focusing on here and now.

"Come on," Shun turned to leave the studio's production area, "Tell me da latest on this bitch of a nigga Doug." T-Mac followed him to the office. There were still a few ends that needed tied and it was better to concentrate on these. In this day and time slippers count.

In the floor board of the 77' Cutlass Supreme, was a box of No-Dose. Doug looked at his watch. For the last couple of hours, it seemed like his watch was looking at him. He was tired. Still he continued to survey the streets of his condo. In his hand was a Starbucks cup. This was his medication for the day. Even though he felt like a truck driver, he was wide awake and ready. So far, none of the dreadheaded son of bitches had showed their faces. The summer morning was drawing people out in numbers. Some were heading to work, while others were enjoying the cool breeze. His stomach was starting to growl and that was something he couldn't ignore. The last meal he'd eatin was yesterday around lunchtime. It was time to fill the voided spot. Plus, in this Far North Dallas area, a car like this would draw unnecessary attention. Attention he didn't need or want. There was no reason to see a police officer at this point. There was time enough for that.

Doug glanced around some more. Nothing that sent his warning antennas up. (I'll give it just a bit longa!) Doug told himself. His stomach was starting to get the better of him. He tossed the empty container in the backseat and leaned against the headrest. When it was evident no one was coming, Doug turned the ignition and pull into gear. The sound of his phone made him mash the brakes. He grabbed the phone and spoke into the receiver. "Ahhh, who callin? Czar."

"Who?" Doug asked while pulling the lever back into park. "Da nigga out da Cliff. I fucked wit' Vipa befo' he pasted." Czar answered Doug searched his brains trying to put the name with a face, then he snapped his fingers once the recognition clicked. "Yeah, Yeah." He said more to himself. So, what's up?" Czar inhaled, then coughed briefly before speaking. "Man, I need ya. You holdin' down da candy store Vipa had, huh? I can't really get at cha over da horn tho'." More coughing. "It's worth 35 grand." Doug remembered the transaction and from the sound of the constant coughing, Czar was trying to rescore. Being a big name in Oak cliff, also made him picky at who he messed with.

Activity was growing around him and it would be in his best interest to get moving. "How you get my numba'?" Doug asked. "I been havin' it when you got at me." Czar paused. "Nigga ain't no slick shit. I thought you might be holdin' it down since that bullshit went down...but what's up?" Czar replied.

"Where you at?" Doug asked another question. He still wasn't sure of how to handle this. "Right now, I'm feeling my belly wit' grill cheese an' waffles at da Waffle House off Harry Hines." Czar chuckled. At the sound of food, Doug's stomach started to growl again. "Stay there! I'll talk to you then, I'm gone swang through. I'm jus' comin' from helpin' my uncle so I'm lookin' bad."

"I don't give a fuck how you look baby." Czar countered. "Jus get here so we can do some talkin aight''?"

"That's what's up." Doug hung up, then pulled off. It didn't hurt to make a little money while this was developing. (Money make yo' world go 'round!) No need to let those last pounds sit in the storage.

It's hard to fight a feeling that's dug deep in your heart. Chip lay with his hands under his pillow and stared at the ceiling. His mind kept wondering about Missy's well-being. It was hard to face the fact, that in that short time, he'd fell in love with her. He wasn't sure why he hadn't packed up and left the city. This shit was becoming worst as the days pasted and by no means was, he is planning on getting caught in the web that was being set. His mind told him one thing while his heart told him another. (Fuck!) Chip jumped out of his bed and begin to pack his things. (If I'm going out. Then I'm going out how I wanna!) He stuffed his Versace bag to the rim, then did the same with his shoes in another bag. When everything was packed and sat by the door, Chip picked up his phone to dial the one person he hated. His baby mamma could be one hell of a bitch to deal with at times.

"Hello!"

A woman said into the receiver of the phone.

"Keisha what's up? I'm a come through an' grab da girls in about an hour, O.K."

"What fo' Chip?" They in there nappin'" He could tell she was in straight black mode, with the neck poppin' and all.

"Check game, I don't have time fo' that shit. Do what I said wit' my girls. I'm on my way." He hung up in her face.

Chip knew by the time he got there his children would be ready to roll. He couldn't understand why she loved to send him through the drama. Chip walked back to his dresser and retriever his .357. Placing the weapon in his waistband, he headed toward the door. There was one thing he needed to investigate, before moving to Sacramento, California.

Fifteen minutes later, Chip sat in front of a small brick house. The neighborhood was just as he'd remembered in weeks prior. The house showed what good money could buy in Farmers Branch. He studied the house. The curtains seemed to have moved but he wasn't sure. Chip placed his hands over his eyes to get a better look. Sure enough, the curtains were moving. He got out the car and hurried to the front door. His pistol sat in his hand, while his ear pressed against the door to listen. "Missy!" He called out. There was a faint sound that got his attention. He stepped back and kicked the door open. The loud sound echoed through the house. "Missy!" Chip called again but didn't enter. There was a muffled sound. "Missy!" He yelled a little louder. Still no response.

Chip took a deep breath and stepped inside the house. His gun was pointed ahead of him as he walked. Movement came from somewhere in the house and that was making him nervous. There was a pool of blood staining the carpet. He focused on that area. "Missy you alright?" No one answered. "Say som'em girl!" He demanded. Chip finally stepped inside the room. Missy was laying on her side, taped to a wooden chair. He raised the chair upright and removed the tape from her mouth. "Thank you, Zachary." She started sobbing.

"It's alright baby... we cool." Chip looked toward the blood and shook his head. Her dog's head was totally gone. "What happened?" He asked. Chip removed the tape as he waited for her to answer his question.

"I'll tell you everything." She wiped her eyes. "First get me away from here." Missy paused, then continued. "Do you have your phone on you?" I must contact my brotha immediately."

"Yeah I do but let's get da hell out of here." Chip grabbed her hand and walked for the door. "We'll get somebody to come clean this place up." When they were safely away from the house, Missy begin to talk again. There's a lot you must know. Please don't hate me for what I'm going to tell you. "She started to cry softly. This would be one of her hardest moments in her life. "Don't worry about that Pocahontas." Chip hit 635 heading toward 35. He had one stop, before he said good-bye to Dallas. "You wouldn't understand if I told you." He hands his phone over. "Here take care of your business. Everything's aight now, hopefully." Chip looked toward the road.

The choices a man must make to direct his destiny. No one ever knew what that choice would bring, he only knew what he wanted, and that he wanted wasn't always the right choice.

Chapter Thirty-Two

All through the night things were quiet. Uncle Jeff hadn't seen any signs of movement. The few loose pit bulls patrolled the yard. They stopped every so often to inspect whatever they heard. Once satisfied, the dogs continued walking the big yard. This morning proved to be different. Uncle Jeff sat in his high-tech home office staring at four television screens. The setup he used with his cameras enabled him to monitor all four sides of his land. Today he was focused on the eastside of his property. It was a wooden area that could conceal a person completely. That's if he didn't know what he was looking for. Uncle Jeff leaned closer to get a better look and smiled. He pushed a button to zoom in closer. Two men lay in army fatigue gear. They were quiet as they moved through the brush. Their movements were very good. At this moment, they hadn't drew the dog's attention. This told the ex-navy seal these were seasoned vets.

Uncle Jeff leaned back in his chair. His nephew hadn't gotten to them, which only meant one or two things. The first being, there was two separate groups. They thought the both of them was hiding out in this house. He shook his head, then studied the screen again. Uncle Jeff was sure there was more. It would be suicide to send only those two men. With one rifle, he knew he could take them out before they knew what happened. He pushed another button to zoom in closer. His eyes focused on the monitor facing the North side of the property. A car sat a mile up the dirt road leading to the front of his house. It was too far to see their faces, but he could tell they were in no hurry to confront him. (Must be waitin' on night fall!) Uncle Jeff took his hat off and scratched the center of his head. He placed his cap back on, stood up and hustled toward the back. There would be just enough time to get things set up before they made their move.

Uncle Jeff walked to the back and pushed an Oakwood dresser to the side and lifted the carpet from the floor. He pulled the handle carved in the floor and raised the plank. The latter that connected to the top dropped into darkness. This was his escape tunnel only used for times like this. It was for situation like the one he was about to create. Uncle Jeff turned away and walked toward the closet. Once there, he filled his duffle bag with clothes. Next, he opened his safe and removed the money. When he was done, he sat the bag by the tunnel. Uncle Jeff glanced at his monitor, there was still no movement. He mouthed a silent thank you and went down the hall into another room.

He pulled a string and lite the small area up. The sight was that of a gun show. There were racks of assault rifles, followed by handguns, military grenades and bulletproof vest lining the wall. Uncle Jeff removed three Dessert Eagles and placed them in his waist band. He moved to a metal case and grabbed an electronic box. Using his finger, he switched the dial to on and watched it glow red. Once sure that there were no malfunctions, Uncle Jeff placed the device in his pocket. He reached back inside the box and removed two separate 8oz cubes of powdered explosives. Now was the time to set the stage for the upcoming guest.

Doug stopped the cutlass at the edge of the curb. He jumped out and hustled to his friend's condo. Doug stopped cold in his tracks once he made it to the door. It was slightly cracked and seemed spooky, even in the day time. Doug pushed the door inwards and called out. "Chip!" Nobody answered. "Chip you aight in there nigga?" When there was no answer, he removed his weapon and stepped inside the apartment. His eyes examined the room. There was no sign of force or a struggle. Quickly Redman's presents were extinguished from his mind. Redman wasn't that stupid. There was no way he'd reveal his position for someone that didn't matter one way of the other. Doug continued to walk and examine the room. Once he entered the closet there was doubt what was transpired. Doug smiled. He knew from the start Chip was a coward son of a bitch. If things were to fold at any point, Chip would be the wink link.

Doug stopped in the middle of the bedroom and took out his cellphone. After several rings, he disconnected and punched in a text. (Where you goin'!) was all he asked. Doug shook his head aggressively. (Niggas!) It hurt him to do Chip this way, but it was what it was. The only reason for this stop was to prevent himself from having to go to the label. Chip still ran a Kush house in the south. From the looks of things, he'd packed up and ran. Again, Doug shook his head. Czar wanted to purchase seven pounds of exotic marijuana and that was something he couldn't think of passing up. That would clear out the storage room of Street Approved Records. That was one spot T-Mac didn't pay too much attention to.

Doug looked at the screen of his phone. There was no call. He placed the phone back in his pocket and left the apartment. He causally walked toward the big Dodge Ram truck, trying not to skip in the process. Today was a beautiful day. One problem was almost out the way. The truck wouldn't be needed after today. Doug took the keys from his pocket, found the appropriate set and unlocked the door. Before getting inside, he kneeled to one knee and looked under the front fender. It took only seconds to find what he was looking for. Slowly Doug disconnected the wide box. Everything clear, he jumped behind the wheel and turned the engine to life. Doug pulled next to the old Cutlass and quickly removed all that was needed. The Mac-90 sat in arms reach in the passenger seat.

Doug removed a small controller as he was driving away from the apartments. This held the power to control life and death of whoever sat behind the wheel of the Camaro Chip was in. One touch of a button and the day would seem like a holiday. He sat the gadget in his lap and grab his cellphone again. After a few rings there was a different result. "Ay what up Doug?" Chip yelled through the receiver. Traffic could be heard clearly over the phone.

"Where you at nigga?" Doug asked.

"I'm on my way to get my girls, why?"

(Fuck da games!) "I went by the house. Shidd you movin' or some'em?" Doug asked. (Gone lie, it ain't save you!) Chip said nothing for what seemed like an hour. "Naw man, I jus' want no more parts of this shit." He paused some more. "Didn't take yo' cash so we straight… nobody lost, right?"

(Nigga please!) I guess that's one way to look at it. Tell da girls bye fo' me."

Doug hung up the phone and grabbed the device from his lap. He pressed the button and it turned green, indicating that the system was activated. He hit the switch again and turned the color back red. (One bitch in da trash an' one more to go!)

Shun was sitting in front of the T.V. watching ESPN 1, when the broadcast was interrupted. The announcer was speaking. "I'm David O'Neil live from T.V. 31 your local news station. I'm here at the scene of a car explosion, which contained six individuals in three separate cars. The explosion happened at the exit of 35 frwy and Ledbetter Ave. At this point the fire department can't say what caused the explosion.

"But they do know that it was likely the cause of an extreme C-4 explosive." Shun shook his head and continued to listen. "At this moment two cars have been extinguished. They can tell two small frames are inside one of the cars. There's no identifying the bodies at this time. The other two adults are unviewable..." Shun switched the channel and picked up the phone. T-Mac answered from his office." Street Approved Records, Tracy McDavis speakin'."

"Hey nigga da dam nest thing just happened. He was sure T-Mac hadn't heard yet. Somebody's car got blown up, Some'em about some military explosives. "Shun paused "What you think?"

"In da words of the great Malcom X, I think da roosters have finally come home to roost. "T-Mac replaced the receiver in the cradle.

Chapter Thirty-Three

The bell sounded when Doug stepped through Street Approved Records glass door. T-Mac was the only member of the label present. He raised his head up from behind the desk as Doug neared him. "What it do baby?" T-Mac asked calmly. Doug scratched his head before answering. There was no reason to being about suspension.

"It's cool, I guess. I need to grab some'em from da storage right fast an' go. I'm kinda in a rush" He started pass the desk still talking over his shoulder.

"Have you found that otha producer yet?"

T-Mac said nothing until the man returned. The long distant conversation wasn't something he liked to have with people. The talk of a new producer was only an act to see how Doug would react. That probably would show some unnecessary sign if a music producer was to just pop up. T-Mac wanted everything to be straight across the board until the time was right. T-Mac's face balled up when Doug entered the room again.

"What da fuck is that?" He studied the black bag in Doug's hand. Doug shook his head and smiled trying to defuse the situation.

"It ain't shit, I jus' needed to get it before I fo 'get it's here." T-Mac stared at him but said nothing. Doug looked away from the young man's stare. The more the eye contact, the more he felt he was looking at Viper.

"What did you say befo' you went back there?" T-Mac asked. The sudden change of conversation caught Doug off guard. He thought for a brief second, then looked up quickly. Too much was going through his brains at one time. "Ah, have you found anotha producer yet? We need anotha beat maker to keep da cheat off me. "He laughed momentarily.

T-mac agreed. "Yeah as a matta of fact, I have. It a group though. They call themselves Beats from da hood. Real gutta shit. I like 'em too. Everything they touched been live. You heard that song, Special Times by Stacy Breeze an' D-Boy."

"Hell yeah. It's that slow jam." Doug shook his head. "Yeah that bitch crushin'. D-Boy on some young Jezzy shit. Good pick up!" He sounded excited.

"Man, I gotta run but I'll holla back in about two hours." Doug throw the deuce up and stepped to the door.

T-Mac watched the man until he was out of sight. That was Chip's truck he was driving. Doug was starting to get sloppy with his game. He was insane to come to the label like that. T-Mac understood though. Everyone thought he was just a naïve little boy, playing a big man's game. T-Mac laughed, (Good you niggas sleeping on me like that!) T-Mac picked up his phone and dialed. "Yo' Czar!" He listened, then smiled. "Man, you kno' what you doin'. He jus' left outta here. That must be what he came in here fo'. "More listening."

"Now that's yours... my gift to you. I'll have yo' money when you arrive. Ahh use da back. Come in through da garage. I'll be waitin'. Aight, about 10 o'clock. One love." He disconnected the line.

There was one more call to make. This time he used the record label's
Line. "Hello this is CEO Tracy McDavis of Street Approved Records. I'm callin' to talk to a Mr. Peter Tyree. Yes, I'll hold. "He needed to complete the distribution deal with Universal. This was a major step in the right direction. T-Mac glanced at the clock on the wall. There was just enough time to finish this conversation and set his office up for tonight's entry. "Hello Mr. McDavis, I've been expecting your call." Business always came first, and the rest would follow.

There was too much going on. Doug was living on the edge. He drove carefully to the Oak Cliff part of Dallas, Texas. Keeping in mind not to pass the speed limit so he wouldn't draw any attention to himself. He exited 67 freeway on Camp Wisdom Rd. Doug turned left, going under the frwy and headed in the direction of Houston School Rd. He stopped at a four-way crossing, looked both ways, then continued straight. Lancaster was just a few ways up, so he pressed the gas a little harder once Ledbetter was in view. Doug braked the big truck and pulled loose his cellphone. He dial and waited. It didn't take long before the line was answered. "Ay who this on my chirpa?" Czar asked. People could be heard in the background.

"This Doug baby. I'm in da cliff. Where you wanna meet at?" Doug watched his rear-view mirror. There were cars approaching him from behind. He couldn't stay here too much longer.

"Hey, my nigga, you kno' where Sweet Georgia Brown at?" Czar asked.

"Yeah. What's up?" Doug clicked his hazard lights on, allowing the on-coming cars the opportunity to go around.

"I'll meet you there in a minute. That's my wife's shit so it's a cool spot to do use, feel me?" Czar hung up and Doug quickly redialed his uncle's phone. Almost immediately it was answered, "Hey what's up son?"

"What da word on them boys?" Doug watched as more cars approached him. He still was in a hurry. "It seems like I have company."

"I'm on- "His words were cut off by his uncle's stern order." LISTEN SON, do not come here. I will not talk to you to much ova this phone but I'm finna head to da spot. "Uncle Jeff paused to let his words sink in his nephew's head." Do what you gotta do an' meet me there." The line went dead. Doug contemplated for a moment about going to his uncle's house anyway but that would only mess up what the man was trying to do. The man was a little slower but as fast as the average master's degree holder, when it came to planning out a situation. They'd just have to talk about it when he made it to Chi-town. Doug turned his hazard lights off and entered traffic. Shortly after, he arrived at the restaurant. There was a pearl white 500 Mercedes-Benz and a blue one. Both sat on 22-inch chrome Ashanti's. He pulled next to the white one and got out.

Czar stepped out the passenger side of the car wearing a throwback Lakers jersey, Guess pants, and some purple Air Max. His jewelry shined brightly against his dark skin. Doug took his time as he walked from behind the truck. "What's jumpin' baby?" He looked side to side surveying the scenery "Ay baby you wanna deal here or you wanna hustle at da house?" Czar asked, then added. "It's just a block away but this my chicks shit so it's cool, feel me?" Czar waved in that direction. His fingers were crossed. This wasn't exactly a good spot to kidnap a nigga. Doug watched the two men as they fumbled around in the dumpster. Something wasn't sitting right with him about this situation. He pushed the thought away. This nigga didn't need any money, so it shouldn't be any foul play. He looked at the men again. (Maybe they're his watch boys!) Doug told himself. He shrugged it off. "Let's jus' get this ova now. I got some mo shit to get into." Doug stared at the men sitting in the second Benz. No one moved a muscle.

The princess cut diamonds in Czars mouth shined when he smiled. "I guess, we do it here then." Doug looked toward the truck just as the two men moved to him from the dumpster area. There was no doubt in his mind he could've killed both of them, but the cold muzzle of Czar's gun froze any hope of trying. "It's like this Doug. You gone go wit' me or you die where you stand." He paused to look around. Nobody was watching. "Yo' choice!" The men pushed Doug to the rear of his truck, in order to conceal themselves from the passing by traffic. Their activities wasn't to strange for this part of the city, so they could move as usual. "Search da nigga!" Czar ordered. Two Dessert Eagles on his vest were found, "Da nigga came prepared." Czar laughed, then nodded toward the second Mercedes. A brown skinned man with hazel eyes opened the truck. "Here Czar... make it quick. People startin' to get nosey." Pop said. He tossed a pair of handcuffs to him. "Let's put a move on it."
Nutty, another one of Czar's men asked. "You want me to drive da truck?"

Czar shook his head. "I got it. Drive da Benz an' meet me at da house. I gotta get rid of this truck." He smiled. "It's been a long time since I did som'em like this. Might as well make me some money off it. Czar hopped inside the vehicle with no other words. With all the cars leaving parallel, Czar took a left and hit the back streets. His attention was caught by the black bag in the passenger seat. There was two. One black and the other brown. He laughed when he saw the Mac-90 in the brown bag. Without looking, he knew what the other bag held. This was turning out to be Christmas." Czar clicked his phone open. "Mike". He yelled through the phone, once someone answered. 'I'm on my way, be ready." Nothing more had to be said. The Chop shop owner was his partner and they were always ready for incoming cars. Doug would be delivered in time and in one piece just like T-Mac asked.

Uncle Jeff looked at the monitor screens. The men were still waiting in the same spots. He reached to the small device on the desk and turned it on. In his hand was a miniature camera that showed the movement inside the house. He walked around making sure he could see every part of the place. Once satisfied Uncle Jeff opened his Closet and activated the generator. If they were going to make a move it would have to be by destroying the power. He glanced at his watch. 6 o'clock. Two more hours before the sunsets. Uncle Jeff grabbed the camcorder and placed it in his bag. He threw the strap over his shoulder. Then begin climbing down the homemade tunnel.

This tunnel would lead him to the underground water sewage of the Dallas city limits. From there, he could exit the creek and walk to the nearest public transportation stop. It was best to be completely out of the area when the house exploded. From two half of pounds worth of TNT, it was bound to be a day to remember. Uncle Jeff closed the manhole and flicked on his flashlight. He began his crawl until it was large enough to stand and walk in. At that point he removed his cellphone and placed a call. No answer to the first, he dialed another and waited. "Hello." A female said.

"Hey baby this yo' daddy. I need you to pick me up in da Chicago bus terminal. Aight sweetheart.... I'll call you when I'm there." The line went dead. He stopped and leaned against the concrete slab of the creek walling. He removed the camera, and the electronic controller. Now all he had to do was wait. Uncle Jeff smiled as he lite his cigar. This smoke was well needed so he was going to enjoy it. ("Try me, ain't no comin' back!") After this he had another ½ a mile to foot before he was safely out the way.

Redman crouched low looking through the field binoculars. To his left was one of Kimdiki's soldiers. The others were creeping through the field on the near side of the house. The man had an assault rifle and a silencer. "Buju, Doug's BMW an' Jeff's truck iz in da yard. At exactly 8, kill da lights."

"O.k., I'm in da car bout a mile up da road." Buju spoke. "I'm takin' da men an' movin' in on feet."

"O. k.... Fundo, can chu hear me?" Redman asked. This was the man with the rifle. "I can hear you Redman." Fundo answered.

"Take out de dogs." Redman said. He turned to the yard and watched the pit bulls. Less than a second later, the animals fell to the dirt. Redman surveyed the yard. Something wasn't right. This was to easy.

The back half of the ground was some sort of target practicing range. It was like a full set- up of the game called got'cha but on a deeper scale. Secondly there was a dog kennel with no dogs. It was like they were ready for a confrontation. This puzzled him some. Redman crept closer and looked at the house. He saw movement in the house, so somebody was there. He figured Doug would hole up in his uncle's house because of where it was located. It would be hard for anyone to get closer without being seen. Redman knew they saw them but what could they do but fight. That was a losing battle. Redman nodded to his warrior to tell them they were going on.

In a low run, they sprinted to the side of the house. When Doug realize the dogs were dead that would cause some panic. Hopefully it would cause them to reveal their position. Even though these weren't the average street thugs, they could make mistakes. "Buju I'm at de house. Chu get ready to come as soon as chu kill da lights."

"I'm out." Buju replied.

Redman put his walkie-talkie up and tried to peep inside. The old man was walking toward the back of the house. He squatted down again. The power would be out in a few minutes and that's when he would make his move. It was time to end all this bullshit.

Chapter Thirty-Four

T-Mac relaxed in his office. His feet sat on his desk top comfortably. He slightly rocked back and forward in the big leather swivel chair. The Gigi shirt was open, displaying the holstered .40 caliber pistol. He focused on the clock on the wall while he spoke rapidly into his cellphone. "Yeah Kim, I been about my business since y'all been gone."

"That's good! What it's been two weeks?" Kim asked.

"Exactly…how things goin' in ATL? Shid I wish I could be there. They say Magic City da bomb!"

Kim laughed. "Boy you jus' like G.T. He went the first night we hit the city."

This time T-Mac laughed. How could a person go to Atlanta and not hit the spots everybody talks about? That's like going to the beach but not touching the sand. It just wasn't heard of. "Kim, I signed anotha artist to da label… His name is D-Boy. "T-Mac's eyes were on the wall. The time read 9:00 p.m.

"Is he any good?"

T-Mac removed his feet from the desk and sat straight up. "I can't believe you asked me that." He faked astonishment. "I'm da one told my brotha about G.T. and look how he turned out."

Kim said nothing on the other side of the phone. That was something Viper never mentioned to her. It was surprising because they talked about all the business side of the company. "Kim you there?" T-Mac asked over the silence.

"Yeah I'm glad to hear that." She replied.

"Guess what else?" He didn't give her time to respond. "I also signed a new production team called Beats from da Hood."

Kim grunted to clear her throat. "What's up wit' Doug?"

"I'm thinkin' about da future. Doug good but we need mo' beats, if Street Approved gone hold it down. T-Mac thought for a second, leaving the line quiet. "Kim check this out boo. I talked to the President of Universal Records an' we came to an agreement, but I told him I'ma wait 'til my lawyer return. We'll go ova da contract then. Now what you think?"

"Wow that's good boy… you've been busy. I mean that's great!" Kim exclaimed. "I kno' you don't have to spoil me. Cîroc on me when you get back. T-Mac said arrogantly.

He stood up and walked to his office mini-bar. "Kim, I got some mo' business to 'tend too. When can I expect y'all back in da city?" T-mac poured himself a glass of Ace of Spade. He needed to calm his nerves. There was a large decision that awaited him. "Well after the last show, we heading back but you know that." Kim paused. Papers could be heard over the phone. "Three weeks, so I'm guessing one more week, if all goes right. G.T. wants to stay awhile longer but I'm tired of this already." She giggled

T-Mac joined in with her briefly. Women where different from men, when it came to partying. Some could go hard but more or less they were content to a few nights and that was just fine. "I feel you. We'll be expecting you then aight."

"Alright stay out of trouble boy and I love you. I'll tell G.T. we talked. Bye." Kim said. "Bye an' da same to you." He disconnected the line.

Tracy McDavis walked around the office sipping from his glass. There was plastic on the floor just like e seen in the Godfather movie. (Like Face said, these niggas livin' like da movies!) He shook his head. It was hard not to kill somebody that was involved wit your family's death. It was also hard to live like a killer, especially when it wasn't embedded in your heart. Real is only the word that the individual decides it to mean. There's a lot of fake people that use the word to sugarcoat what their trying to do at that time. T-Mac knew real was an action that was done and not said. He also knew he wasn't a murderer. His heart and emotions wouldn't allow it to occur. He thought about Shun. Quickly shaking the thought away. This wasn't the time for that. If he wasn't going to handle his business, then there was no reason to put it off on someone else. Those were his family buried in the ground.

T-Mac down the last of his drink and walked to his desk. It was time to think this through, no need to get caught in the middle because he was angry. He a strong end game to assure he could live with himself when this was all said and done with. Again, he glanced at the wall. 9:30 p.m. T-Mac picked up his cellphone and dialed.

It was too late once they realized. They'd entered the house to easily. The place was dark and quiet, all except the humming of a generator. This brought light into the room. They rushed the house from both sides, using tear gas as a scare tactic. With the lights on, Redman knew he'd been tricked. There were no signs of life anywhere in the house. He moved to the monitors. Three of them where watching the outside area. The screen showed the lay out all the way up the road, where they once were. Redman's mind began to turn. He looked around the room to afraid to move. His men stared crazily, not yet understanding the sudden change of demeaner. They still hadn't connected the pieces.

Buju was coming from the back of the house when the voice cracked over the amplified speaker. "When you come fo' somebody, make sure it's da right mu'fucka. I neva did like you pussy ass Jamaican. Da way you killed that innocent women an' smiled, neva sat right wit' me No sir.... Doug told me all about it." Redman and his men stood there listening. Each man was in his own thoughts. This situation wasn't looking to good. They all understood the ineffable. Death was around the corner and the rifle was looking them in their face. "You see some of the things my nephew did fo' money, wasn't to my likin' an' I stayed clear because a man has to learn fo' himself...Yes sir but this time, it was me that helped you. Not a good moment in my life eitha. Whut's that sayin' you like to say when you got da upper hand son..." Redman's blood in his face drained. With nothing to lose, he made a play for the door...." Say hello to yo' family, where eva' they are." Redman and his crew never made it. His last thought was one word before the gigantic flash erased the flatland. That one word was (FUCK!) Uncle Jeff closed the camera screen and begin walking. He reached inside his pocket and removed his cellphone. "Dallas Fire Department."

"There's a large fire in da wooded area of Southland, can you send someone out to check on it." He hung up and redialed. The line was picked up on the third ring. "Hello."

"Hey youngsta, my word is bond. Da job is complete an' I'm leavin' Dallas as we discussed. I'm sorry about da drama in yo' life but there's no bringing back what's done." He paused. "Jus' keep yo word now. A man is only how much his words is worth. Uncle Jeff went silent for a moment. "An' thanks fo' callin me. I could do life in prison." He hung up and walked toward the nearest bus stop. It was time to leave Dallas, Texas forever.

T-Mac hung up the phone and walked to the storage room of Street Approved Records. He raised up the garage door. Waiting was a pearl white Mercedes -Benz 500. The car crept slowly into the open space. T-Mac let the slide door back down. Czar stepped out the driver side, while his deuce Pop, stepped out the passenger side. They walked to the trunk and raised it up. Doug was handcuffed with duct tape over his mouth. "Tak'em out Pop!" Czar commanded. "Here he is. So, what's up from here?" T-Mac shrugged his shoulders, then handed him an envelope full of bills. "It's all there an' thanks bro. T-Mac said. "I can help wit' this baby. I know" His words fell short. T-Mac shook his head to Czar. He had given his word to Jefferey Hicks and he was going to keep it. T-Mac called the old man and told him that his nephews' life was in his hand and if he wanted him to live then he'd better complete his part.

Uncle Jeff had agreed to take care of Redman just as long as his nephew was spared his life. He didn't want him thrown out like some old trash. Now T-Mac was having second thoughts. T-Mac walked to the garage and raised it up. "Gone an' leave. What I do from here is only fo' myself an' I to kno'"
"I felt that." Czar hugged T-Mac and got in the car. He yelled out the window as he was bagging out. "Call if you need me baby. I'll be here asap." Czar through up the deuce and disappeared into the night. T-Mac let the garage down and relocked the chains. (Shoot! Shoot! Shoot!) The words kept echoing through his head. His finger tightened on the trigger. "Nigga you dead!" He yelled at the top of his voice.

Chapter Thirty-Five

They sat in the first bench behind the District Attorney's desk. This was the third day of the trial. Everyone was patiently waiting for the prosecutor to present his opening argument. It was the State v. Douglas Hicks. He was being charged with two counts of capital murder, conspiracy to commit murder, tampering with evidence, and organized crime. If convicted, he faced death by lethal injection. Kim and Tracy were right behind the DA's desk. She held his right hand caressing it gently as her eyes grazed over the courtroom like a lioness in the jungle. All the employees of the label were on the back row in numbers. With everyone focused on this moment. Tracy McDavis shook his head, the leaned down and kissed Ja'Zarri, who was holding on tightly to his left hand. He knew through all the drama, she'd stayed firm and supportive. Even when it was hurting her to be open minded.

D.A. Rufas Johnson was one of the most respected prosecutors in the state of Texas. He'd personally agreed to represent this case. Slowly Mr. Johnson got to his feet. He looked around the courtroom calmly, stopping his gaze on the jury box. For seconds he just stared at them. Using that time to straighten out his Raphel Lauren sports suit. The color, a off tan, made him seem more then the part he was about to partake. "In this case you will hear some heartbreaking tells about a man that was not from a not so great past but- "He paused as he walked parrelle across the court room. The word (but) hung in the air like a kite in the air." ... was a rehabilitated person in this community. He gave to charities, fought for young programs, and continued to be a family man. The tell you will hear, shows you how people like Douglas Hicks need and want for money, fame, excitement..." Mr. Johnson paused in front of the defendant's table and starred" ...would plan the murder of Vince and Samantha McDavis and later would plot on the life of their heir, Tracy McDavis."

Tracy listened closely, ever so often, looking at Doug, who sat next to his attorney. District Attorney Rufas Johnson was during a good job painting the picture for the jury to see. "My first witness will be some people we all respect very much. Mayor of Dallas, Dave Kinney. "A few gasps were heard when the mayor's name was called. This was becoming bigger by the minute. Mayor Kinney sat in the witness chair, crossed his legs, and loosened his tie to relax.

"How are you today Mayor Kinney?" Mr. Johnson asked.

"Fine under the circumstances."

Mr. Johnson nodded. "Can you please explain to the court your involvement and how you found out about this plot against the deceased."

"Being that Vince McDavis, was an active member of my charity for kids camp." Mayor Kinney licked his lips and added. "It disturbed me about how he was murdered. I talked to his younger brother and was led to believe someone close to the CEO had planned this attack."

"Please continue sir. This is a very serious situation as you well know." Mr. Johnson said after the mayor's long pause. "I talked it over wit' the now owner an' his attorney. We decided that inside surveillance was necessary to get a better outlook on what was going on an' why. "Mayor Kinney said.

Tracy looked at the man as he told detail by detail and explained everything perfectly to the jury, giving them the understanding, that this whole thing was a planned move to get to the bottom of the unsolved murder. The tapes were played, allowing the people of the court a chance to hear the conversations, as they took place. Tracy looked at Doug again. For some reason the man's poker face was painted like Mona Lisa. You could see, he still had hope of beating the death penalty. That was until, the caption of the Dallas Police Department, took the stand. DA Johnson was playing hardball from the beginning. "Good morning Captain Romeo." Mr. Johnson said. "Please explain your position and how it fits into this situation sir."

Captain Romeo was all professional when he told his part. He talked about the mayor asking him to place this case on the high priority list. Also, Captain Romeo explained that an anonymous letter, faxed to their office, gave them the extra push to act on this situation. He went on to tell about Tracy's involvement. "The young man had more than enough reason to shoot Mr. Hicks, when he caught him breaking into his place of business. But give credit to Mr. Davis, he contacted us immediately, while he held the assailant at gun point. "Tracy smiled as the Captain nodded toward him. It felt good to get revenge but not lose your soul doing it. Tracy knew he wasn't a killer, so it didn't bother him not to have blood on his hands. He thought about Plies words." If you not from da hood, then stop impersonating' us!" In his heart, Tracy wanted to but, in his mind, he couldn't stoop to these creatures' level.

He looked around the courtroom. Many family and friends were in attendance to show their support. His high school coach saluted him with his hands. After a brief survey of his surrounding, Tracy turned around to listen to the DA speak. "Can we please pause for recess before I give my closing argument?" The judge banged his gavel and declared a twenty-minute break. The two guards begin to escort Douglas Hicks out the courtroom when the unthinkable happened.

Doug moved fast, throwing an elbow to the jaw of the office to his right. Sending him falling to the floor. Next, he grabbed the pistol from the, late reacting old officer. Everyone in the room screamed at the sudden action. They screamed, ran, and dove toward the floor, not yet knowing what would take place. Nobody seen the shot, nobody saw whose life was taken, nobody paid attention until the courtroom was silent. The Louis Vuitton olive green suit lay on the floor covered in blood. Blood sat around him. The guards were yelling at the top of their lungs, trying to gain control of the situation.

"People calm down and exit the area!"

Each officer kept screaming over and over the same instructions. Kim and Ja'Zarri were wiping the sweat and tears from their face as they stared down at the dead body. Tracy grinned. He wasn't the least bit sad or disappointed that Doug tried that A1-Quada move. Suicide was his way to deal with what was going on. A coward's way out. It was better that way. Things would end today once and for all.

Tracy stayed silent as him and the two women exited the courtroom. He kept his head bowed down, not wanting to talk to the many reporters outside the building. His mind drifted back to the agreement he'd made with the man's uncle. The man never knew about his ace in the hole-Mayor Kinney. Together they'd put into rotation the perfect scenario. Tracy touched Kim's shoulder.

"It's all behind us now ma'" He held his girlfriend closely as they got inside the chameleon painted 600 Mercedes.

"All there is to do now is look to da sky…Vipa an' my momma smilin' down. They deserve that." Tracy said She looked to the sky and spoke.

"Thank you for watching over us." Viper was dead, but he was far from forgotten. She closed her eyes and rode the rest of the way listening to the classic rock station. Phil Collins, I can feel it in the air, play smoothly.

EPILOGUE

Tracy McDavis lay in bed reading the latest issue of Hip Hop Weekly. Street Approved Records was now connected with Universal and that gave them the push needed to climb the charts rapidly. Not only was the underground scene still getting major recognition, but the commercialized music was also on high demand. Street Approved Records had several songs on the rap playlist. G. T's Street fo' Life album was second on the chart behind only Kanye West. D-Boy's 2 Street 2 believe was making some noise too. It barely missed the top 10 albums of the year. Tracy looked at the ceiling and smiled. He placed the magazine down on the bed of the dormitory, then slowly walked to the window. The University of Connecticut was a nice school. He liked the choice. The decision, more personal then anything else, shocked a lot of people.

All the problems were thousands of miles away. It was a nice feeling to be out of Dallas, Texas. Coming to Connecticut was the change he needed to get his mind back on track. The basketball program, to the educational department was enjoyable. Tracy shook his head. This year he was eligible for the draft and to make matters worst, he wasn't sure that he was going to enter. Money was the least of his worries. He turned 20 and drove a 600 Mercedas. Again, Tracy exhaled. Life never stopped throwing twist into view. He continued to watch the people down below. Everyone was taking advantage of the 68-degree weather outside.

Tracy walked back and sat down next to his magazine. He smirked when his roommate entered the room. The man wore the same excited face expression he'd wore a year ago, when he'd stepped on campus. Tracy was why the man was here. He'd chose this to be close to him. Tracy couldn't be happier about the decision. "What's up dawg? You still in here?" Shun asked, smiling like a kid in a candy store. "It's so many snowbunnies out there a nigga ain't gotta hunt." He chuckled. Tracy joined in. "I was da same way but Zarri ain't tryna hear that." He said.

"I'm about to call Kim at da label an' then we'll bounce." Tracy picked up the phone and placed the call.

The call was processed and moments later the line was answered. "Hello Street, Approved Records, CEO Kimberly Jones speaking."

"Damn girl you sound just like you runnin' shit." Tracy said. Kim giggled.

"It takes some getting use too...so, how are you?" You know your nephew trying to walk?" "No, I didn't but that's good to hear. I see da charts." Tracy added. "Ya'll on da rise."

"Yeah that's the only way to survive in this game."

"How's G.T." Tracy asked. More laughs. "He the same person, just in the studio daily. I'm glad you asked hold on." Kim commanded. The phone went silent and a deep voice came on the line. "Nigga what's da deal? I'm keepin' an eye out fo' ya." G.T. said. "Ya'll got knocked out da Final four last year, what's up can I put some money on you this year or what?"

It was good to have a friend like this. Sometimes we forget what's important to us and start chasing our tails. "Yeah bet da house. I got some help this year." Tracy winked at Shun. They talked about the car explosion that claimed Zacherey Bell and his two daughter's life. An employee from the Dallas Police Department by the name of Missy Gola died also. All this was connected to Douglas Hicks and all of this was showed to the world.

Tracy shook the thought away. So much chaos formed from greed. His uncle, Mayor Kinney assured him everything was over, but Tracy wasn't so sure about it. Jefferey Hicks was still out there. With him lurking, there wasn't any going to sleep. The thought would always be there.

"So, what we gonna do?" Shun asked, interrupting his thoughts. "I gotta get a feel of da campus."

T-Mac raised up and grabbed his basketball. He chest pasted it to Shun. "Let's go work on yo' game cause yo' left sloppy. We gotta win this Championship for my boy." Tracy McDavis exited the room, leaving his problems behind. They were over but far from forgotten.